WEBB OF DECEPTION
A CARTER WEBB THRILLER
BOOK 1

JOE LOPA

LIQUID MIND PUBLISHING

Copyright © 2024 by Joe Lopa. All rights reserved. No part of this publication may be copied, reproduced in any format, by any means, electronic or otherwise, without prior consent from the copyright owner and publisher of this book.
Liquid Mind Publishing
This is a work of fiction. All characters, names, places and events are the product of the author's imagination or used fictitiously.

CARTER WEBB THRILLER SERIES

Webb of Deception

Webb of Shadows (Coming soon!)

ONE

HIS HANDS PRESSED against his face as he rubbed them up and down his rough, prickly cheeks. A long day's work left Keith drained. The mall, where he was due for a family portrait, was the last place he wanted to be. His stomach rumbled as the smell of Auntie Anne's pretzels consumed his nostrils. Another reminder that he'd rather be home with a bag of Doritos and a Miller Lite. Thousands of people crowded the walking paths as the Christmas décor had taken over every square inch of each store front. The sound of Christmas music blared through the speakers as Keith visualized his already depleted bank account sink lower.

He heard Jeremiah groan. Keith turned and looked at his only son struggle to contain his annoyance at the hand-knit sweater he was stuffed into. The annual tradition was a burden on both men but catching the look from his wife out of the corner of his eye, Keith knew it was his duty to try to make the best of the circumstance. Having already fielded his wife's earlier complaint about how he had failed to back her during times like these, he was desperate not to receive part two of that lecture series once they got back home from this evening's outing.

"Just cool it with bitching and moaning for a minute, would ya?" Keith gripped his son's shoulder, his tone reflecting his disdain for the hypocritical advice he was dishing out. "I'm already in the doghouse with your mom about this whole thing. I'd like to go a night without having my ass chewed before bed."

"But these sweaters—they're hideous. I mean, what if someone from school sees me?" Jeremiah pleaded.

The whininess of his son's voice was that of a nine-year-old rather than the fifteen-year-old starting quarterback of the freshman football team.

"C'mon. If not for your mother, do it for me."

"Oh, stop it. I barely ask a damn thing of you as it is." Gina, his wife, glared at the pair of them.

Obviously, his efforts to keep the negotiations with his son below his wife's earshot had failed miserably. Looked like he'd be in the doghouse for another night. He bottled his frustration, which of late had started boiling over to anger. He let out a groan as he rubbed his fingers through his unkept hair.

"Thanks for shaving too, hun. Nothing like a family photo with dad looking like he just rolled out of bed."

Her words and the tone she delivered them with were nails on a chalkboard to him. They seemed to come more frequently in recent months. The long, slow-burning candle of their relationship was flickering at the end of its wick. To their family and friends, their relationship was anything but. The tediousness of maintaining the façade was becoming more difficult, and tonight was becoming another hole in the wall of their crumbling marriage.

Keith snapped out of his despondence, releasing a loud exhale. He did as he always did at times like these: he kept his mouth shut. He took up alongside his son, slowing his pace and allowing his wife to take the lead. The two followed her through the mall's corridor. The destination, the JCPenney photography studio.

"Why do we have to wear these stupid sweaters anyways?

They're hideous." Jeremiah continued his volley of complaints, even after receiving his father's elbow jab.

"My mother your grandmother knitted you that sweater." Gina shot a look over her shoulder without breaking stride. "I don't ask for much. Seeing us in these sweaters on the Christmas card will make her day."

As they entered JCPenney, Keith was smacked in the face by the odors of too many different perfumes lining the wall next to the main entrance. He did his best to hold his breath as he passed by the beauty counters as they made their way toward the escalator located in the middle. The short trip down to the first floor was made longer by the tense silence they were shrouded in.

As they passed through the athletic department, Keith saw an opportunity to break the awkward tension dividing his family. He reached into a bin and grabbed a football. Jeremiah's glum face broke into a devilish smile at the sight of the pigskin handed to him.

Jeremiah bent slightly at the knees and extended the ball in front of him as if he was preparing to receive it from the center. "Blue forty-two, blue forty-two! Hike!"

Keith darted forward, passing his wife, and feeling the disapproving look in her eyes as he zigzagged his way down the aisle.

Jeremiah dropped back into the pocket, securing his back foot on the tile floor. He cocked the football and released it. The ball moved in a tight spiral, sailing over his mother's head and that of an unsuspecting shopper like a heat seeking missile to its intended target.

Pushing forty years old, but still thinking he was twenty, Keith wasn't about to let his son down by dropping the perfectly delivered pass. His legs didn't have the *oomph* of the gridiron days of his youth, but he powered through, knowing his efforts would have repercussions tomorrow. Keith's father had never made time for him, especially when it came to sports, and he didn't want to give Jeremiah the same stockpile of disappointed memories.

He could see his son looking on with anticipation. Keith expended the last bit of his reserves, picking up his pace. It wouldn't be enough, not without diving. Thankfully, the path of the ball had brought him to the bedding section of the store. With his landing pad in sight, he launched into the air. He brought the ball into his chest and landed on the padded queen mattress. His antics caught looks from the other patrons.

With all the grace he was able to muster, Keith rolled from the now disheveled bed and jumped up, his arms raised in a celebratory V above his head. His son sprinted forward, and the two connected in a mid-air chest bump. He knew this stunt would cost him later, but for the moment he was a hero to his son.

"Sick catch, dad!"

Off in the distance in front of them, Gina stared back at them with her arms crossed. "Are you done embarrassing me?"

"C'mon, grinch. We're just having some fun," Keith fired back. He regretted it the moment the words left his mouth.

Gina instantly shot a dirty look in his direction. "Ok, well fun's over. It's picture time. I want this to look nice and seem like we're actually a normal family. Now fix your hair. Both of you!"

Winking at his boy, Keith brushed his dark brown hair to the side with his fingers. They both looked at the pillows that were thrown around and the balled-up comforter on the ground. Jeremiah looked over at the bed and then back at his father. Keith could see the concern on his boy's face as they'd just messed up the store's display. A shopper walked by, only looking out the corner of their eyes, but saying nothing. Lifting his finger up and placing it over his lips, Keith tossed the ball to the ground as the two snuck out of the area before being caught.

"You couldn't just give me a daughter?" Gina said under her breath, but loud enough for the two to hear.

"Oh, stop it, we're just having fun."

Gina pointed ahead to the studio. Several oversize photos of families posed with big smiles lined the entrance. Keith could hear his wife's inner monologue, wishing she could trade places. There was another family waiting on a bench a few feet away from the receptionist's desk. They weren't in matching sweaters, but they shared the similar look of annoyance.

"Ten minutes is all I'm asking," Gina said. She then gave a roll of her eyes and a forced smile to the other mother. A bond forged in the comparable frustration.

"Hi, Daigle family for a 6:00 pm appointment." Gina relayed to the teenage female receptionist.

Looking through the computer to locate the appointment, the receptionist stared at the screen. "Yup, here it is. Looks like you still owe the fifty-dollar payment." The girl looked at Gina.

"No, no, dear. I used a Groupon. It's already been paid for." Gina said, narrowing her eyes at the young worker.

"The code you used wasn't accepted, so you may have to re-enter it."

"But I don't have the code, I threw it away. It was a gift. I entered the code, and it accepted it. Then, I threw it away."

The teenager sighed at the comment and looked toward the ceiling. "I can only tell you what's in the computer ma'am."

Keith stood back, as he could see his wife starting to get flustered as she shuffled through her large purse. Not wanting to deal with the drama and wanting this over, he stepped in. "Here you go," Keith said as he handed over his credit card.

"Keith!" Gina snarled at him.

Keith threw his hands up in mock surrender and then cast an apologetic smile to the girl behind the counter. He took the wrong side and knew it. "If we find the code later, can I have this credited back to my account?"

"Yes, sir." The girl stated as she began writing a phone number on a piece of paper. "Just call this number and they'll take care of it."

"Appreciate it."

Away from the receptionist, Gina leaned in and spoke in a harsh whisper, "You always have to humiliate me when we're in public, Keith, don't you? Always looking for someone else to take your side. How about you take mine for once and just let me do what's right?"

"What are you talking about? I'm just trying to make this go as smoothly as possible."

"Yeah, while making me look like an asshole," Gina rolled her eyes.

Closing his eyes and turning his head to the left, Keith swallowed his emotions yet again.

"Daigle Family."

Raising her hand and smiling, Gina and her crew made their way toward the back of the studio. With lights all around the thick red shag rug, the backdrop of Santa on his sleigh flying through the night lit up.

The high energy female photographer threw fist bumps at everyone in the family. Dressed as if she was going to an ugly sweater party, her pigtails bounced as she jogged over to the family. "Yeah! Let's do this! I'm loooving the sweaters. You guys are too cute. I'm sure this was all dad's idea, right?" She said with a wink.

"Boy, you sure read that one right," Keith chuckled, pointing back at her.

Positioning the family in front of the corny winter themed background, she held her fingers up in a box shape trying to frame the family. Moving Keith slightly to the left to ensure a clear shot of Rudolph at the head of the sleigh. "Gorgeous."

"Man, JCPenney's really getting their minimum wage payment out of this fruit loop," Keith mumbled to his son.

"Enough." Gina gritted through her teeth.

"Okay, smile!" The overly enthusiastic photographer yelled.

In complete unison, the family all perked up and smiled at the lens as the flash bounced off the walls of the studio. Rapidly clicking the shutter release, several photos loaded into the memory stick.

"Easiest family of the day. You guys are great!" She shouted, throwing up another round of high fives.

Rolling her eyes at the photographer, Gina said, "That's the first time we've ever gotten a compliment like that. Trust me."

Keith had finally hit his breaking point. "Will you stop it, hun! Geez, we did what you asked."

Shock flashed on the photographer's face, and she scurried away to remove herself. Keith's face flushed as he clenched his teeth in annoyance at his wife's always disappointing responses.

Making their way back to the front of the store, they approached the computers and punched in the code given to them to view the pictures. As ten images popped onto the screen, Keith looked over his wife's shoulder as Jeremiah sat in a chair scrolling through TikTok. He let out a small chuckle as he observed. "Every freaking one is money. Perfect. Nothing to worry about hun."

"Yeah, for once I have a photo of you where you don't look drunk."

Throwing his hands up and shaking his head, Keith walked away, joining his son.

After twenty minutes of scrolling through the same ten photos that looked exactly the same, Gina finally made her choice and ordered this year's Christmas card.

"Let's go," Gina said as she walked past the boys.

The family made their way back through the South Lake Mall toward the parking lot. Each had their eyes glued to their phones, completely ignoring one another.

Once in the parking lot, Keith clicked the button two times on his key fob to unlock the doors of their 2014 Honda Pilot. Loading into their seats, he slid the shifter to drive and made his way out of the parking lot.

Absentmindedly approaching the four-way intersection, the light turned red, catching Keith off guard.

Slamming the long-worn brake pads, the Pilot slid forward, coming to rest just past the stop bar.

"What the hell, Keith!"

While his heart began to slow from the quick sympathetic dump, he felt the impact of another vehicle striking their rear bumper.

7

Gina let out a scream as Keith focused into his rearview seeing his son's surprised look staring back at him.

"Just a minor fender bender, no problem," Keith said, endeavoring to keep his tone calm.

"Did you remember to pay the insurance bill this month?" Gina snapped at him.

Biting his bottom lip, Keith slowly looked over at her and made eye contact.

"Gina, I missed one insurance payment eleven years ago. Can we drop it now and deal with the accident we were *just* in?"

He then turned his focus to the side mirror and saw the vehicle that struck him pulling up beside them.

Stopping next to the passenger's side window, Keith noticed the driver was a man as he lowered his window at the same time Keith did the same.

"By golly, I'm so sorry. Is everyone okay in there?"

Smiling back and raising his hand, Keith said, "Yeah, we're good."

"Let's pull over right here and exchange information," the man said.

Acknowledging him with a nod, Keith spun the wheel and turned into the poorly lit parking lot of an abandoned gas station.

Keith pulled behind the 1988 Ford LTD Country Squire station wagon, which was complete with wood trim. It looked like it came straight out of a 1980s movie set.

Keith briefly found it odd that the station wagon pulled to the rear of the gas station, but quickly refocused as the wagon came to a stop.

Shifting his vehicle into park, Keith tugged the metal door handle towards him.

"All right everyone, hang tight while I get Ned Flanders information."

"'Hi diddly ho neighborinos'!" Jeremiah yelled from the back seat without taking his eyes off his phone.

Keith smiled, exited the car, and shut his door.

Walking up toward the driver's side of the man's vehicle, the driver popped out and threw his hands up.

"I am so sorry. I'm such a klutz."

"It happens. That's why they call them accidents, right?"

Shaking his head and running his fingers through his wiry mustache, so thick it almost looked fake in the poor lighting, the man locked eyes with Keith. Keith noticed that the guy seemed to almost look right through him.

The man's just an odd duck, Keith thought.

"Well, let's take a look at the front of my Mercedes to see what kind of damage I'm dealing with." The odd man said as he awkwardly chuckled at his own joke.

Coming around the front, Keith crouched in front of the headlight, running his hand across the front of the vehicle. Not feeling any dents or seeing any scuffs, Keith shrugged his shoulders as he leaned in for a closer look.

"Well, I'm sure it'll be just fine, Keith."

Keith's heart dropped as his name came out of the man's mouth.

Something was wrong.

Feeling his blood pressure rise and his heart accelerate, Keith caught a glimpse of an object coming crashing down toward his face.

Lights out.

TWO

CARTER WEBB LOOKED through the windshield at the large housing complex that was littered with trash and overgrown grass. The spray-painted tags of the local gangs adorned several of the building sides. Gripping the steering wheel, he pulled himself up from the reclined driver's seat. He opened the window and spit out the piece of tasteless Juicy Fruit gum that he had been grinding up for the past sixty minutes.

With the gum no longer working to stave off his craving, the need for nicotine immediately returned. He gave in to its call and popped open the center console. Webb flipped the top of his Marlboro Red box open and slid the lung dart up from the pack. After lighting it and taking a drag, he blew the smoke into the bitter cold air.

The vibration of his phone rattled at his thigh. He slid the iPhone from his pocket and viewed the screen. *Jonny Edwards* was displayed across the top of the screen.

Edwards, his boss for the past few years since Webb's untimely departure from the South Lake Police Department. It had taken some adjustment, converting his old life into the role he now played, but

Edwards treated him well and made the transition easier than he anticipated.

As good a boss as he was, Edwards had his negatives. The most glaring being his need to micromanage every aspect of an investigation. His need to know at all times everything that was going on, annoyed Webb. He countered by only relaying things he felt his boss needed to know. This tit for tat had been a game they'd played since first taking the position as the defense attorney's investigator.

"I've got nothing on my end." Webb put the call on speakerphone and blew out the remnants of his last drag. "I'm taking a wild guess he hasn't checked in with you yet?"

"Damn, this guy's killing my chances of properly defending him. How the hell are we supposed to help him out if he never shows up to an appointment?"

"He already paid the retainer. It's his dime." Webb's voice was raspy, a reminder of his third failed attempt this month of quitting was taking its toll.

"I wouldn't be stressing if this trial wasn't next week. Make a stop at his place and see if you can get him to come in. You two have history. I'm sure he'll be happy to see you again."

Webb's lips tightened. Webb looked down at the cigarette hanging loosely between his fingers. He fought the urge to take the last drag. Before his willpower caved, he flicked it out the window and shut it.

"Aye aye, Captain." Webb ended the call without bothering to tell his boss that he was already outside of the residence of Luis Velez, in the same spot he'd been for the past hour trying to locate him.

Webb grabbed his jacket from the passenger seat. He put it on inside the warm car and zipped the heavily padded Columbia all the way up to his chin. Pushing the door open, he stepped into the cold mid-December air. Fall had been too short. The picturesque kaleidoscope of colors that dotted the New England landscape had transitioned into gray skies and barren trees. The smell of sweet decomposing leaves was accompanied by the pungent odor of burnt marijuana as he stepped from the sidewalk into the concrete courtyard of the Frog Hollow housing project Velez called home.

It was a few minutes after one in the afternoon, and the majority of the residents were just rising. Young children, no more than eleven years old, circled the area on their bikes. Webb knew from his experience as a narcotics detective that these kids were lookouts for the dealers they served. Years from now, these same kids would likely rise in the ranks and replace those now in charge. The gang life, the dominant subculture here, typically came with an early retirement.

Webb didn't acknowledge but felt their watchful eyes cautiously evaluating his every move. Two were already on their cell phones, thumbs hammering away. He picked up his pace as he moved toward Velez's home, hoping to close the gap in the event one of those kids was shooting off a warning of his arrival.

Webb stopped a few feet from the door to the apartment and scanned the exterior. The blinds were closed. No movement, making him hopeful he hadn't been spotted. The only sound came from the wind. It bit his cheeks.

Stepping onto the small concrete platform, he pulled the storm door. A gust of wind swept the door from his grip, slamming it against the siding.

So much for the element of surprise.

Grimacing, he banged against the steel door. Even through the thick gloves, the impact stung his hand.

"Who's there?" A woman called from the other side of the door.

Webb didn't answer. He plugged his thumb against the peephole and rapped on the door again more forcefully than before. He heard the metallic chain lock slide, followed by the release of the deadbolt. In the silence that followed, Webb heard the woman curse.

The door creaked opened just enough for the woman inside to peer out. Iris, Velez's girlfriend stood there wearing a Looney Toon's flannel pants and a hoodie. Her eyes were wide, worry dotting her face until she saw who was standing before her. Her face seemed to relax a fraction at seeing Webb. "Ain't seen you round this way in a while."

Webb shrugged. "Been busy."

"What d'ya want, Webb?" Iris's face hardened again.

"Where's your little boyfriend on this fine afternoon?"

"Not here."

Webb noticed Iris give a fleeting glance behind her. The micro gesture would've likely been missed by most, but to Webb's trained eye it was like a neon sign pointing telling him she was lying. She made to close the door. Webb inserted the tip of his boot in between it and the frame, grateful the steel tip of his work boot minimized the impact.

"What's your deal?" Iris flashed with anger. She eyed Webb's boot, muttered something under her breath, then tucked her hair to the side and broke eye contact. The tone in her voice changed when she spoke again. "He's tryin' to do right. Maybe you could cut him some slack."

"Maybe you tell me where he is, and I'll think about it."

"He said he was heading over to his attorney's office. Something about his trial. Why don't you head there and get off my damn stoop?"

"No can do."

"Why's that? Didn't fill your harassment quota for the month?"

"You're lying."

"I ain't no liar."

"Your body says otherwise." The trace of a smile crept along his lips. "You've got a tell. Everyone does. Just got to know what to look for. Like a poker player watching for the bluff."

"That so? Then, why don't you tell me what my tell is?"

"It's your eyes. Every time I ask you about Luis, you break eye contact and look down and away."

Iris stiffened. "That don't mean shit."

His smile broadened. "The more you try to conceal it, like you're doing now, the easier it is to see."

Iris clenched her jaw and shook her head while throwing her hands up. "You don't know squat. Just trying to trip me up, is all."

"Even if I wasn't able to see through your bullshit, I already knew the lie as soon as it left your mouth." Webb leaned his weight against the door, angling to get a vantage point to see past her into the apartment. "Funny thing about his meeting with the attorney: I was just on the phone with him. Guess who didn't show up?"

Iris cursed. Her shoulders went slack. The defensive posture of seconds ago melted away. She opened her mouth to speak but didn't.

"Let's try this again. Is Luis in the house right now?" Webb's smile dropped from his face.

"Is Luis in the house?"

The classic lie without the lie, answering his question with a question of her own. In Webb's world, it was confirmation enough. No doubt in his mind that Luis was home. The longer he stood idle in the doorway the greater the risk of allowing him to flee unnoticed. Webb, no longer bound by the procedures that came with wearing a badge, pushed the door wide and slipped by Iris.

Webb hadn't taken two steps across the worn laminate planks of the living room when he heard footsteps of someone scurrying through the kitchen. Velez was on the move and heading toward the back of the apartment.

"C'mon Luis, don't do this!" Webb yelled.

It'd been a while since he'd been in a good old fashioned foot chase, and the thought of it secretly excited him. Adrenaline cranked through his bloodstream, preparing him for the hunt.

The crash of the metal door slamming against the wall echoed through the sparsely furnished apartment. Webb saw Velez' back as he exploded out of the back door and sprinted off into the heart of the housing project.

Webb pursued.

Velez, wearing the black and yellow of his gang, looked like an oversized hornet. His thick frame which had earned him the street name Gordo belied his capacity for speed. Webb put his wheels in motion, his boots hammering the frozen pavement as he began gaining ground.

Velez' feet slipped on the ice-coated concrete of the basketball court, but he managed to keep his balance. He whistled at the lookouts on the bikes and pointed back in Webb's direction. The unspoken command delivered. The junior thugs drove directly at Webb, blocking his path and redirecting him to the left.

His new path took him behind a set of apartments which backed up to a line of trees separating the complex from the road beyond. Webb didn't have Velez in his sights but knew the project well enough to know there was only one way out.

The cold air burned Webb's chest. He cursed himself for not kicking his habit. The acrid taste of his last cigarette taunted every breath. His face took the brunt of headwind as he huffed heavily, causing saliva to cover his face.

Webb slowed to a jog as he neared the end of the complex and finally came to a stop behind the last apartment in the row. He took a second's pause to catch his breath before peeking around the corner.

Velez burst into view. His stride had shortened, and his pace had slowed. Webb listened to the rasps escaping the man and was glad to see he wasn't the only one winded by the sprint. Velez didn't look to his left, his eyes dead set on the ground in front of him, only offering the occasional glance over his shoulder.

Webb waited for his opportunity to emerge from hiding. Velez did exactly as he'd predicted and headed to the right, but instead of taking the road, he made for the woods. Webb couldn't let him hop the fence. He shot out from cover and resumed his pursuit.

Velez was a foot from the fence when he turned. Locking eyes with Webb, he gave a solemn shake of his head before spinning back to the fence. He gripped the pole and pulled himself up the chain link. The girth of his midsection caught at the top. Velez was suspended for a moment and then began flailing. The frantic action freed him, sending him over. Velez landed square on his back, releasing a loud gasp. He bounced across the hardpack and scrambled to his feet.

Webb looked on with surprise at the resilience of his prey. A smile spread across his face as he reached the fence, the thrill of the hunt returning. In the cold trenches of the housing project, Webb couldn't think of anywhere he'd rather be. He threw both hands out and wrapped them around the top bar. Webb flung himself over and landed on his feet, the treads of his boots striking the ground with a crunch.

Velez looked back over his shoulder, his eyes a blend of frustration and fear.

Webb pursued Velez down the driveway of a single-family home. He then pivoted like a football player trying to juke a would-be tackler and began sprinting back in the direction of the street. Webb lunged, but he was off balance and miscalculated his effort. A split-second later, he slammed sideways onto the icy asphalt.

Webb pressed himself up from the ground. He saw that Velez had slowed. He could also see that the street thug was struggling to remove something from the front of his hoodie. He watched the suspect's hands closely. Criminals often made furtive movements to rid themselves of evidence, or, in a worst case scenario, reach for a weapon.

Webb stood, planted his feet, and placed his hands in front of him.

Velez freed his hand. A metallic snap filled the silence between them. The gray light of sky glinted off the switchblade hovering at his waist. He took a step forward with the blade held out in front of him. Sweat dripped profusely from the big man's forehead. His breath was ragged, but his eyes were as sharp as the weapon in his hand. Luis Velez was a cornered dog with gnashing teeth, ready to bite.

Webb stepped wide, trying to keep his distance while angling himself for a better position to defend himself. His right hand drifted slowly to his hipline, his eyes vigilantly assessing and reassessing the situation. Webb felt the butt of his semi-automatic pistol protruding out from the holster at his waist. Shifting to conceal his movements, he raised his jacket enough for his hand to slip beneath. The gun was cold to the touch, but the feel of it against his skin gave him a subtle reassurance. This is not how he'd intended things to go, but, in Webb's life, things rarely did.

"C'mon Luis, let's not do this, man. You don't want to go down this road with me. It won't end well." His Glock was now free of its holster and bootlegged behind his lower back.

"I ain't going back to jail, Webb." Velez spat the words. "You're gonna to have to kill me."

Webb recognized the desperate stare of Velez and knew he wasn't bluffing. Surrender wasn't on the table. Webb slowed his breathing and fought to control his heart rate. He'd need a steady hand and clear mind for the fight coming his way. Webb brought the gun into view but kept it down by his thigh.

Velez tracked the movement and took stock of the weapon. His eyes went wide and immediately darted in all directions as if expecting to be surrounded by a swarm of cops. Without a word, Velez charged at Webb.

The scene before him played out in slow motion. The strange shift in time allowed Webb to cancel out everything around him and focus solely on the approaching threat. Instinctively, the gun in his hand rose up toward his target, but something engrained deep in Webb's brain through countless confrontations gave him pause before firing.

Velez was unsteady. His sneakers didn't give him the same traction as Webb's boots. A subtle advantage, but one capable of turning the tide, one that wouldn't require taking a man's life. Something Webb had experience with and not one he sought to repeat.

Webb planted his right foot and bladed his body to minimize the target he presented. Velez was a runaway train, fully committed to his attack. Velez lunged with the blade leading the way.

At the last possible second, Webb sidestepped the hulking gang member's frame. Velez had over extended, unable to react to the sudden change in direction. The knife nicked the side of Webb's coat but didn't find its mark.

In a blur of violence, Webb countered. With the blade hung up in his jacket's lining, Webb slammed his elbow into Velez's face. The impact sent the big man backward, his feet slipping out from under him. Rage had locked his hand to the knife. His refusal to release his grip while crashing to the ground caused his arm to bend in the opposite direction. Webb heard the loud pop.

Velez released his hold on the weapon and the blade fell to the ground, skittering away from them across the icy driveway. Webb didn't allow the opportunity to be squandered and pounced. He pressed himself down, temporarily stabilizing Velez while he holstered his sidearm.

"Yo! You messed up my arm!" Velez squirmed.

"I gave you fair warning how this was going to end." A nonchalant Webb said, in stark contradiction to the panicking man beneath him. "Better to have a broken arm than a bullet to the head."

"I'm cool, man. Ease back. You win."

Webb knew better than to accept the words of a man who, only moments before, tried to impale him. He snatched the set of handcuffs that hung from the rear of his belt and ratcheted the stainless-steel bracelets on Velez before releasing the pressure, bringing him into a seated position. Though no longer allowed to legally take people into custody, Webb was not concerned about the lifelong criminal filing a complaint with the police.

"I heard you … were out … of the game. Heard … you got fired." Velez's words came sporadically between rasps.

"Guys like you and I are never out of the game." Webb shrugged. He felt the adrenaline subside, followed by a wave of exhaustion.

"Ain't that the truth?" Velez said, raising his eyebrows.

"But you heard right; I'm not a cop anymore." Webb shook his head.

"Then what's with the gun and cuffs? You just rollin' the hood for old times' sake?"

"I'm an investigator for Edwards, your attorney."

"No shit." Velez shook his head. "I thought you were all about puttin' guys like me in jail. Now you're playing for the other side? Never thought I'd see that."

"Pays the bills." Webb lifted Velez off the ground. The big man winced at the movement, favoring his injured arm. Webb did a quick scan of his surroundings; just because Velez was in custody didn't mean Webb was out of the woods yet. He was on Velez's turf, and that meant he had the home team's advantage. However, the lookouts were gone now, and the courtyard was a ghost town.

"You could've just called."

"Would you have answered?" Webb waited a beat, knowing the answer. "Plus, we wouldn't have had this chance to bond."

"What's this all about anyways?"

"Your trial starts next week. And unless you plan on pleading guilty, we need to prep you before you go before the court."

"It's all bullshit. It didn't go down the way they're sayin' it did."

"All the more reason to meet with Edwards." Webb pulled Velez up from under his arms, while keeping his good arm secured in a rear wrist lock to prevent him from running. "Let's get you cleaned up. We'll take a look at that arm once we get to the office."

"I'm starving too, man. Can we grab some grub?" Velez asked. The anger-driven, knife-wielding gang banger was suddenly transformed into a needy child.

"We can see about food once we're settled." Webb eyed the heavyset gangster. "I can't have Gordo turning into Flacco."

Webb walked Velez out of the Frog Hollow housing project and over to his car. He looked back in the direction of their chase. Even though he couldn't see them, he could feel the hateful glares of those watching him as he placed his captive in the backseat.

As the door was closing, Velez looked up at Webb and spoke in a whisper. "Thanks for not shooting me back there."

"I'm glad I didn't have to. I try to avoid killing people if I can."

"I owe you."

"Just don't put me in that position again and we'll call it even."

"Not how it works in my world." Velez was serious. "I owe you a life debt. 'Round here, that means something. You need anything, I'm there."

"For starters, let's get you to Edwards. Murder isn't something you can run from." Webb closed the door, circled around to the front, and slipped inside.

He started the engine. Heat bellowed from the vents, washing away the layer of cold. Webb put the gang leader's stomping grounds in his rearview but couldn't shake the residual effects of the near fatal showdown.

Killing, regardless of its justification, was not to be taken lightly. Survival comes at a price. Webb knew this better than most. He glanced at the man who'd narrowly escaped the reaper's scythe and was glad not to have added his death to the burdens he himself already shouldered.

THREE

AFTER SITTING in the idling Toyota 4Runner for several minutes, Richie James took a deep breath and turned his vehicle off. Looking at his dark, spiked hair in the rearview mirror, he ran his hand across his clean-shaven face. James looked out the window at the police vehicles parked throughout the lot as officers were set to begin their tour of duty. James opened the door; the brisk air greeted him as he set out to begin the newest chapter of his career.

As he walked through the parking garage, the clip-clop of his dress shoes echoed off the concrete walls. He cocked his head and pulled at the tie secured around his neck. After three months of training in Ohio, it was James' first day back at the Police Department and his first day with his new unit.

A group of four patrol men walked up the ramp as they exited the department after their third shift tour. While conversing back and forth with one another, they all looked up and gave James a half-ass nod of the head to say hello.

James had transferred to South Lake PD a few years earlier and was given the opportunity to join their elite unit after only three years. The move that James had clearly earned had ruffled a lot of feathers in the department. Mostly by those who find anything to complain about. Knowing it's easier to catch more flies with honey, James ignored their attitude.

"Morning fellas. If anyone has a road job and needs anything out there, just let me know. Have a good one." James said with a friendly smile and upbeat energy. The officers smiled and thanked James.

As he reached the door, the vibration from his pocket alerted him to an incoming call. "Hey babe, what's up?"

"Just making sure you made it to work okay. I know it's your first day back and you have a lot on your mind," James' wife Marie said.

James laughed. "Damn babe, you have me feeling like a freshman going to his first day at high school. It's just work. How are the kids?"

"I know, but I, I mean we sacrificed a lot with you leaving for all that training. It's obviously important." She replied before continuing. "Kids are good. Gianni is freaking out because Cole and Joey won't let him catch with them as usual."

"Every freaking day with them. Tell them to let him play or their iPads are gone for the week," he said, shaking his head. "I'm just walking in now, I'll give you a call later," he said and ended the call.

James took a deep breath and pulled the handle of the door. Stepping inside, he made his way toward his new office. The Deception Unit was located on the second floor of the department. The office space was located at the far end of the hallway, away from everyone. Purposefully separated from the other, it was done so because of the sensitive nature of the cases worked and the need for minimal interaction with victims and witnesses involved in those investigations.

As he walked through the office door, his new boss, Sergeant Dom Dealto, stood by the printer. He looked up as the copier spit page after page into the receiving tray.

"About time you got back from training," Dealto peered over the glasses resting on the tip of his nose. "How'd they treat you in Ohio?"

"Man, different world out there. Slow is an understatement. I'm used to the Northeast. Fast-paced, direct, loud. You know, assholes." James laughed.

"Yeah, no shortage of those here," Dealto replied.

"It was good, though. Schooling part was tough, but so much easier without family around. No distractions."

"Yeah, I agree with that. I wish someone had told me Polygraph School was that intense. I thought I'd just wrap people up with some wires and say abracadabra. Turns out, we're all Physiology and Psychology majors. But glad you got through it. Now the real fun begins." Dealto jutted his chin toward an empty desk tucked inside the corner cubicle near a window overlooking the street outside the front side of the building. "This will be your desk. Detective Michaels should be in any minute. It's a good team here. We all share thoughts and bounce ideas off each other. It's an essential part of investigations we handle in this unit."

The briefcase his wife had bought him felt awkward in his hand. She'd told him that it would make him look more professional, that he wasn't a patrolman anymore and needed to look the part. He felt like an imposter, playing a role he wasn't sure he was ready for. James always wanted to be a detective but making the switch from patrol officer seemed odd.

The entire department was old and ready to be torn down and rebuilt. The old wood desk was L-shaped, with drawers on each far side. Dual monitors sat in the corner with a rolling chair that had twenty-year-old coffee stains embedded in the fabric.

"From what I heard back when you transferred here, you came out to Connecticut because your wife got a job here. Is that right?" Dealto asked.

"Yup. Her marketing firm was really taking off in the New York area. They wanted to expand out to Connecticut, Jersey, and Mass. She went to college at the University of Hartford, and after graduating decided to stick around the area."

"I don't hear that often. Not too many people leave Hartford and come back." Dealto chuckled. "How'd the fam hold up while you were away at Poly training?"

"As good as can be expected for a guy who left his wife for months to deal with their three kids. All boys. Every day is a pay-per-view WrestleMania event in my living room." James shook his head, rolling his eyes. "My wife got fed up really quick. I've been riding the blame train since my return. Not sure when it'll end."

"Well, don't expect that resentment to go away anytime soon. I went fifteen years ago, and my ex-wife still brings it up and my kids are all out of the house." Dealto rubbed his head.

"Great. Sounds like I've got something to look forward to."

"Don't know what they told you about this unit, but we're different from any other in the department." He surveyed his cubicle kingdom with pride. "Not many could do what we do, nor would they want to. Maybe you've heard it already from your buddies down in patrol, but none of them have been where you're sitting and don't have a clue as to what really goes on here."

"Definitely some conflicting reports. But I've always been one to form my own opinions."

"Good. It's one of the qualities we look for in our people." Dealto's expression grew serious. "What we do here matters. In my opinion, we handle the toughest cases and face off against some of the city's worst offenders."

"It's why I put in."

"I'm not sure what they told you about your selection, but I'm guessing not much. Application, testing, oral boards, all of that aside, you were hand-picked. I knew you were the guy we needed to fill the vacancy."

"How so?"

"I've got people I trust, people who know the caliber of officer I'm looking for. Word of mouth is a far better litmus test than any standardized process. And you came highly recommended."

"Thanks." James fiddled with the handle on his briefcase and the room began to feel hot after hearing the unfamiliar praise.

"Don't thank me. Prove you were worthy of it. Don't make me regret my decision to bring you onboard."

"Will do."

"You've been through the school, but I'm not going to know how good you are until you really get rolling in the interview room. Our job is to take on the high-level cases. Homicides, abductions, child pornography, and anything involving our local government. We'll also be handling both the criminal and pre-employment polygraphs. Each is uniquely important."

"I'm here to do my part." James felt like he was giving some type of military, yes sir, no sir, three bags full routine, but couldn't stop himself.

"We don't like to lose, and we don't lose often. It's something I pride myself on. Understand?"

"I don't like losing either."

"Our unit has the highest case closure rate in the department, averaging around ninety-five percent, give or take. This doesn't come by way of luck. It's achieved through tedious work, methodically approaching every investigation, and looking at every possible angle."

"It's what I prided myself on when working the beat."

"Good, because we break most of our cases through hard-fought confessions from seasoned criminals. We squeeze them until there's no juice left. Eventually, we get what we need." Dealto sized up James. "This job comes with demands that will test you and your family's resolve. It's not easy, but the reward of solving one of these cases is worth it."

Dealto moved off in the direction of the back of the office and waved for James to follow. Stopping next to a large filing cabinet in the backroom, he pulled open the top drawer. "Each drawer is a different year. All the folders up front are closed cases. The ones in the back are still open, or our cold cases, so to speak. As you can tell, there aren't a lot of them."

The card reader outside the secure door to the office buzzed a flustered Detective Michaels in. He made a beeline for his desk, head down without making eye contact with anyone, taking special care to avoid Dealto's glare.

He offered up a barely audible, "Traffic was a real bitch today." before ducking below his cubicle wall and taking his seat.

Dealto rolled his eyes. James got the impression Michaels wasn't exactly the boss's favorite. Dealto continued without skipping a beat. "Any case this unit gets will have a lead detective. But like I said, we do our best to work on everything as a unit. Michaels has been up here the longest, so I'll have you shadow him for a little bit, until you get your footing."

Michaels threw his hand up while ruffling the newspaper he was reading. James knew very little of Michaels, but knew he was one of the old guard. His face snarled at the comment of being shadowed by the new detective. But James knew that the good ole boy network was thinning and guys like Michaels fought tooth and nail to hold on to traditions of the past, like giving the cold shoulder to a rookie detective until they'd proved themselves worthy.

Dealto was about to continue his office tour, when the radio sitting on Michaels's desk crackled to life. "Sergeant Dealto, contact dispatch," the voice on the other end said. Dealto's face flushed red. He fished his cellphone from his pocket and cursed to himself. James caught a glimpse of the three missed calls.

"Dammit, had it on silent." Dealto snatched the radio from Michaels's desk and keyed the mic. "This is Sergeant Dealto. Go ahead."

"Lieutenant Backes has been trying to reach you. He'd like you to give him a call on his cell phone?"

Dealto acknowledged and returned the radio to the desk and stalked off toward his office without a word. James, not sure if the sergeant was done with him, gave a slow follow. He kept the door to his office open, ignoring the fact he left James standing there as he pulled his cell and placed a call. "Sorry I missed the call. Just showing James around the office."

The sergeant grew quiet as he listened to the man on the other end of the phone. Dealto's face became a bit more serious, his responses coming in a staccato of *uh-huhs* before ending the call with "Yes sir. No problem, we're on it."

James was happy the role of the good soldier had shifted to his new boss.

Dealto let out a long, slow exhale. "Well, looks like our little welcome tour is going to have to wait. The best way to learn is to drink straight from the firehose kid."

Michaels sauntered toward the coffee maker with mug in hand.

Dealto leaned past James and stuck his head out of his office. "Michaels, the coffee's going to have to wait."

"It's Monday morning. How am I supposed to work without my liquid IV?"

"Cut the shit. We got a hot one. You're taking the case."

"I'm not on deck for a new case."

"I'm switching the lineup. You're at bat now."

Michaels muttered something under his breath, before yielding to Dealto's request and returning to his desk. He made a show about slamming his mug down.

"James, I want you stuck to Michaels side for this. He may be a grumpy bastard, but he knows his way around a crime scene and can teach you a lot."

James heard the impact of Dealto's last comment hit home with Michaels. James pretended not to hear the string of whispered expletives flowing from the man he'd be shadowing. His first case in the unit was getting off to a rocky start.

"Grab your stuff," Michaels said.

James walked over to his desk. He looked down at the briefcase and popped it open. He saw a note from his wife stuck to his notepad. *We're proud of you.* The simple words gave him a flood of confidence as he retrieved his things. He called over in the direction of Dealto and asked, "What do we got?"

"Apparently, some guy over on Acorn Street called dispatch to report what appears to be a family murder scene. Lives next door. He's good friends with the father and they work together. Two days went by, he didn't show up to work," Dealto slung his jacket around his back. "He peeked inside and sees the whole family lying on the floor. Patrol just arrived on the scene and locked down the area." Dealto led the way out of the office.

James came up alongside Michaels. "I'm looking forward to working with you on this."

"Watch and learn, kid." Michaels cocked an eyebrow, as if sizing James up. "Whatever you do, try not to piss me off."

"Noted." James felt an even blend of nerves and adrenaline coursing through his veins. The door to the office closed behind them. Being a detective was something he'd always dreamed of becoming. He'd know soon enough if he was cut out for the reality of it.

FOUR

A SLIGHT BEAM of light crept through the window blind of the office, reflecting off the mahogany desktop. Dressed in expensive leather furniture and books stacked against wall cases, the high-end attorney clearly had plenty of success in the past.

Defense attorney Jonathan Edwards was simply known as Jonny to the client he served. Webb sat to the right. Velez sat across from them, the expression on his face was a stone wall to the questions being lobbed in his direction.

"Listen, you have to understand what you're looking at here. I'm trying to help you. I shouldn't have to send my guys out looking for you." Edwards explained.

Velez slumped down in the chair, pulled his phone from his pocket and scrolled. Clearly annoyed at the situation, knowing exactly what his future could look like.

Velez shrugged his shoulders up and slightly shook his head, dismissing the statement.

"Put down the phone and let's work through this. If you don't want to spend the next ten plus years in jail, you have to tell me something. You paid me a lot of money. I'm not a miracle worker. I need all the details if we're going to get you out of this. You can't just throw money at me and expect the charges to vanish," Edwards urged.

Looking up at Edwards and then over at Webb, Velez slipped his phone back into his pocket and sat up.

"Okay." Velez said, letting out a large sigh. "What do you want to know?"

Edwards sat down behind the large mahogany desk and shuffled through the pages of the police report.

"You were found three blocks from the murder. You had the gun on you, and it matched the ballistics. Several witnesses saw you running from the scene. And all you've told police, and us for that matter, is you don't know anything." Edwards asked.

Webb watched as Velez began rubbing his right hand up and down his thigh, unconsciously. Without making eye contact, he replied, "I don't know what to tell ya."

Edwards didn't respond. He turned to Webb, who closed his eyes and shook his head.

"How am I supposed to help you if you deflect all these questions and treat me like an idiot? You have to be honest, Luis." Edwards pushed.

Luis rubbed his hand around the top of his head while shaking it back and forth.

"What do you want me to say, Jonny? The cops got the wrong guy this time."

Edwards threw his hands up and looked over at Webb for some assistance.

"Luis, you're lying. Again, you need to tell Jonny the truth so he can help you through this. This is for his knowledge, not the courts." Webb said, attempting to loosen him up.

"Yo Webb, for real this shit don't feel right, man. How do I know you ain't still a cop?"

"That chapter of my life is over. I'm not a cop anymore. Come on man. I've known you for years. I've put you away for years. You can call me a lot of things, but you can't call me a liar. Besides, you know I always looked out for you back in the day."

"True, true. You were a pain in my ass, but you always did shit the right way."

Webb looked back over at Edwards and nodded, signaling him to continue his questioning.

"Just tell us what happened. The unedited version." Edwards continued.

Velez was staring right back at Edwards and paused momentarily.

"Alright. So, you know the line of work I'm in. That guy was a client of mine. I hit 'em off almost every week with a hundred grams." Velez said as he squirmed around a little in his chair.

Shaking his head as he ran his hand across his mouth, Velez sat back in his chair.

"Ya'll aint gonna believe my story, man. My girl didn't even believe it."

"Luis. You know the kind of wild things I've seen out on the streets. Just try me bro," Webb pushed.

Taking a deep breath, he continued. "So, I meet up with Toon, that's his street name, like I always do. For some reason he said he needed to meet in a different spot that day. I didn't really think nothin' of it at the time."

"Did he ever switch locations like that in the past?" Webb asked.

"No. Never. It was like clockwork with us. But I just thought the spot was hot. Dude was always a loyal customer, ya know?" Velez said. Pausing again briefly, he continued. "He says to meet him over at his brother's house on Goodrich Street. Quiet street and the house is tucked in the cul-de-sac. It was only a few blocks away, so I walked down there. As I approached the back porch, the dude tried to rob me!"

Edwards smirked in complete disbelief at his client's story.

Velez threw his hands up and popped out of his seat. "See! Why bother if you ain't even gonna listen?"

"Okay, okay." Webb said as he stood up and walked around the desk toward Velez. Sitting partially on the desk in front of Velez and blocking Edwards's view, Webb tried to calm him down. "Pay no attention to him right now, Luis. People tell him lies every day. Talk to me. I'm listening. Sit down and just continue. You walk up to the back porch, and he tries to rob you. Is that right?" Velez slowly sat down while nodding his head. He didn't say a word.

"Was he alone, Luis, or was his brother there?" Webb asked.

"Alone," Velez mumbled. "I don't think there was anyone even in the house."

"Alright. So, you get there, see Toon. And then what?"

"He had his hand tucked inside his jacket and pulled out a gun. He was apologizing, telling me he had to do it."

"What do you mean 'had to do it'?"

"I don't know. He was just like, 'sorry dog, I have to, I have to.' He just kept saying it as he walked toward me."

"Is that when you shot him?" Edwards chimed in.

Shooting a dirty look over at his lawyer, he didn't say anything and turned back to Webb. "No. I didn't have a gun on me. Webb, you know I don't mess with guns, man."

"I know. Was never your thing. Although, pretty dangerous being a dealer with no gun to be honest."

"Nah, I throw hands Webb. I don't need no gun. If it's my time, it's my time." Velez said while balling his fists up in front of him. "Besides, you know the higher ups wouldn't okay that shit. I ain't messing with them like that."

Edwards glanced over at Webb with a confused look.

"You been around a little bit. This really shouldn't be a surprise. Most of these kids don't just decide they want to deal one day, then go out and do it. There's a structure to this if it's being done right. These guys up top are real businessmen."

Edwards chuckled as he listened to Webb and said, "Damn Luis, you working for Don Corleone himself?"

Webb shook his head at the blindness his boss had to the way the streets really worked. But this was normal among people who haven't been where he had.

Nodding his head, Webb gestured for Velez to continue.

"When he got close, I grabbed the barrel of the gun and pushed up trying to get it from him. Then we started struggling over it."

Velez was quiet again, clearly reliving the incident in his head by the way his eyes lost focus. Webb knew that no matter how much a thug someone may appear to be, taking someone's life was not normal for many. Webb allowed the silence to fill the room.

"I was kind of crouched over and we both had a hand on the gun. Next thing I know, Bang! It went off. Toon just instantly dropped." Velez said as a single tear rolled down his cheek.

Webb reached out and put his hand on Velez' shoulder. "It's okay Luis. You clearly didn't want that to happen. Now, tell me what happened after the gun fired."

Gruffly wiping the tear from his face with the palm of his hand, Velez sniffed and sat up in his chair. "I freaked out man. I took the gun and just ran. Thought I could get rid of it. I don't know, my brain was racing. Next thing I know, cops everywhere. That was that."

Edwards looked over at Webb, making direct eye contact. It was clear to Webb that he was trying to gauge whether he was believing the story or not. Webb pursed his lips and nodded, knowing the story was true.

"Okay. You did your part, Luis. Now Jonny and I have to do ours. I believe you. But Jonny here has to prove it. We have some work to do, and we only have a week," Webb said, shaking his head. Reaching his hand out to shake Luis' hand, the two came together with a firm grip.

"I know there won't be a next time," Webb said while staring Velez in the eyes. "But if there is, come see us. We're going to have to work a miracle here to prove this over the next six days."

Velez looked defeated. "Is it even possible?"

Edwards stood up and chimed in. "If Webb believes what you're saying, then it's the truth. There's no one better than him at determining that. I can't promise we'll get you off, but I promise I'll do all I can."

"That's all I ask, man. I ain't no killer, but," Velez fought back tears. "I wasn't about to lay down that day."

"Understood. We'll get to work." Edwards confirmed.

Webb walked Velez to the door and handed him a business card, reminding him to keep in touch. He watched Velez leave, closed the door, and sat back down. It was time to discuss the conversation with Edwards.

"If I didn't know any better, from the way you spoke to him back there I'd think you and Luis grew up in the same neighborhood."

"I become a mirror image, in mannerisms and dialect. It helps the process and subconsciously builds rapport. My acting skills have improved over the years."

"Well, that certainly caught me off guard. I just don't understand how you always know for certain when these people are telling the truth."

"Years of experience, my friend. The voice can say one thing, but the body doesn't lie. It can't. When you lie, the body leaks out the truth. Just have to watch closely."

"Whatever you say, Webb. I'll continue to leave that part up to you. You haven't steered me wrong yet."

"Did Ariana get everything back through Discovery yet?"

"Yeah, came in last week."

"Good. I'm going to go grab the file and start looking through the photos as well as the Medical Examiner report."

"You sure about this, Webb?"

"Are you questioning me, boss?" Webb said with a cocky grin.

"It's just a lot to take in, man. My week is shot now."

"That's why you get paid the big bucks," Webb replied with a chuckle. "I'll give the ME's office a call later. I still have some connections over there. Based on what he's saying, the entry and exit wounds should be consistent with that. Also, if it was close range, there would likely be some flame burns or singed hair. I'll see what I can come up with.

Running his hands through his hair, Edwards blankly stared at Webb. "Looks like I'll be clearing my schedule and begin digging in."

"You're a good lawyer." Webb dropped the casualness from his tone. "A long time ago, when I was still on the job, you told me you got into this profession to ensure an innocent person wasn't sent away for a crime they didn't commit. If there was ever a case that fit the bill, this is it."

Edwards looked up from the file spread across the desk. "Let's just hope you're right."

"I am. It's proving it to a jury of twelve that's the challenge." Webb cracked his knuckles. "Time to flip some rocks. The truth will be hiding under one of them."

FIVE

THE UNMARKED FORD TAURUS drove to the end of the cul-de-sac. Neighbors stood outside gawking at the disruption of their neighborhood, while others simply pulled the blinds to the side and peered from their living room. Police vehicles were an unfamiliar sight to this quiet street that bordered the suburbs.

James exited the rear of the vehicle, blowing warm air into his hands as the cold day immediately struck his core. He was anxious to get started and wanted to prove his worth to his new team.

"Sarge, you want me to start a canvass?" James asked. Out of the corner of his eye, he caught an eyeroll from Michaels.

"Slow down, kid. We just got on scene. I know you're anxious, but we have a way of doing things around here." Dealto reached back into the vehicle and pressed the button, popping the trunk open. "Grab a notebook from the crime scene bag so we can start an entry log. Just follow along with Michaels and let him take the lead."

James gave a frustrated sigh. He reached into the trunk and sifted through the large crime scene tote. In the bottom left corner, he located a binder with the words *Crime Scene Log* printed on the front.

Pulling the binder out, James flipped through the pages. All the city's biggest crimes in recent years were logged in this book.

"Let's go kid. It's not time to read a book," Michaels said. James tucked the binder under his arm and slammed the trunk shut, then joined the other two detectives, and they made their way toward the home.

Walking up the driveway, James observed a blue ranch style home with a large picture window in front. The landscaping around the front door looked like it hadn't been maintained in some time. The west side of the city located by the reservoir was the only area with single family homes. A place officers didn't visit often due to the low crime rates.

The three detectives walked down the cracked, uneven walkway toward the front door.

"Well, if it ain't funky cold Medina," James said with a smile while extending his hand and walking up the concrete steps.

"Oh, I didn't know you talked to peasant patrolmen like me still," Medina responded while shaking James's hand.

"C'mon you think I'd forget about my favorite training officer?"

James' shoulder pushed forward as Michaels shoved his way by him. "Give the logbook to him, James," Michaels said while pointing at Medina. "No one comes in or out without logging into that book. Understood?"

"Whatever you need Detective," the unfazed Medina replied.

Dealto followed right behind his detectives into the home. "Who was on scene first?" He asked.

"I got here first. Waited for my two back up officers before we approached," Medina responded.

"Okay. Give me the quick rundown before we dive in."

"I was first on scene and met up with the complainant who was waiting at the end of the driveway. He was a mess when I got here. Poor guy hadn't heard from them in a while and stopped by to check on them. Peeked in through the blinds and saw the whole family dead on the floor. Freaked out and called 911," Medina said.

"Did he come in the house at all?" Michaels chimed in.

"Nope. Wants no part of it. He'll already never unsee what he already saw."

"When's the last time he heard from them?" Dealto asked.

"He's tight with Keith, the dad. They were supposed to meet up two days ago, and he hadn't had a response from him since he didn't show up that day."

"Anything else important?" Dealto continued.

"Not really. We forced entry and conducted a protective sweep. Once the home was clear, we locked it down and LT called you guys."

"Okay, thanks Josh."

James walked toward the three victims who were lying in the middle of the living room floor. They were all on their backs side by side. He knew they did not all fall like this and were clearly staged. James leaned down next to the father, looking him up and down trying to find any clues.

"Up kid. Away from the body. We have a particular order we do things," Michaels snapped.

"Sorry. Got some quick tunnel vision there." James' face flushed at the snappy comment of his training detective as he quickly stood up.

"Well, refocus. The first thing we do is a walk-through of the home. Look for some points of entry, items out of place, or somewhere a struggle occurred. Things of that nature." Michaels said sternly, without making eye contact.

James walked the interior of the home and checked all the doorways and windows. There did not appear to be any forced entry, which would be unusual if this were a random killing.

"What do you see here kid?" Dealto questioned while pointing to the kitchen table.

James bit his lip and thought to himself for a moment. "Ahhh. I don't know. A chair that's a little out of place, maybe?"

"Ok. What about down below here on the corner?"

"Honestly, I got nothing."

Michaels walked up and rolled his eyes at James' response. "The chair was pushed back this way. In the corner there, you can see some of the baseboards pulled slightly off. Just prior to the table, that free standing cabinet is pulled out a bit, no longer even with the wall."

"Okay, so what does that prove?" James responded with squinted eyes. "The bodies were dragged in through the garage. They were hitting off items as the suspect, or suspects pulled them, throwing them out of place. So that gives us our likely entry point. But looking at the door, it looks clean." Michaels explained.

"You think the killer knew them?" James asked.

"That or he was casing them. Still a lot to cover."

Dealto led them back to the front door. He stood in the threshold and turned back. "Michaels, I'll make the call over to the States Attorney to give them a heads up. Can you have the patrol guys start a neighborhood canvass and have one of them get a good statement from the complainant? James, go grab the camera from the car and we'll start getting all our photos." Dealto instructed, while sliding his phone from his pocket.

James, excited to continue the investigation, bolted through the front door and dashed to the unmarked like Barry Sanders breaking away from a defense. As he reached the car, he popped the trunk from his key fob. He reached into a plastic tote and grabbed the Nikon D500, which was much nicer than the cameras he was used to in patrol.

With the camera strap slung around his shoulder, he pulled the collar of his jacket up to block the frigid air.

James pulled a placard from his bag and wrote the case number, location, and his name on it. He placed it on the ground, focused his camera on the corners, and snapped his first photo. He then circled the entire exterior of the home, taking shots from every corner. While he had never photographed such a serious scene, he knew more photos were always better than fewer. He started each shot from a wide angle, then medium, and finished with a close-up shot.

"Make sure you get a picture of the street sign over there and then get in here so we can get rolling," Michaels shouted from the front door.

James pointed the lens at the sign and pressed the shutter release halfway until the words on the sign were clear. Once the exterior photos were complete, he made his way back to the front door. While walking up the steps, he made eye contact with Medina, who rolled his eyes in disgust at the cocky Michaels.

James smiled at the gesture of Medina who was still guarding the entryway.

"Stop there. Take a shot from outside the door. Then come in and snap one from each corner of the room. Go through the home taking photos in the same manner. Be sure to do the garage as well. When you're done, we'll lay our placards down and take those photos. I'm going to get started on a sketch."

James nodded his head and methodically made his way around the home as Michaels had instructed, doing his best to pick up little details as he went along. While in the garage, James noticed that the Ford Explorer was backed in and slightly crooked. He found it odd but couldn't figure out why.

James slowly walked back to the front of the home. His eyes scanned the walls and floors, taking mental notes of everything he saw. This was his first day on a big case and he wanted to be sure he caught every detail possible. James informed Michaels when he was finished.

The two detectives then placed markers around the items out of place as well as a few blood smears located on the kitchen tile.

Michaels directed James back to the bodies and had him begin taking photographs of anything noteworthy.

"You can see the lividity has set in. I feel fairly confident in saying they've been dead for longer than twelve hours. But if they were dragged in here, the timeline is going to be a little harder. We'll know more about that at the autopsy." Michaels said. "But I'm sure they weren't killed here."

"Looks like dad got cracked pretty good over the head. What do you think he got hit with?"

"Hard to tell. There are very few lacerations around the wound. I'm guessing some sort of flat object like a shovel." Michaels paused before continuing. "Now check out mom's eyes. Anything look odd?"

"She's got those weird dots around them. Is that what you're talking about?"

"Yup. It's called petechiae. Commonly found in victims of strangulation." Lighting up the woman's neck with his flashlight, Michaels pointed out the bruising around the area to James.

"Be sure to grab photos of all that. I don't see anything else important. I'm going to call the ME's office to come grab the bodies. When you finish that, grab the swabs, and start collecting DNA from the door handles, table area, and counters."

Michaels exited the home, leaving James alone inside. Still crouched over by the victims, James couldn't help but have an eerie feeling being alone with three dead bodies. Having been in the home of deceased elderly people while in patrol, being alone with a slain family was different. The hair on the back of his neck stood at attention as he knelt next to them. He looked them all over thoroughly to be sure he didn't miss anything.

He focused on the mother. Her hands were resting on her chest with one hand on top of the other. The father and son were both lying with their arms by their sides. James knew the bodies had to be posed by the killer, but he wanted to figure out why the mother was placed differently. James leaned toward the mother's arms and noticed something resting inside her top hand. He couldn't quite make it out. "Michaels, can you come back in here right quick?"

"Okay, we'll see you in about forty-five minutes," Michaels said just prior to hanging up the phone as he walked back into the room. "Yeah, what's up?"

"Check this out." James said.

Dealto came back inside, shaking off the cold. He looked over at his detectives. "You boys need anything before I cut out?"

"Looks like she's holding on to some sort of ball or something," James said.

"Looks like a pearl," Dealto said. "You didn't tell me about that Michaels."

Michaels shot a nasty look in James's direction. "Must have missed it, boss."

"James, take a photo first, then see if you can pop it out."

James stood back and took multiple photos of the victim from different angles and depths. After taking his close-up shots, he pulled a pen from his pants pocket. He bent down next to the woman. The object sat between her thumb and pointer fingers with a closed fist. James pressed the pen into her stiff hand to pry at the object. Like a cannon shooting out of a rocket, the round white object popped out of her hand and landed on her stomach.

Dealto reached into his rear pocket and drew on a set of rubber gloves. "I'll grab it." With two fingers, he grasped the object and held it up near the ceiling light.

"Definitely looks like a pearl of some sort," James said.

"Seems to have some holes in the side like it came off a necklace. Did we see any more of these around the house?" Dealto asked.

"Nothing, boss."

The three men stared at the pearl.

"Let's just bag it up and get it out to the lab. Maybe it's nothing, or maybe it'll lead us somewhere. Either way, good work, kid." Dealto said.

"I'm on it," James dipped his head.

"You guys finish up and wait for the ME's office to get here. LT's going to give me a ride back to the PD so I can let the captain know what we have." Dealto said, tossing his keys to Michaels as he left the home.

Michaels waited until Dealto was beyond the tape and out of earshot. He turned to face James. His eyes were darker than usual. A scowl formed. "Hurry up with that and go get those swabs done. I don't want to be here all night."

James fought the urge to address the senior detective's attitude, but ultimately thought better of it. He'd been a rookie before. Patrol had its pecking order too. He'd survived it. He'd survive this, too. Everything he'd worked toward led to this point and he wasn't about to blow it because some burnout "has been" is looking to take out his misery on the new guy. He gave a slight nod of his head. "Measure twice, cut once."

"What's that supposed to mean?" Michaels asked, squaring his body up to James.

"I used to work construction. Boss always told me to take my time and do things right the first time." He pulled on a pair of sterile gloves and picked up the kit. "I plan to do just that. As long as it takes."

SIX

WEBB SAT at the desk to the side of the jury as Edwards made his final arguments. Based on the information gathered from the Medical Examiner's Office, the case of self-defense seemed very plausible. In his job as a police officer, Webb had sat on the other side of the courtroom, racking his brain to confirm he'd done all he could to put away a criminal. Now, finding himself on the other side helping the defense almost felt dirty to him. He continued to tell himself he was doing the right thing. Velez leaned sideways toward Webb and waved him in. "I don't know, man, this jury ain't giving me good vibes," he whispered.

"Trust the process, Luis. We've done everything in our power to give the facts of the case. After that, it's out of our control."

Velez leaned back and began anxiously gnawing on his fingernails while looking over members of the jury.

Dressed to the nines in a perfectly fitted dark blue Armani suit and sporting Gucci shoes, Edwards walked back and forth in front of the jury with his hands in his pants pockets.

Webb watched as he masterfully laid out his arguments

surrounding the self-defense argument of his client. He was smooth, calm, and convincing.

"You see ladies and gentlemen, it's no secret why my client was there that day. He doesn't claim to be an upstanding citizen of this city that works a hard nine-to-five job. No. My client is honest about what he does and why he was there." Edwards paused, looking up at the jury. "But does that mean he deserves to be robbed? Does that mean he has to sit there and possibly be shot?" He approached the counsel table and reached over as Webb handed him a folder. Edwards held up the folder while gazing at the jury and nodding his head. He pulled out a picture he had previously submitted to evidence and held it in front of them.

"As I showed you previously, this photo located from a neighbor's Ring Cam shows a grainy still photo of the incident. Yes, it's hard to make out what's happening. But it does seem pretty clear my client has his hands up. Why? Why would a man with a gun put his hands up? I'll tell you why. Because he didn't *have* a gun and he was the victim that night. The DNA analysis showed both men's DNA on that firearm. If anything, you must have a lot of doubts that my client showed up to rob this man that night."

The jury sat stoically, not giving off any visible reaction to the statements.

Edwards turned back and pointed at Webb, while finishing his remarks.

"Carter Webb. This man laid out our interview with Mr. Velez. Carter is a well-known expert in the fields of interview and interrogation as well as detecting deception. He said with certainty that Mr. Velez was telling the truth in this matter. This is not just some guy that works for me. Webb is well known for what he does and is highly respected. He has testified in hundreds of court cases as an expert witness in the field of interview and interrogation."

Webb looked back and observed Sergeant Dealto sitting behind the prosecution, rolling his eyes at the statement. Dealto and his team had arrested Velez. Finding themselves in a trial was rare for them.

Again, Edwards walked forward and stood before the jury, resting his hands on the railing of the jury box.

"Ladies. Gentlemen. My client did not show up that night intending to harm anyone. My client showed up and found his life in danger. He did what he had to do to survive. The fact that someone lost their life that night is a tragedy. I feel awful for the man's family." Edwards then turned and nodded his head toward the victim's mother sitting in the crowd with her head down sobbing. "However, my client simply acted in self-defense. I just ask that you take all the facts I've presented into consideration, as I have no doubt my client is innocent." Edwards turned from the jury to face the judge. "I rest my case, your honor."

Edward strutted back to his seat, sat down, and crossed his legs. The three men waited to see if the prosecution would provide a final rebuttal.

A visibly nervous prosecutor stood from his seat, tugging on his suit jacket. "The state rests its case."

The judge gave some final instructions to the members of the jury. He slapped his gavel down and dismissed all in attendance until deliberation was complete.

As the jury stood and left the courtroom, Webb looked over at Velez. Beads of sweat covered his temples as he gnawed at what was left of his fingernails.

"Come on boys, let's go grab a coffee downstairs while we wait. I don't expect this to take too long." Edwards emphatically said while squeezing the shoulder of Webb.

The men made their way to the coffee shop on the ground floor of the courthouse. Webb and Edwards grabbed some caffeine while Velez chose to sit by himself in the hallway with his hands covering his face. The small café was equipped with five small round tables, with two that were occupied. Webb located a table in the corner, pulled out a chair across from Edwards, and sat down.

"Feel good?" Webb asked, swirling his coffee cup.

"I do. Not only because of everything we uncovered last week, but your testimony just sealed the deal. Always does. You're my Mariano Rivera."

"Well, if that's the case, I'll be looking for that big off-season contract," Webb smiled.

They sipped on their coffees for the next ninety minutes while they came up with a game plan for a new client. While in mid conversation, an alert from Edwards's watch caused them both to pause and look down at his wrist.

"It's time. Jury's ready," Edwards said while reading the message.

"Quicker than I thought." Webb stood, grabbing his empty cup and tossing it in the receptacle.

As they left the small café and made their way to the hallway, they found Velez still sitting in the exact same spot. Webb came up in front of Velez and took in the blank look on the man's face.

"They're ready for us in there, Luis."

Velez took a deep breath while rubbing his palms up and down his thigh. He released a large exhale and stood.

The hallways were empty, as everyone had already made their way back into the room. Webb pulled open the large wooden door, holding it open for Edwards and Velez to enter.

The people in attendance all turned and stared as the three men made their way down the center of the room. Webb felt their eyes burning a hole through Velez, knowing his fate would shortly be sealed. Edwards, Webb, and Velez positioned themselves behind the counsel chair and waited. The jury entered from the rear and sat in the box as they awaited the magistrate.

"All rise," the marshal announced as the judge emerged from the rear of the court and made his way to the bench.

With a file tucked underneath his arm, the judge sat, turning himself forward prepared to conclude the trial. The occupants of the courtroom sat back down as the anticipation could be felt throughout the room. The room fell completely silent.

"Welcome back everyone, I'm informed that the jury has reached a decision. Is that correct?"

"We have." The presiding juror responded.

"And is it unanimous?"

"Yes, it is your honor."

"Has it been signed by your foreperson?" The judge asked.

"It has."

"Please give it to the bailiff."

The paperwork was passed down from the jury and into the judge's hands. A few moments passed as he read it over.

"This is the jury's verdict as it relates to case 20-14764b, State vs. Luis P. Velez." He briefly paused before continuing. "We, the jury in the above-entitled manner, count 1, Connecticut General Statute 53a-217 Criminal Possession of a Firearm, find the defendant not guilty. Count 2, Connecticut General Statute 53a-54a Murder. We, the jury find the defendant, not guilty."

Velez immediately dropped his head, covering his face with his hands. His body shook as the tears flowed down his cheeks. Edwards slapped him on the back and smiled while congratulating him.

Still motionless and almost in a trance, Webb stared up at the judge while he read the final rulings. It was an odd feeling for him. The family of the victim bellowed out as they wiped the tears from their faces. Webb wasn't sure if he should be happy or not.

The judge slapped his gavel, establishing order in the courtroom. Bellying up to his desk, he made his final remarks by dismissing the charges against Velez and thanking the jury. He stood from the bench and the trial concluded.

Like a popcorn kernel ready to burst, Velez sprung from his seat, shaking Edwards' hand and thanking him for all he had done. He turned to face Webb while shaking his head in disbelief. "Webb man, I can't even believe all this. I owe you. This doesn't even feel real right now."

Velez turned to the crowd with a look of victory written all over his face. Webb noticed Velez nod his head toward a male sitting in the front row. The large burly man wearing a long black trench coat, stood up and approached Webb. A familiar face that Webb had seen from past investigations. Webb knew him as one of the higher ups within Velez' crew, but someone that was hard to catch. The man extended his hand towards Webb for a handshake.

"We appreciate everything you did here today, Mr. Webb. My boss would like to meet with you over dinner. We'll reach out with the particulars," the man said, nodding his head as if Webb had no choice.

Webb stared at the man while his head processed all the crimes he had been likely involved in. The request made him very uneasy. His brain felt like a game of ping pong as he battled with what he was doing. But he was no longer a cop and knew he could get away with handling things differently now.

"Anytime. It's my job. Glad I could help. We'll see you around." Webb said with a fake smile. Throwing some files into his black backpack, Webb slung the bag over his shoulder as he made his way out of the courtroom.

The marble tile echoed throughout the high ceiling of the hallway with each step he took. After a long day of trials, the courthouse had emptied out. The sound of the metal bar clacked as Webb pushed the exterior door open into the cold winter day.

"You know, for a real smart guy, you really are an idiot, Carter!" A voice yelled out from his right.

The old, familiar voice flowed through his ears as Webb turned. Dealto's voice was distinct, sounding like a character straight out of A Bronx Tale. With the brim of his fedora tilted down just above his eyes, his coat flapped backward as he stormed toward Webb.

"Whoa, whoa, take it easy," Webb said with a smirk as he took a step backward.

"Haven't you learned a thing since you got your ass fired?" Dealto yelled, pointing his finger at Webb's face.

"Yeah, I learned that you still don't know how to seal a case to put someone away," Webb shot back while slapping his old boss on the side of his arm.

"I see you working with these scum bags. Taking that dirty money. Hope you sleep well at night."

"Gotta pay the bills somehow, boss." Webb said, making sure his tone dripped with sarcasm. "Your case just happens to be the low hanging fruit that's easy to pick."

Biting his lip, Dealto shook his head at Webb with disgust. "I caught your cheating ass once. I'll do it again, Webb. Just remember that."

The words still cut deep. Webb remained calm, not allowing Dealto to see him bothered by the remarks.

"Sounds good, sir. It was really great catching up. We should do this again sometime." Webb threw his hand out to be shaken, just to annoy his old mentor.

Dealto's face became flushed as he turned and left without saying another word.

Webb watched Dealto stomp away. He dropped his hand and slid them both into his pockets while turning to make his way toward the parking garage. Webb knew he could make people believe whatever he wanted, but deep down, he couldn't fool himself.

SEVEN

JAMES STOOD up from his desk, one of four cubicles in a square smack in the middle of the room. The office was small which forced a cohesiveness between the detectives. A long filing cabinet against the wall was packed with current and unsolved cases spanning several decades. He walked over to the copy machine, tucked in a corner by the door. The search warrant slid into the top and scanned into the department server.

"How long do these companies usually take to get back to you?" he asked the two detectives.

"Depends on what carrier," Detective Lisa Shaw remarked.

"Lightening. One of those pre-paid ones."

Shaw rolled her eyes. "They're the worst. I assume you spoke to someone there and told them you needed it fast, but they couldn't care less. Fast to them is a day or two."

James pulled the search warrant from the feeder and shook his head. Tossing the paperwork on his desk, he sat down and twirled on his chair. "Told the guy we just processed the scene yesterday and need the info ASAP. Seemed like a good dude."

"You'll learn. They don't care. Be careful what you say about the case on the phone. You have no idea whom you're talking to. They need only the absolute basics."

James opened his email, attaching a copy of the search warrant to send off to the cell phone carrier. As the swoosh of the email signaled the message was sent, he minimized the box and opened his internet browser. Google appeared on his screen, and he typed in *Keith Daigle South Lake, Connecticut.* Several results came up, including multiple social media pages. James had always loved sifting through these treasure troves of information. He wanted to know more about his victims, and social media had always served him well. The result at the top was of a New York Giants background and the Keith's profile picture was of his family. They all looked so happy as they stood on the beach somewhere in front of the ocean. While scrolling through his posts, James' desk phone line rang. The caller ID notified him it was from the Main Desk. He pulled the receiver from the base. "James."

"Hey, there's some guy down here who says he has an interview scheduled with you," the main desk officer replied.

"Thanks, I'll be right down." James hung up the phone and began shuffling some case notes around and looking for a pen. He heard the metal door handle thrust downwards as the office door swung open. Dealto came storming through, wearing a long jacket with a suit underneath. The scowl on his face told the story of how his morning had started.

"How'd the verdict go, boss?" Shaw questioned.

Dealto took a deep breath and turned toward the group. He placed his hands on the long file cabinet in front of them. "So, when I walk into the courtroom to see that turd cry when they read the word 'guilty', guess who's sitting over there with the defense?"

"Jonny Edwards was representing him, right? He's a cocky SOB, but that guy is good," Michaels chimed in from the corner.

"No, not him. I knew Edwards was representing him. He's got a new sidekick. Mr. Carter Webb himself."

Michaels stood up from his desk as his jaw dropped. "No freaking way. He's gone to the dark side?"

"Yup. Can't say I'm that shocked. Classic Sociopath. Only cares about himself. I had heard he was helping Edwards out on occasion but didn't know he was getting involved in trials. When I heard he testified, I knew we'd be in trouble. The guy could sell a ketchup popsicle to a woman in white gloves."

James just took in the banter, as he never had a relationship with Webb. The two had crossed paths a few times early in James's career, but that was all. James never cared for the drama and kept himself out of all the details surrounding the termination.

"Where are we at on the Daigle case? Anything new?" Dealto asked, changing subjects.

"I was just about to head down to grab Tommy Marino. He was our complainant. I have to dig more into this family. Hoping he can steer us somewhere."

"Good. Keep me posted. I'll be in my office," Dealto gave the filing cabinet two staccato smacks before walking away.

James grabbed his case folder from his desk and made his way toward the elevator. While taking the trip down, he formulated a list of questions he wanted answers to while speaking with Marino. The doors separated in the middle, and the main lobby came into view. James took a half step out of the elevator to make sure the door did not close. He waved Marino over.

Slowly standing from his chair, Marino made his way toward James. A middle-aged man who was balding with a thick goatee and glasses, his face was easy to read. He was taking this incident really hard. This was going to be a difficult interview James thought. James shook Marino's hand as he entered the elevator. "Sorry for your loss, Tom. I couldn't imagine what you've been going through the past day or so."

Marino just shook his head and remained quiet. The quick ride up the elevator was quiet and awkward. James didn't want to say too much yet, allowing Marino time to process everything going on. The two walked out into the hallway and entered the Deception Unit office. Tucked in the far corner was a single interview room. James flicked the switch to activate the camera in the room and the two men sat. Not wanting to dig right into the details, James took some time to establish rapport and get Marino comfortable. He wanted to do all he could to keep Marino from shutting down when they got into some of the uncomfortable details. "So, you were saying you and your wife moved up here about four years ago. You guys been tight with the Daigle's for a while?"

"Yeah. Almost immediately when we moved in. Keith saw me hanging my Redskins flag up in front of the house," Marino said with a laugh. "He just started tearing into me. We were both big football fans. That was that. We've been close ever since."

"Now, now, Tom. They're called the Commanders. Please show some respect," James said, poking fun.

"Ahhh," Marino groaned, waving his hand forward. "I'll never call them that."

James smiled, sitting back in his chair, and crossing his legs before continuing. "How was their marriage? Any fidelity issues or anything that has ever raised any flags for you?"

Marino threw his hands up. "That's so hard to answer. I racked my brain all night about how the hell this could have happened. Every relationship has its issues, you know. I knew them well and saw some arguments. But nothing crazy. I feel confident saying neither of them was cheating."

"That's good to know," James said, rubbing the newly growing stubble on his face. "What kind of arguments have you heard? Being closer with them, those things will bleed out in front of people you're tight with."

"Yup, they sure do. I've seen a few over the years. Gina was tough on him, man. Not trying to speak ill of the woman, I loved her. But she liked things a certain way. Liked to wear the pants if you know what I mean. That always bothered Keith. He never really fought back, though."

James shook his head in understanding and jotted a few notes. "There's a lot of relationships with those power struggles. You said he wouldn't fight back. Did he ever talk to you about that?"

Marino shot back almost immediately, "He did. Keith was a funny guy, man. We had a ton of nights just crushing beers and BS'ing. He would complain about her all the time. Nothing crazy, mostly money related stuff. Gina didn't like him spending."

The subject of money piqued James's interest. This was a huge topic in all relationships that could spiral out of control quickly. "That's another big issue in relationships. I hear that." James said, then pausing before he continued. "How'd Keith handle that?"

"He was usually really good about it. Gina didn't know, but he had a separate account on the side he used to get the things he wanted."

"What kind of things?"

"Used to be just sports related memorabilia and whatnot. But to be honest, when this betting stuff became legal in Connecticut, Keith kind of went crazy with that."

James' eyes widened as the words came out of Marino's mouth. Was he on to something? "How so?"

"I don't know. He won big on his first bet. He got all fired up after that. Was always chasing the big win but couldn't grab it again."

James uncrossed his legs and leaned forward in his chair. "Tommy, was Keith having money issues with his gambling?"

Marino shook his head back and forth. "Nothing crazy I don't think. He got into some trouble about six months ago. Guess he borrowed money from a loan shark. But he told me that was all paid off."

"How much did he borrow?"

"Only like five grand or so. At least that's what he told me."

James's brain was spinning a million miles an hour as he finally felt he had some sort of lead to move on. Marino didn't seem to see the significance of this. Probably better that way. "Oh, well that's

55

good," James replied softly as his head slowly nodded. "Any idea who he took that loan from?"

"I don't know the guy's name. I went with him when he picked up money one time. I forget the name of the restaurant he met him at."

"You saw this guy?"

"No. Keith went inside by himself. Think the guy works there or owns it or something. We got takeout from there. I have a menu at home. I can call you later with the name, if you want?"

"Yeah, why don't you do that? I just want to make sure I look at everything and talk to everyone. Never know what's important. Ok, Tom, just give me a call when you get that info. Appreciate you coming by."

James concluded the interview and escorted Marino back toward the elevator, anxious to let the team know what he found out.

The doors to the elevator closed and James scurried back toward the office. Exploding through the office door, he found everyone standing and already looking at him. "I think I got something."

"I think you do too, kid," Dealto said. "We were watching the second half of that in my office."

"It has to be something, right?"

"Maybe. You need to call him in like ten minutes and get the name of that restaurant. I don't want to sit on this. This is all we're working with right now."

James quickly made his way back to his desk and checked the time. Staring at his watch as the seconds ticked by, he waited to make the phone call. He couldn't help but think he might have just busted the case wide open.

EIGHT

"THANK YOU SO MUCH, Tommy. Again, I appreciate all your help today. Reach out if you need anything or if you think of something else." James was so excited when he hung up that the phone bounced back off the retriever. He jumped up from his desk like a Jack-in-the-box, turning to his team.

"Let's hear it," Dealto ordered.

"Stadium Market on the east side of town."

Dealto slowly closed his eyes and grinned, letting out a small chuckle. "That's Sal Tarascio's old place. After he died, his son Carmine took over. Kid's a piece of work. Got his hand in every kind of money scheme there is."

"Everything but making a good chicken parm," Michaels chimed in with an awful Boston accent.

"Let's head out there and put some eyes on the place," James replied.

"It can wait until tomorrow, Columbo. Let's cut out for the night," Michaels said while rolling his eyes.

"He's right, Michaels. I don't want to leave and give this thing any time to grow. That's not how we do things in this office." Dealto, with his hand held up in Michael's direction.

Shaw rolled her chair back and threw two fingers in the air to gain everyone's attention. "I'll go with him. I was supposed to go out to dinner with my fiancée, but he'll live."

Dealto interrupted her as she spoke, waving his hand and shaking his head. "No, no. I'll go with him. You guys can turn it in for the night. Just keep your phones on."

James pulled out his desk drawer and retrieved his department issued Glock 19, badge, and handcuffs. He placed them on his desk, undid his belt, slid his tools on, and buckled back up. "You want me to drive, boss?"

"Already got my keys, I'll drive."

James pulled his radio off its charger and slid it into his back pocket. He snatched his jacket from the back of his chair and threw his arms through the sleeves while he walked. The two men made their way down the hallway to the parking garage. Reaching their vehicle, they hopped in and left the station.

"I need to stop at Dunkin first to grab a coffee," Dealto said.

"No problem, I could use one too."

James's brain was still turning as they made their way to the coffee shop. He was developing so many different angles in his head but didn't want to blurt them all out in front of his new boss and sound stupid, so he opted for the safe approach. "What do you think, boss? Do we have a connection here or what?"

The department's senior sergeant raised his shoulders and shook his head with a skeptical face. "Maybe. I don't like to think in absolutes. I like to dig in, build my facts and go from there. At this point, anything's possible." Dealto leaned forward and pushed the power button to the radio. Dean Martin's Mambo Italiano played through the speakers. While pointing down and nodding his head, Dealto said, "Now this is music kid. You're probably my son's age and listen to that garbage."

James laughed and looked over at the fedora, brown trench coat, shoulder holster, and suspenders Dealto was wearing. He looked like a police officer out of a 1940s movie. "No shocker to me this is your type of music. For what it's worth, my father loved this stuff too. Dino has always been one of my favorites."

"Well, that's one gold star for you. Your dad is clearly a good man," Dealto replied with a wink.

The tires screeched as the Ford Taurus entered the parking lot. Dealto stopped the car at the drive thru and waited for service. The speaker crackled and the worker requesting their order sounded like the teacher from Charlie Brown. "What do you want?" Dealto asked.

"I'll just take a medium light and sweet."

Dealto stared at him with disgust and then turned back to the speaker. "Yeah, I'll take a small black coffee. And the little boy here will have a light and sweet." Dealto glanced back at James as he spoke.

"What? That's how I like my coffee. I'm still in my thirties, man. I can't drink it like you."

"That's not coffee. That's a candy bar, kid. Your star is being removed."

The vehicle crept up to the window and James immediately pulled a twenty from his pocket and handed it to Dealto. "Well, I guess that means I have to buy then."

Dealto nodded. "Smarter than you look." With coffees in hand, the detectives made their way to the restaurant.

AFTER A SHORT FIVE-MINUTE DRIVE, Dealto pulled across the bustling street and parked in a large commuter lot on Franklin Avenue, approximately seventy-five yards away from *Stadium Market*. It was an old school looking restaurant with a retro brick exterior and neon lights which provided a cool vibe. Dealto turned the headlights off and both men sat silently for a few moments, both watching the restaurant's front entrance.

"You guys were saying this place used to be good back in the day, huh? What happened?" James asked.

"It's not that it's not good anymore. The food is still decent. When Sal died, his son took over, but that kid's always been mixed up with the wrong people."

James felt stupid that he had never heard about this place being mixed up with crime. He thought with his short time in patrol; he had had a pulse on everything going on within the city. "I never got any info about this place being involved in anything."

"You wouldn't," Dealto's face was deadpan. "This isn't low level stuff here, James. Carmine is the real deal."

"That's annoying," James said, shaking his head. "Always thought I knew what was going on when I was pushing the black and white."

"You have to understand, kid. There are levels in the street. The big-time criminals, they're businessmen. Normal guys just like us. Families, big houses, the whole nine. Those guys, the smart ones anyway, blend in with society."

"That's crazy. I've been doing this job for a while and never really saw any of that movie type criminal. Kind of knew it was real, but never got to investigate one." At that moment, James found himself becoming more and more attached to this case with every step he took. "What kind of stuff are they into over here?"

Dealto's eyebrows rose as he shook his head and threw his hands up. "Not really sure. We've gotten information about them many times, but it never leads to anything. Drugs, guns, thefts, gambling, homicides, you name it, but nothing ever leads back here. Can't pin it."

While the sounds of Frank Sinatra rang out, James watched as a man came walking down the sidewalk, smoking a cigarette while on his cell phone. He reached behind the back of Dealto's seat and slid binoculars out from the pocket.

"What do you see? My old eyes don't work like they used to," Dealto asked as he squinted his eyes.

"Just some guy walking up. Want to get a look at him." The expensive Nikon's were pressed to his eyes as he rolled the bar in the middle until the man came into focus. The man's back was to James. He watched as the guy dropped his cigarette, twisting his foot on top of it. The miscreant put his phone into his pocket, turned, and greeted another man who had exited the restaurant.

"Look familiar?" Dealto asked.

James was pretty sure he knew the cigarette smoker, but before jumping to a conclusion, he deferred to his boss. "Why don't you take a look and confirm?"

Passing the binoculars over to Dealto, the sergeant raised them to his face. While squinting through the lens, he let out a quick laugh. "Well, well. Carter Webb. You have got to be kidding me."

"I thought so. Didn't want to throw that out, though."

"Carter flew off the deep end when he left, but this is just wild."

The two men continued to watch as Webb and the unknown man talked outside the restaurant. James could barely make out what was going on without the binoculars. Webb stood with his hands in his pockets and his shoulders shrugged upward, fighting the cold night. "Looks like the other guy is getting something from his jacket pocket," Dealto said while watching closely. "Yup. He's got a letter size envelope he's handing over to Webb."

Trying to focus his eyes on the men while his boss looked through the scope, James watched as Webb looked around prior to accepting the envelope. He then reached out and took it, lifting the tab to check the contents.

"Can you tell what it is?" James asked.

"Not really," Dealto replied. "But it sure as hell looks like money to me."

Webb then tucked the envelope inside his jacket pocket. The two men turned and entered the restaurant, disappearing from view.

"What do you think?" James asked.

"The more time that goes on since Webb left, the more I think he really may be dirty." Pulling the binoculars from his face, he looked at James. "The guy was probably the best detective I've ever worked with. Human lie detector. Had a drive like no one I've ever seen. Wouldn't let a case go until everything was combed. Almost psychotic. But maybe the guy really did just have us all fooled."

James' phone vibrated in his pocket. He dug in to retrieve it and found his wife's name on the display screen. "Hey, what's up hun? I'm busy, what do you need?"

"What do I need? The boys have basketball practice in twenty minutes. Are you coming home or am I supposed to do everything?" While she talked, he heard what sounded like wild hyenas fighting in the background.

James looked at his watch and cursed. "I completely forgot. I can't believe it's so late already. Can you take them for me?"

"You're the coach!" She yelled back.

"I'll get ahold of Adam. He'll handle practice tonight."

Dealto put his hand out in front of James, shook his head and whispered to him. "No. We're good here. You have to go. Say 'yes dear, I'm on the way,' and hang up."

Not wanting to listen to his new boss, but not wanting to say no, he listened. "Ok. I'm leaving now. I'll be home shortly." James hung up the phone and placed it on his lap in disappointment. Adjusting himself in his seat, Dealto sat back and took a deep breath. "Listen, my generation took this job way too seriously and could never give it up. Don't let the job take away everything you're working for."

"It's one night boss, she'll be okay."

"No, it's one night *now*. That turns into multiple nights, and multiple practices, games, recitals, and dinners missed. That takes a toll on a relationship. My wife left me almost twenty years ago. I don't blame her. My kids hate me for it. Just look at me as the ghost of Christmas future if you keep it up."

James listened to what his boss was saying, but still didn't agree with it. Being his first big case and a chance to prove himself, the investigation was extremely important to him.

As Dealto turned the ignition, James looked up as Webb came

popping out of the restaurant and jogged down the sidewalk. "Whoa, hold up boss."

Dealto watched through the binoculars, as James squinted his eyes in an attempt to see what was happening from afar. Webb made his way to the small alleyway next to the restaurant. Approaching an older dark colored Honda Accord, Webb pulled the handle to the driver's side door and opened it. He leaned inside the car as if he was putting something in or getting something out. The door was then shut.

"I couldn't tell what he did," Dealto lowered the binoculars. Webb then re-entered the restaurant through the front door.

"Let's stay for a few more boss. My wife really doesn't care," James pleaded.

"Nope. Your divorce isn't going to be on my conscience."

Shifting the vehicle into drive, Dealto exited the parking lot. James kicked his foot against the floorboard like a two-year-old who was denied a piece of candy.

NINE

THE CLUNKING NOISE of the loose tie rod could be heard as he turned his vehicle off the main road and into the quiet neighborhood. He made his way toward the ranch style home set slightly off the road. The sun had just set with the sky still giving a slight glow, creating a silhouette around the trees. Looking up at the home while rubbing his fingers around the corners of his mouth, he checked for any movement inside.

The high pitch squeal of the window reverberated through the car as he lowered it, leaving it open just enough to hear a dog barking in the otherwise silent dusk evening. The exterior light was shining next to the front door of the ranch, which provided a view of the Christmas wreath and a small Santa character waving at visitors. Shifting his eyes to the right, he stared into the large picture window in the middle of the westside wall. The lights were on in the living room, which gave a direct view into the interior of the home. He did not see anyone.

He jabbed at the power button, turning on the AM radio station, which was playing the local news.

"The murder trial of a young man from South Lake concluded

yesterday afternoon," the commentator said. *"After three days of testimony, the jury had heard enough. Following a quick deliberation, Luis Velez was found Not Guilty on all counts."*

The man reached down, spinning the volume slightly upwards.

"You were in the courtroom yesterday, Mike, what do you think of the verdict?"

"I wasn't surprised at all. Listening to the defense provide everything they had gathered was really powerful. The state seemed completely unprepared for the angle Attorney Edwards and his team had come up with."

A slight grin curled into the cheeks of the man as he listened to the broadcast.

"I was talking with a friend of mine from the police department, and he told me the testimony of Carter Webb really sealed the jury's mind in his opinion."

"Yes, I would agree. For those listening that are unaware, Carter Webb was previously employed by the South Lake Police Department as a detective. He was a highly decorated officer responsible for some of the city's biggest arrests. Today marks the three-year anniversary of his termination."

The man squinted his eyes as he glared at the radio.

"After being unable to close a case on a one-year-old homicide investigation, Detective Webb allegedly was caught planting evidence on the scene in order to make an arrest. He was fired almost immediately after a short internal investigation."

Almost zoning out listening to the story, he looked up as the headlights of a vehicle traveled toward him. The wheels spun to the side as it turned into the driveway. It was her. The long blonde hair was pulled back in a ponytail and wiry glasses sat on the rim of her nose. Her husband, a larger, balding man, was sitting next to her in the passenger seat. She pulled the small sedan up the driveway, and the garage door opened. The brake lights lit up the walls. As the car parked, the door lowered.

. . .

HE TURNED BACK to the radio to refocus his attention on the news.

"I have to be honest, as competent a job as the defense did, I just can't seem to understand how the state dropped this case. The evidence was overwhelming when the arrest was made. Velez was found in possession of the murder weapon just blocks from the incident. While I never went to law school, I feel even I could have won this case," the reporter laughed.

Having heard enough, he tapped the power button to turn it off. Pushing the door open, he stepped out onto the black pavement while quietly pressing his door shut. He began walking toward the home as his shadow filled the street.

Not wanting to be noticed, he moved up the side of the property, which was void of any streetlights. Tucking himself behind a large pine tree, he watched through the window to see her enter the home. It was unclear if the couple was alone or if their daughter was in the back seat with them. His shoulder pressed against the bark of a tree, he watched as the wife entered the kitchen and placed her purse on the counter. She walked to the rear of the home, disappearing from view, the husband emerged with their teenage daughter close behind.

They were all home.

Carefully making his way through the wooded area, he struggled to avoid stepping on any branches as he quietly moved closer to the home. His eyes scanned the home for the illuminated red light of a camera that could capture his presence, but there were no signs of any. He slid his body across the siding and peered inside the garage window. No one else was with them.

Once it was clear, he moved away from the window and looked to the front door. His fingers combed through his greasy hair as he walked toward the door. Now standing in front of the wreath he had seen earlier; he pressed the lighted doorbell to announce his presence. A male's voice could be heard yelling to his wife that someone was at the door. He heard her respond, "I'll get it."

He gripped his jacket and pulled it outward and cleared his throat. The foots steps grew louder as she approached. The outline of her body appeared through the frosted glass as the deadbolt slapped the metal plate. As the door slowly swung open, she stood in front of him.

He watched as her eyes locked on his face, and he relished seeing her look of shock. She grasped at her chest and exhaled, staring back at him.

Looking her directly in the eye, he said, "Can I come in?"

TEN

AFTER BEING DROPPED off by Dealto, James jogged over to his car in an attempt to make it home in time for practice. The heat from the vents blew onto his chilled face as the leather he sat on became hotter from the seat warmer. He took the backroads home to avoid any traffic. The radio was turned off, and the car was completely silent. James could not get his mind off the case and wanted to make his next move. Patrol cases were always easy for him to investigate. The majority of calls he would respond to were active. Domestics where a husband assaulted his wife. Thefts from stores. Fights outside of a bar. Things that he could dissect right away and reach a conclusion. Long term investigations were going to be different and difficult for him. James hated leaving things undone.

The winding roads were dark as he navigated through them on autopilot, not truly paying attention to his driving. His brain was scattered like satellite TV searching for a station in a snowstorm.

How much could Keith have owed to a bookie that they would kill his entire family? If the goons at the *Stadium Market* were real criminals and businessmen, wouldn't they just take the father out and spare the family?

James found himself pulling up to his garage door, having no recollection of the drive he just made. The clock read 6:58 on his dashboard. He slid the shifter to park and jumped out. Jogging to the front door, he swung it open and yelled inside. "Cole, let's go, we have to hurry up!"

With eyes glaring directly through his soul, his wife stood in front of him. "He was picked up twenty minutes ago, hun. The practice is being handled," Marie snarled.

James threw his hands up in frustration and slammed the door shut. Walking back to his vehicle, he turned it off, retrieved his backpack, and reentered the house. "Why would you do that? I would have gotten there."

"No, you wouldn't have! You're the coach, for crying out loud. You have to show up for practices."

"Marie, I don't need you to tell me how to coach a game you know nothing about. Please." James knew she was right but wasn't ready to surrender yet. His new assignment was slowly taking priority in his life.

"We've only been here a couple of years. No one knows you as a head coach and no one cares where you played high school ball."

"Will you leave it alone, Marie! I run around all over this state trying to make sure we get everywhere the kids need to be. I don't need to hear this nonsense."

Pushing James to the side, Marie stomped her way into the laundry room. "Oh, and the laundry fairy came again today. Lord knows you don't know how to wash your own clothes."

Not the norm for James and Marie, but James felt she was all over him lately and he had enough. He turned to fire back, taking a deep breath as he was about to unload on his wife.

"Daddy!" Gianni screamed as he came sprinting down the hallway in his SpongeBob pajamas.

"There's my little man," James said completely changing his tune, hoping his son hadn't heard the argument.

Leaping through the air, Gianni crashed into James' chest as he caught him.

"How was school today, bud?"

"Good. It was too cold to go out for recess, so we had to stay inside."

James placed his boy back on the floor and ran his hand through his straight blonde hair. "Ahh, that stinks. I'm sure you and your friends came up with something good to play anyway."

"Yeah, we played a big game of dodgeball. My team won," Gianni said with a big smile before turning and running back toward his room.

"Go get your reading done before it's bedtime!" Marie snarled, taking her frustrations out on her innocent son.

Gianni didn't turn back, clearly pretending he didn't hear his mother's orders.

"Leave him alone. He'll be fine for one night without reading," James snapped back.

"It must be nice being the fun parent all the time. This house would collapse without me."

The comment ran true, but James rolled his eyes and moved past it, not wanting to argue. He made his way to the kitchen, suddenly feeling the need for a drink. He swung the pantry door open and scanned his bottles of bourbon resting on the top shelf.

It had been a long day.

While the majority of his time had been spent conducting interviews or doing surveillance, his brain had never stopped working on the case. This type of mental exhaustion was something he never really experienced while working patrol.

The muscles in his calves burned as he propped up onto the tip of his toes. James reached up, using all five foot seven inches of his frame to grab the bottle of Basil Haden staring at him. Sliding the bottle across the smooth granite countertop, he snatched a rocks glass and pulled open the French door freezer to retrieve one large ice cube. The glass echoed as the ice dropped inside.

The cork popped as he pulled it out, sending the promise of relaxation throughout his body. A splashing noise gushed as the bourbon poured out the tall three fingers. As he tilted it up to stop the pour, he could feel his wife's eyes burning a hole through him. Clearly, he underestimated how quickly she could fold laundry.

"It's a Wednesday night. Is a drink really necessary?"

James inhaled through his nose as his hand rubbed up and down his face. An argument was the last thing he needed. Not responding to the comment, he slid out a chair and sat at the table. Grasping his glass, he took a large swig of the drink, gritting his teeth to ease the burn as it went down. The smoky cinnamon flavors brought instant relief. "Marie, I don't want to argue. I had a long day. I just want to relax and get some work done."

James unzipped his bag and removed the entire case file for the homicide he was working on. While it was against policy to remove these files from the office, James couldn't get his mind off it.

"Are you bringing work home now, too? Really? The whole reason I agreed for you to go to polygraph school was because you told me your hours would get better, which would allow more time with the kids."

His head sank and he closed his eyes. James knew his wife was not going to go away quietly.

"First of all, you're not my mother. I don't need your permission to go anywhere," James said, still looking down. Refocusing back on his files, he continued. "Secondly, this is a once in a lifetime case. This is the type of case that could change the trajectory of my career."

"Well, is it worth ruining your marriage over?"

"Ruining my marriage. What does that even mean? You clearly have got some things you need to get off your chest. But understand that absolutely everything I do is for you and the boys."

"You could've fooled me, because it sure seems you are only concerned about yourself."

The words rang through James' ears, as they had a hint of truth behind them. While his family meant everything to him, he felt he was being given an opportunity to prove his worth within the police department. He closed the folder and slid it back into his bag, zipping it shut.

"I'll be in the basement working," he whispered. Slinging one strap over his shoulder and grabbing his drink, he rose from his seat and made his way down the hall.

The metal chain slid against the housing as he unlocked the door. He twisted the handle and descended into his man cave, the only place his wife refused to go. He knew he should have gone down there from the beginning. Retrieving his folder, he sat on a leather chair while tossing down another large gulp of his bourbon. He placed the glass on an end table next to him and dove back into his work.

James figured there had to be a connection between the family's murder and the gambling debts, but the whole thing didn't make sense to him. If Carmine Tarascio was really running the streets at a high level, this type of crime would cause too much noise for a guy like him. The screen on his laptop lit up the room as he pulled it out and pulled up the state's judicial website. He ran Carmine's name through the database for pending cases and convictions. As he reviewed the results, it looked as if he had no pending criminal cases, and his last conviction was almost five years ago.

This wasn't making any sense.

He sunk down and leaned back into the soft leather seat. James reached over and grabbed the glass, which was now surrounded by condensation. He tilted the glass to his lips and downed the last of the bourbon. Exhaling to avoid the burn, he put the glass down and stared at the wall. His brain was turning, but nothing was happening. The vibration of his phone pulled him from his trance. Michaels' name was written across the screen and James was oddly excited to be getting a call from his new arrogant partner. "Hey Michaels, what's going on?"

"Go kiss the wife and kids, then make your way back to the office ASAP."

"What are you talking about?" James asked as he stood from his chair.

"Patrol just responded to another homicide. I don't have all the details yet, but it sounds pretty similar to the one we're working on. The boss and Shaw are already on their way."

James' heart rate accelerated at Michaels' words, and he grabbed his bag. "Holy shit. I'm on my way."

He leaped up the stairway, skipping several steps on his way. He ran down the hallway and grabbed his jacket while making his way to the door. As he passed the laundry room, he caught a glimpse of Marie kneeling on the floor in front of a mountain of socks attempting to find matching pairs.

James paused at the laundry room door long enough to poke his head in. "I have to get back to work, I'm sorry. Long story,"

Marie shook her head in disappointment. "Whatever you have to do. Thanks for stopping by."

Before she'd finished speaking, James had already left, the front door slamming behind him.

ELEVEN

HE WALKED through the parking lot of his apartment complex after parking in the rear, out of sight. The large brick building was very plain-jane looking. It hadn't been updated in over twenty years, still equipped with payphones outside and several flood lights that needed to be replaced. Webb didn't care about its appearance. A place to rest his head without breaking the bank is all he needed. He gripped the satin handle and pulled the door open, entering the large foyer. Raising the top of the mailbox to apartment 856, he looked inside. Nothing, as usual.

His hands dug through his pockets as he sifted for his keys. Unlocking the secure building, he made his way to the elevator. A group of three residents chatted with one another in a small sitting area while Webb attempted to avoid them while passing by.

"Hi Carter, how's everything?" The young millennial with bleached blonde hair squealed at him.

Webb simply nodded and continued toward the elevator. The other residents didn't know much about him, which seemed to bother them. They were a tight-knit group who scheduled several building activities together to create a "family" atmosphere. Webb couldn't care less.

Quickly snapping at the button with a light hammer fist to avoid any conversation, the number eight illuminated. Webb kept his head down as he waited for the doors to open. The events over the past few days had been running through his head nonstop, making it impossible to think clearly or relax.

The chime of the elevator echoed off the marble floor and walls as the double doors separated. Shifting his eyes upward, he luckily found the car unoccupied. Conversation avoided. As the elevator reached the eighth floor, the doors opened, and he made his way toward his corner apartment. This had been home ever since leaving the police department.

While walking, deep in his thoughts with his body on autopilot, the vibration of his phone bounced off his thigh. His ex-wife Pam, whom he had remained close with, was calling. "Well, good evening Ms. Mazur. Always a pleasure seeing your name on my phone."

"Oh, stop it, Carter. It's probably the only name you've seen on your phone in the past fifteen years besides cops and snitches." Pam replied with a laugh.

"You ain't wrong about that," Webb replied while finagling with his key in the lock. Pushing the door open, he tossed his keys onto the black leather couch directly in front of him. The poorly furnished apartment screamed single man.

"So, sounds like you're a big celebrity again. Getting thugs off for murder now I see," Pam playfully poked.

Webb paused in his response as he walked toward the rear of the apartment and processed her punch. "Hey, at least one of us is able to get an innocent man off for murder."

"Ouch. It's like that Mr. Webb," she laughed again. "You know, I can still get you a job over here at the courthouse. We can always use another good inspector."

Webb smirked. "Nah, you guys don't pay enough to corral this bull. Besides, I trust you got it all taken care of. I just like to punch back when someone throws a stiff one at me, you know that."

Sliding the mortise lock over, he made his way out to the large private patio. His view overlooked the City of South Lakes' downtown area, which was still under quite a bit of construction as the local officials were attempting to revitalize the area. His fingers slid into his jacket pocket, pinching together his box of smokes and matches. Placing the filter of a cigarette to his lips, he snapped a match against the concrete wall, and touched it to the end of the cigarette. The smoke flooded into his lungs as it lit, and he exhaled the remains into the cold night.

"I heard that! I thought you quit?" Pam scolded.

Webb shrugged his shoulder and said, "Yeah, well turns out nobody likes a quitter."

"What's going on? You don't sound good. Something on your mind?"

His index finger tapped onto the cigarette to release the excess ash. Webb didn't know how to respond. Pam was the only one on the planet that could see right through him. "Just work stuff. It's complicated."

"Everything's complicated with you, Carter."

She was right. He lived solely in his head with his thoughts, talking to no one about them. "Comes with the territory, my dear."

"Carter, we've known each other since high school. You can play your word games with someone else. Don't give me that nonsense. Just because we're not married anymore doesn't mean you can't talk to me about what's going on."

Webb took the words in and lifted the cigarette to his lips, taking an extra-long pull from it. The smoke poured through his nose as he exhaled. Pursing his lips, he nodded his head. "I don't remember talking to you about this stuff when we were married either," he said, trying to deflect her attempt to get him to open up.

"You know it's impossible to progress in life if you don't change, Carter. You are the smartest, most talented, and hardest working person I know. That takes a toll on you. I'm just worried about you. I can hear it in your voice. Just talk to me," she pressed.

Webb's mind was still racing with thoughts, barely hearing what Pam just said. Grabbing a retro metal outdoor folding chair by the armrest, he pulled it backward and plopped into it. Resting his head on the back of the chair, he gazed into the dark night.

"Are you even listening to me?" Pam asked.

"Of course, I am. You were just telling me how wonderful a job I did getting that poor man off for murder. Then something about being famous. Yeah, I got it all," continuing to deflect. "What's going on with you? How's the dating world?"

The large exhale of annoyance vibrated his eardrum as he held the receiver to the side of his head. Pulling the phone away from his ear, he knew he had struck a chord. "What? Off limits?"

"It's just not important, Carter. Contrary to what you say, you know I still really care about you. I just don't want to see you go on another bender. That was really hard for me to watch."

The six months following Webb's termination sent him into a dark hole. It was Pam that helped him pull himself out and find some kind of new purpose. Being a prosecutor, she had a good relationship with Edwards and was able to help him land his new job. This wasn't the same type of breakdown, but he could feel himself sinking again.

"I know you care, Pam, and I really do appreciate it. You're probably the only one who's always looked out for me. But seriously, I'm okay. That trial just really burnt me out, that's all."

The short pause on the other end let Webb know she really wasn't buying his reasoning. "Okay. Just know I'm here if you need anything."

Webb leaned forward in his chair, smirking. A visualization of Pam popped into his head and his heart fluttered. "Anything?"

"Knock it off, Carter." Pam said through a slight laugh.

"So, how's work going for you? Any big trials or cases you're working on?"

"I'm swamped. We're running about three prosecutors down and the state's hiring process is so slow. Feel like I can't breathe."

"I told you when you moved from the private sector to the state this would happen. There's no reward for working hard. You know half those shlubs don't do a quarter of the cases you do. Why bust your ass?"

"Coming from you that's comical. You know damn well that sitting back and not working hard isn't in our DNA. Besides, I care too much. Get too emotionally attached to some of these cases. These people need to be locked away for good."

"I know I know. Just frustrating to see. So, who's on tap? Any of my old school criminals?"

"Not really. So many young kids. These eighteen to twenty-five-year old's are just a different breed. They don't care about anything." She paused. "I did just get an assault involving Sean Aldieri. You remember him?"

Webb's eyes widened as she said the name. "Yeah, one of the old goons from Darling Street."

"Yup, that's the one. I guess he's mixed up with Tarascio and his crew now. Almost strangled a guy to death with a cell phone charger cord. Weird case."

Webb knew Aldieri was running with Tarascio but didn't want to draw any attention to the matter. But he didn't like her working on anything involving them. "Listen, watch your back with those guys. They aren't to be played with. Just do your work and don't do any extra digging on them. Please."

"Wow. I've never heard something like that from you. Sounds like you really know them."

Sitting up in his chair, he took another rip from the cancer stick hanging from his lip. "No. I know the type, though. Just promise me you'll be careful."

"I will. Hey, why don't we meet up next week and get some coffee? It's been a few months."

"Sounds like a plan. I'll text you soon and we'll set something up. Let me know if you need anything. Take care." Webb ended the call.

He stood from his chair and stretched his body out while yawning. One more drag of his cigarette, pursing his lips, he exhaled. Holding up the half-smoked cigarette, he dropped what was left and stomped it out. The cold air seeped into the apartment as he opened the door. He locked the deadbolt behind him and looked around the room. The cold feel of the place lacked the warmth of a woman's touch. Webb was always a minimalist, but he did miss the comforts of the home he and Pam had built. He always tried to keep her out of his daily thoughts, as it only reminded him of his past mistakes.

He peeked his head into the spare bedroom as he walked down the hallway, which had been turned into a home office. Flicking the light switch, he leaned against the door frame, gazing at his desk. A stack of case jackets sprawled across the middle. Sitting on top, written in thick black Sharpie was "20-72913." The numbers were etched into his brain and would forever haunt him. The walls were now covered with cork board and several photos and newspaper articles were pinned to them. His head sank and he slid the switch down before walking away.

His feet shuffled across the floor as he walked into the kitchen. Swinging the fridge open, he grabbed a Miller Lite. The carbonation hissed as he twisted the cap, lifted up the twelve ounces and took a big swig. While in mid gulp, his phone began to ring from his rear pocket.

"C'mon Jonny, don't you got anything better to do than to bother me? My boss isn't supposed to be calling me during off hours," he groaned into the phone.

"Oh no, that's not the way this works, Carter. I pay you too well for you to send my calls to voice mail," Edwards jested. "Listen, I know we talked a little about Velez and the guys he's working for. Well, one of them reached out. They were impressed with our work, to say the least."

Webb let out a large exhale. "Yeah, no kidding."

"Big time. They scheduled a consult with us for tomorrow morning. I need you there. This could bring in a lot of work."

Webb thought about the statement as it radiated through the phone. "I don't know, Jonny. I'm not sure that's the kind of work I want to get involved with. Velez was one thing, but this can get out of control real fast."

"Don't worry about it. I'll handle that part. But you have to be there. They insisted. I just wanted to give you a heads up, so you're not thrown off when they come in tomorrow."

Webb closed his eyes and slowed his breathing. He just told Pam to steer clear, and here he was about to jump in bed with the mob. He felt like he could see the devil on one shoulder, and an angel on the other.

"Okay. I'll be there."

TWELVE

JAMES PUSHED the engine of his Toyota to the limits as he sped through the intersection. His car coasted under the yellow light as he checked his rearview mirror. He didn't bother to stop at the station to grab his firearm, being too eager to get to the scene. He grabbed the container of gum from its home above the gear shifter, pressed his thumb to the plastic front of the gum pack, snapped out a mint flavored piece. As he chomped away, he cupped his hand over his mouth, breathed, and sniffed. No bourbon aroma present.

Yellow caution tape was wrapped securely across the front of the home, knotted off at each end of the chain link fence as he pulled up on scene. Ramming his shifter into park just before the vehicle rolled to a full stop caused the car to jerk forward as James flew from his door like a confetti popper. He ran his fingers through his hair to look presentable with his right hand, as he lifted the yellow tape with his left and ducked underneath.

"Man, were you monitoring the radio at home or something? Michaels just hung up the phone with you." Dealto said with his head leaned back and hands in the air.

"Hey, new assignment boss. Always got to be ready."

"Well, let's go, I was just about to go find the sergeant to get the rundown."

They worked their way up the concrete walkway and climbed the few steps to approach the door. Scribbling their names in the crime scene log that Michaels already had set up, they made their way into the home. James saw standing in front of him his old street boss that he had spent two years on the midnight shift working for. The two hit it off shortly after James transferred to South Lake, finding a common connection. Each had three young boys at home.

"Sergeant Hebert, what's going on, boss? Looks like you picked the wrong day to grab an overtime shift, hey?"

"Every freaking time, James. It's like a black cloud just follows me around." Hebert said with a grin, giving James a fist bump. "But I'm on my last three, have to pull some good overtime years here to bump that pension."

"You're crazy man. That's blood money. You need to be home chasing them boys around the house. Not worth it." James shook his head. "So, you want to give us the rundown here?"

Hebert waved his hand and signaled the men to follow him toward the rear of the home. As they walked, he said, "So if you look through this window right here," He pointed to a home directly behind the crime scene. "That resident can sort of see right down into this house. She said the family had been sitting at the kitchen table for the entire day. Just thought something seemed off and made a call."

Dealto squinted his eyes while rubbing his finger against the stubble on his chin and scanning the home. "What happened when patrol showed up?"

"Routine stuff, for the most part. Rang the bell, and knocked, but nothing. Walked around the outside and peeked through the rear window. The family was just sitting at the table, completely unresponsive. They saw what looked like blood on the floor, so they called a few more units. They forced entry and cleared the home. No one inside but the four family members who were dead."

"Where's the scene?" James asked.

Hebert nodded his chin to the opposite side of the home and began walking. James and Dealto followed as they made their way across the large sprawling ranch style home. James noticed a photo hanging on the wall and stopped to point at it while they walked down the short hallway. "Damn, is that a young Pasquale Romano?"

Dealto squinted at the photo of a father and his young daughter before he pulled his head away from the frame so his eyes could focus. "Yeah, sure looks like a young Patsy to me," Dealto rubbed his hand over his mouth. "We seem to already have ourselves knee deep in the Tarascio crime family. I sure hope we don't have to deal with another. Never liked Patsy and his crew."

They continued through the home, careful not to touch anything. The Detectives entered the kitchen area. The room was an open floor plan with a large sitting area in the rear corner. Looking over to the table, James stood next to Dealto and observed the crime scene.

"Oh man," he mumbled, but the silence of the room caused his voice to reverberate.

"Yeah, no shit. Never seen anything like this one. I don't know what's happening around here lately, but things are getting weird." James looked back to see Hebert had been trailing behind them. Everything seemed to slow down around James, feeling dazed. He slowly turned back and scanned around the table, looking at each family member. His sight became blurred, with only slight focus in the middle as the tunnel vision began. Sounds disappeared and his body temperature rose. The horrific scene in front of him sent him into a mental tailspin.

Dealto slapped the back of his hand to the young detective's chest, snapping James back to reality. "Let's go get geared up and process this thing. Michaels is talking to the neighbor and making the appropriate calls."

James didn't move, staring at the horrifying scene.

"Hello! McFly!" Dealto snapped his fingers in front of James's face.

James snapped out of his daze, shaking his head to clear the fog. "Yeah. My bad. You have everything in your car?"

Dealto nodded and handed the keys to him while they made their way back outside. James double tapped the key fob to release the trunk lock as they walked up to the car. He reached for the crime scene bag, removing the camera and began taking all of his exterior shots.

"Get all your interior preliminary shots and let me know when you're done. I'm going to get ahold of Michaels to see what he's got. Then we'll go in and start processing."

James made his way back to the home, wanting to be sure he went above and beyond for his new boss. While moving closer to the crime scene, he felt an odd sense of anxiety as he approached. As he crossed the threshold of the kitchen, he took his wide view shot, without yet focusing on the family. His chest expanded as he took a deep breath and approached the table.

Even being the young, yet-seasoned officer that he was, these types of incidents weighed heavy on the mind. The coping mechanisms of joking about gruesome scenes only last so long before the brain boils over, and the intrusive thoughts take over.

His heartbeat slowed and peripheral vision blurred as he looked over the family. It looked like the front of a Christmas card. A mother, father, son, and daughter all dressed in holiday sweaters around the table. A cooked ham in the middle with side dishes around it. They all sat upright in their chairs as if waiting to enjoy the festive spread together. The father held a carving knife in one hand and a fork in the other. The pasty color of their skin and the soulless look on their faces were haunting to look at. He snapped at the shutter release rapidly while taking photos from multiple angles and ranges, attempting to avoid truly taking in the scene before him. After taking the last shot, James scurried out of the house.

The hair on the back of his neck stood up as he walked through the home towards the front door. Entering into the cold, he took a large inhale through his nose and out through his mouth to gather his thoughts. With his phone in hand, he fired off a text to Dealto, letting him know he'd completed the photos and was ready to process. The moisture from the sweat filled latex gloves stuck to his hand as he ripped them off, discarding them in the garbage. He sifted through the evidence bag, being sure to have plenty of gloves, DNA swabs and several numbered evidence tents with scales. Slinging it over his shoulder, he saw Dealto walking toward him from the neighboring home.

"Anything good?" he asked his boss.

"Not really. Seems like a pretty normal family. This neighborhood isn't exactly tight with one another, so no one has much info on them. The guy over there, though, in the blue house said the wife's father owns Romano's over on Franklin Ave."

James watched as Dealto raised his eyebrow while making the last statement, clearly looking for him to pick up on what he was saying.

"Pasquale's place," James said with a sigh. "Shit. A mob boss's daughter getting murdered is a recipe for disaster. You think this is some kind of turf war between the families?"

"I don't want to speculate about any of that yet. Always take all the facts you can gather before jumping to some conclusion. Keeping your mind open to all of it and using your facts will serve you better as you go. Plus, making assumptions with some heavy criminals like those is something we want to keep under wraps for a bit. Let's just keep it in the back of our minds and process this scene."

Both men reached into the box for gloves, being sure to double up to prevent cross-contamination.

"Anything stick out to you while taking the prelims?" Dealto asked.

"Couple things. Several areas around the home would indicate struggles in multiple places. Some small, smeared blood stains I want to be sure to swab."

Prior to heading to the kitchen where the family coldly sat, the men placed their placards around the evidence in the home, numbering each and photographing them. With a cotton swab wet with distilled water, each blood smear was lifted and placed back into its packing with the proper labeling. James watched as Dealto hummed the beat of 'That's Amore' while looking over the family, attempting to find anything that stuck out to him. His calmness in such a horrific scene seemed odd, but this was likely just another day at work to him James thought. A day he hoped to reach.

Dealto stood behind the father, looking him over. He looked back up at James and said, "You already got all the photos of them, correct?"

James nodded.

Softly moving the man's head around, Dealto began inspecting him for any signs of trauma that would give him some idea of the cause of death. After briefly looking over the father, he did the same to each member of the family. "Not a ton to go by from what I can see. Some defensive wounds on the hands that we'll have to snap photos of. But looks like the autopsy will have to give us a more in-depth look."

Dealto's eyes lasered in on something as he tilted his head while looking at the bowl of corn sitting next to the ham.

"I can already see the look. Talk to me, boss."

He slowly walked around the table toward the bowl, reaching in and pulling out a single item that was surrounded by the kernels. He held it between his thumb and pointer above his head while inspecting it.

James stepped towards Dealto and looked over his shoulder at the white pearl. It was identical to the one they pulled from the last homicide. "That can't be a coincidence, can it?" James asked.

"I don't know kid," Dealto responded, placing the pearl back into the bowl of corn and stepping back while scratching at the back of his head. "I shouldn't have lifted that before you took some pics. It caught me off guard. Take a few and let's bag that up."

"Sarge, this has some strange serial killer vibes to it."

Dealto's head slowly bobbed up and down. "It sure does. Let's take it all in and lay out the facts as we go. It looks like we have work ahead of us."

THIRTEEN

THE BASEMENT of Romano's Italian restaurant was quiet. The laughter of the families enjoying their meals hummed through the floorboards overhead. A dim, low hanging light swung slowly back and forth over Sandy Albino, one of Tarascio's top henchmen. The smell of roasted garlic filled the air of the damp, concrete room.

Albino sat on an old wooden chair, with his hands tied at the wrists behind him and his ankles duct taped together. His baby blue button up shirt was now a darker shade due to the rivulets of sweat trickling down his whole body. Blood poured from his nose into his mouth as he slowly looked up at Pasquale Romano. His lips tightened, and chest rose as he inhaled. He aimed blood infused spit at Romano's shoes and released it through the air. Looking back up, he said, "I ain't tellin' you nothin', Patsy!"

Romano sat in front of his prey and grinned slightly while looking at the phlegm dripping from his shoe. Rubbing his fingers across his mustache, the heavy-set mob boss looked away, canvassing the room. His muscle stood silent by the bottom of the stairs, having not moved once during the punishment that had been going on for over an hour.

Romano stared at a large white sink to his right. He sat stoic and unmoving as he watched the faucet slowly drip. With a loaded Beretta 92X tucked in the small of his back, he contemplated firing a 9 millimeter round into Albino for his disrespect. However, he needed information, so staying calm was necessary. The beating was justified. He turned back to Albino, staring into his eyes with quiet rage.

Albino, with his head tilted upward and eyes shifted to the top of his sight, stared back. His face was battered and bruised, but he gave the appearance of bravery.

The fat Romano leaped from his seat with the uncanny agility of a young athlete and grabbed Albino's face. With his hand squeezing both cheeks, he leaned in as drool from Albino's mouth rolled down his hand.

"You think I'm some kinda punk? You trying to test me, you little worm? You're gonna talk, or you're gonna take a dirt nap." Romano gritted through his teeth as Albino began to breathe heavier. As he moved closer, he whispered into his ear. "Don't think I don't know about your little girl scout daughter. She seems like a good kid. Daddy's problems shouldn't be hers."

He pushed Albino's face back as he released it from his grip. Romano closed his fist and reared back, crushing Albino's nose. His head snapped to the right as blood splattered to the floor. Romano moved away from Albino as he collected himself from the blow. He'd struck a chord with him.

"You're a sick bastard!" Albino yelled as his face flushed.

Romano walked toward the sink, turning the knobs. As the water gushed out, blood poured from his hands as he lathered with soap. Calmly, he shook the excess water from his hands and reached for a white towel. Rubbing his hands against the cloth, he turned and stared into Albino's eyes. Tossing the towel on the counter, he began tucking his shirt and rolling his sleeves down. Sliding his cufflinks through the wristlets of his Brioni dress shirt, he extended his arms and twisted his neck.

He ran his hands through his slicked-back black hair and turned toward his guard. The man removed Romano's sport jacket from a hanger and placed it on his boss. Brushing at the sleeves to remove any lint, he slapped Romano on the back and said, "All good, boss."

Romano nodded.

The wooden steps creaked as he climbed his way back to the restaurant for his meal. He pushed the door into the restaurant's kitchen to see the hustle of the staff chaotically working as they prepped dinner service. After closing the basement door and securing the lock, he slowly sauntered through the chaos. Without care, he sunk his fat finger into a pot of sauce, tasted it, and nodded with approval. The employees all greeted him with gestures, smiles, and hugs. He was royalty.

The double-sided swinging door pushed open, and he entered his domain. With live music softly playing, families sat and enjoyed a meal with their loved ones. Completely oblivious of the actions that had just occurred right below them. Two beautiful mid-twenty-year-old women stood and waved from the corner booth. One blonde, one brunette, but both out of his league. Shaking hands with guests as he approached his table, the women kissed his chubby cheeks when he sat between them.

The general manager wasted no time approaching and greeting his boss. "Good evening Mr. Romano. I've selected a lovely Chateau Lafite Rothschild 2002, for you tonight. It's a wonderfully pure and dense Cabernet Sauvignon. Will this be okay, sir?"

Romano nodded and flicked his fingers toward the man, then continued rubbing the thighs of his groupies.

The pop of an expensive bottle snapped as a young waitress arrived with a clean wine glass. A glass which was of much higher quality than that given to guests. Filling it halfway, the general manager placed it in front of Romano and stepped back. "Chef Giuseppe has prepared a delicious Fiorentina Steak, served with fluffy Idaho mashed potatoes. Will that do for tonight, sir?"

Romano again nodded. "That would be great, Pierre. Thank you," he replied while focusing on his women. The stem of the glass sat between his fingers as he raised it to his lips, preparing to enjoy the women, wine, and food.

Scurrying around the corner to the booth, one of his top men placed his palms on the table and leaned toward him.

"Come on, Dan, can't this wait?" He mumbled, clearly seeing the alarm on his man's face.

His man shook his head.

Kissing each woman on the cheek, he shooed them away. "Ladies, please." The women slid smiling from the booth, rubbing his chest through the opening at the top of his shirt as a farewell.

He turned back to his crony, gesturing to one of the now open seats. "Sit,"

"Boss, the jakes is outside. Parked across the street. Looks like a high-ranking detective. He's alone."

Romano shrugged, smiling. "Okay. Send him to me if he needs to talk. Not a problem."

The wine circled around the glass as he studied it in front of his face. He took a sip and swallowed it down while sniffing the blackberry aroma that wafted up.

The smile on Romano's face disappeared as he looked up to find South Lake's Lieutenant Mocarsky approaching from around the corner. A man he was familiar with from past investigations. "Dave, always a pleasure to see you in my restaurant. To what do I owe the visit?"

Mocarsky shook Romano's hand and asked to sit. Romano gripped the lieutenant's hand and lightly smacked the back of it before gesturing for Mocarsky to join him.

"Business is looking great, Pasquale. Got the place full tonight."

Romano looked at the dining room that didn't have a single empty seat. "Good food, my friend. They all come if you do it right. Can I get you something to eat?"

"No, no, thank you. My wife packed me some leftover meatloaf. She'll kill me if I come back with it."

"That's good. You have a woman that cooks. She's a keeper." Romano grabbed his wine. "So, I assume this isn't a social meeting. How can I help?" Mocarsky squirmed in his seat.

"Mr. Romano, I hate to be the one to bring this to you. No one should have to hear this. This is the worst part of my job," Mocarsky hesitated, rubbing his temple.

Romano remained calm and took another sip of his wine. "You guys have a tough job, David. Regardless of our past dealings, I respect you guys. It isn't easy." Romano watched as Mocarsky took a deep breath, sat forward, and folded his hands in front of him.

"Sir, your daughter has been murdered. We found Marie and the whole family in their home. We don't have any leads at this point. I'm so sorry."

Rage and grief flowed through Romano's soul. Who had done this? And why? He didn't want to cause a scene or allow his emotions to be displayed. He simply sat in silence and assessed the last statement. Regardless of his career criminal lifestyle, no one should have to accept losing their child.

"I don't expect you to say anything, and I'd rather not get into details quite yet. You need to take time to process it and call me so we can sit down and talk. We'll get to the bottom of this. You need to grieve the loss of your daughter right now." Reaching into his jacket, he slid his business card in front of Romano. "I'm sorry, Pasquale. Whenever you're ready to talk, call me. This is a top priority for us."

Romano closed his eyes, shaking his head back and forth. Reaching out, he shook Mocarsky's hand. "Thank you, David. I need to talk to my family, and I'll call you. I appreciate you coming down and telling me in person. It means a lot."

Romano sat alone as Mocarsky left the restaurant. His mind ran wild. He was angry and needed revenge. On whom didn't matter to him. He gently dabbed his lips with his linen napkin and rose from the booth.

As he walked toward the rear of the restaurant, his mind couldn't process what he had just been told. The guests in the restaurant were merely faded images as his vision tunneled. While on autopilot, his hand shoved the kitchen door open, as he reached for the key to unlock the basement door. Crossing the entryway to the stairs, his mind focused on one person that could be responsible. Carmine Tarascio.

His steps quickened as he descended the stairs. Sliding his sport coat to the side, he gripped the Beretta and pulled it from his pants. Albino's face paled and eyes widened as Romano closed in on him. With one swift motion, he raised the firearm over his head and sent the butt crashing down across the side of Albino's head. "Are you ready to talk now? Huh!"

Albino's head crashed to the side as he barely remained conscious. Slowly coming back forward, he looked up into Romano's eyes and blew him a kiss.

Romano's vision turned red.

The squeak of a silencer was the only thing that could be heard as he twisted it to the end of the barrel. He pressed it to Albino's temple and pulled the trigger.

FOURTEEN

PARKED in a shopping plaza in the downtown section of South Lake conducting surveillance, Webb held his phone as he scrolled through old text messages from a former CI. He positioned himself in the middle of the lot, surrounded by two vehicles to blend in. Sex workers walked back and forth in front of the store fronts, looking for their next customer. His phone screen was interrupted by a phone call from an unfamiliar number. He took a moment to decide if he wanted to pick up, then pressed the accept button.

"This is Webb," rolling his eyes preparing for an automated response.

"Hey, Mr. Webb, this is Richie James. Not sure if you remember me or not?"

Webb -of course- remembered James and was fully aware of his new position at the police department. With a few allies still on the force, he had a small pipeline into the gossip. Knowing he was likely working on the recent homicides; he was very interested in why James was calling.

"Yeah, I remember you. Transferred over, one of my last polygraphs before leaving. How you doing?"

"Eh, been better. This job gets crazier and crazier, man."

"Oh, yeah. I'm aware."

"Listen, I was hoping we could meet up sometime soon. Won't take long. I just need to pick your brain about a few things. Dealto doesn't seem like your biggest fan, and I don't want to piss off my new boss. If you're willing to, I'd like to make it somewhere outside of town. The people that really knew you said you were the best investigator they've ever known."

Webb knew this was a good opportunity to get some inside information about the recent string of homicides but didn't want James to know he was aware of what was going on. "Yeah, I heard you were working with the Deception Unit. Good for you kid. A lot of work up there," Webb refrained from answering the question.

"It definitely is. I like it so far, feels like I'm doing real police work. Anyways, you think we can meet up?"

Webb sucked at the filter of his cigarette and blew out the smoke, creating a lingering cloud inside the vehicle. "Yeah, I can do that. I'm actually about to take a break. Want to meet me over at Quinn's in Southington? Little dive bar off the beaten path on Cross Street."

"I know where that is. Be there in about fifteen, twenty minutes. Appreciate it."

The phone disconnected and Webb looked back at the building where he was conducting surveillance. What the kid really wanted, he didn't know, but this was a good opportunity to gather information.

He flicked his cigarette out the window and shifted into reverse. The car bounced through the parking lot potholes as he exited the lot, making his way toward the bar.

He became focused as he drove, eager to learn the details of the case South Lake PD was working on. There was a difference between what the public was told about a crime, and what actually occurred. He knew the Deception Unit was likely solely handling the case, so James should have all the intricate knowledge Webb needed to know about what leads they were working.

Arriving at the local dive bar, he slowly backed into a parking space. Webb entered Quinn's and walked to the back of the bar, pulling up a stool and waving the bartender over. "Let me get a tall Miller Lite," he threw his credit card down. "You can keep the tab open."

The bartender pulled the beer from the tap and slid it in front of Webb.

Webb gripped the frosted glass and took a large gulp. He placed it back on the bar top and saw James enter the front door. He raised his hand to catch his attention and waved him over.

"Detective Webb, how are you?" James asked as he reached out for a handshake.

"Detective Webb retired some time ago. Call me anything but please."

"Yeah, unfortunately. Wish I'd had a chance to work with you, man. Heard so many stories about you."

"If they were good stories, they're completely true. If not, total lies," Webb answered with a slight grin.

"All good stuff, Webb. Most of it, anyway," James gave a head tilt. Pulling the stool next to Webb back, James saddled up to the bar and signaled the bartender. "Let me get a Four Roses single barrel on the rocks, please."

Webb leaned back and looked at James. "Damn. That bad, huh?"

"No, no. I just like a little bourbon to get my head right." James looked down and noticed Webb's pack of cigarettes on the bar. "Camel Crushes, huh? Picked up a new habit, I see."

"Eh, more of a hobby." Webb's grin widened.

James didn't make eye contact with him. His body was shifted away, small beads of moisture rested on his temple, and it was too cold to be sweating.

James's sweat glands were not attempting to assist in thermoregulation, but rather responding to his stress. Webb was intrigued.

"Have to find your Zen kid, I get it. You said you're in the Deception Unit now? They send you to polygraph school already?" Webb knew of course that he had gone, but he was playing stupid trying to establish rapport.

"They did. It was great. Never saw myself getting into something like this, but it's fascinating."

Webb studied James as his knee bobbed up and down with what appeared to show nervousness. Webb cut to the chase. "Talk to me. What've you got going on?"

James tilted his glass up and swallowed the bourbon down in one gulp, exhaling as he placed the glass on the bar. "Well, before I get too much into it. I'll obviously get crushed by Dealto if he knows I'm meeting with you. What the hell happened between you two that led to you getting fired?"

Webb didn't need any new friends, so he didn't want to rehash the whole incident with James. Webb decided to give enough to the kid without really telling him anything. A common tactic used by suspects to distract inexperienced interviewers from the actual question. "We're both cops, that's all. Ego takes over sometimes. I wanted to take a case one way, Dealto saw it another. There was a little pissing match between us that ended with me without a job, and Dealto still running his unit."

"Yeah, always a lot of bravado in this field. Gets difficult to deal with when you're all trying to solve the same crime. I assume the case you're referring to is the one I'm hoping to get some answers about."

It was, but James didn't need to know that. Taking another large gulp from his beer, Webb placed it down, ignoring James' last comment. "What do you need?"

"I'm not sure how much you're still plugged into what's happening around the city, but we had a couple of wild murders the past week or so. From what I heard, the case that got you in trouble was possibly related to a serial killer. I feel like I see some similarities in these. Dealto doesn't seem to want to hear it."

"I heard about those cases. Someone was saying they thought it was mob related." Webb pried.

James shook his head and pursed his lips. "I don't know, Carter. It doesn't make sense to me."

Webb wanted James to feel comfortable sharing details, so he slapped his hand on his shoulder and smiled. "I've worked so many cases that don't make sense. Trying to make sense of them at the beginning is a mistake. I'm sure the guys in there told you that. Just start working on the case, collect your facts, and then put the puzzle together. Tell me about these cases, though. What do you guys got? Maybe I can disagree with Dealto again," Webb winked.

James paused, his palms rubbed up and down his temples. "Well, when you disagreed, not meaning the last case, of course, how did you handle it with Dealto? Like, if you had a theory you wanted to run on?"

"It's hard to say, as they were all different. I approached each one different, treating them dependent upon the individual facts and circumstances. I have no problem giving you advice on how I would handle it if I were in your position, but," Webb looked James in the eye. "I can't give you advice if you don't tell me what's going on."

James hesitated; his finger tapped rapidly at the old wooden bar. "These two cases are linked. It's gotta be a serial killer of some sort," James blurted out. "I feel like Dealto is leaning toward this being more of the mob's doing."

Webb remained calm, holding back his excitement about the details he just heard. He swallowed down another gulp of beer and kept his tone casual. "What makes you believe that?"

James's knee started bobbing again. He glanced at Webb before looking away. "Listen, Webb, I don't really know you that well. I need to solve this case. It's my first big one in this unit and as far as investigation, I heard there's no one better than you. But I feel like I could be putting this case in jeopardy by sharing some of this stuff."

Webb threw a hand up and shrugged. "You don't want to tell me, don't. You want advice, I'll give you what I can. If not, I don't care."

Using a bit of psychology to twist up the mind of James, making Webb appear as if he really didn't care, as much as he really did.

James was quiet. Webb washed down his drink and signaled to the bartender for a refill. Pushing the conversation would only frighten the kid more.

"There are these pearls. We found them at both scenes. Identical. They clearly don't belong where they were found and had to be put there on purpose."

Webb paused as the bar tender slid his new drink in front of him before asking, "What makes you lean toward serial killer and not mob-related?"

"I haven't done a ton of research into all the crime families in the area, but there's no way they're leaving behind little hints of their crime. Dealto was telling me how these families aren't dummies. They know what they're doing. Just doesn't make sense."

Webb had heard enough. He downed his second beer and said, "Just keep it simple, bud. Like I told you, it's good to have theories, but gather all the facts you can first."

Webb motioned to the bartender to close his tab. "I have to get over to a meeting at the office. Feel free to reach out, though. I have no problem helping out, just don't let the boss man know."

James nodded. "I have to hit the autopsy early tomorrow anyway. Appreciate you giving me some of your time." Both men stood and shook hands before James made his way toward the exit.

The information Webb just received was crucial.

The question now was what to do about it.

FIFTEEN

JAMES WEAVED his way around the parking lot of the UConn Health center, looking at all the signs pointing to the Chief Medical Examiner's office. With an arrow pointing to the right, he turned his vehicle into the parking lot and saw the building nestled in the back corner. It was a small building located in a somewhat remote area of the hospital grounds, surrounded by trees. He backed his vehicle in between the lines and turned the ignition off.

James had heard about autopsies in the past from other officers and this would be the first he had ever attended. He was intrigued. His foot swung from the vehicle as he opened the door. As he stood up, the smell of sewage attacked his nostrils, causing him to grimace. It was the first taste of what was to come behind the doors ahead.

James grabbed his camera bag from the back seat and slung it over his shoulder. He made his way up the walk and pulled at the metal door handle of the front door, shivering slightly at the temperature difference between outside and inside. An old looking interior with an overpowering smell of Lysol to mask the smell of death. A desk in the middle of the room, with one door with a note that states 'EMPLOYEES ONLY' to his right and an elevator to the left. He was greeted by a receptionist sitting behind the old wooden desk. As he walked toward her, he caught movement in his right-side peripheral vision, and he turned to see a woman standing in the waiting area.

"Detective James?"

Confused, James's eyes flit over the woman, trying to tell if he knew her. The woman appeared to be in her mid-forties, thin, with straight brown hair and dark eyes. Attractive. She was wearing a dark blue business suit and a white blouse. She didn't appear to be a family member of the deceased.

"I'm sorry. I'm usually great at remembering people. Do I know you?"

A soft smile appeared on the woman's lips. "We have not met. I'm Agent Brigette Nelson with the FBI. I was asked to come down and assist with this case."

"Damn. FBI. My first autopsy and I have the feds watching over my shoulder," James smiled as his foot began to tap against the tile floor.

"No, no. I'm just here to assist," she said, shaking her head. "It's obviously intrigued us a little, but I'm not here to step on any toes."

Her words calmed James down a bit. While he was confident in his abilities, when the feds showed up, everyone wanted to be on their game. Interrupted by the elevator doors opening, a woman wearing full scrubs emerged.

"Good morning. I assume you're Detective James and you are Agent Nelson?" The woman said.

"Yes ma'am. Thank you for having us. I didn't catch your name." James said.

"Oh, I apologise. Michelle Clark. I'm the medical examiner. I'll be conducting the autopsy. I assume you've both observed one before?"

"First timer here, but I got the feds on board to show me the ropes." James let out an awkward chuckle as he pointed at Nelson.

"Sounds good," Clark smiled. "Kenyese will grab you some booties, gloves, and masks. I'll meet you downstairs in about five minutes."

As Clark walked away, the two officers approached the receptionist's desk and were handed their personal protective equipment.

"What's up with the booties?" James asked as they both sat to slip their equipment on.

"You don't want anything on your shoes from in there. Go home and track brain matter all over your kitchen floor? No thanks."

"Well, booties it is, then. Thanks for the visual." James laughed. "How long you been with the feds?"

Nelson stretched the thin elastic over her shoes, trying to maneuver the covering around her ankle without grabbing anything for stability. "Coming up on twenty years. Did my first few years in my hometown with a local PD."

"Assume you're out of the New Haven office now, right? Where'd you grow up?"

"Milford, Ohio. Kind of a country girl, so this Northeast thing took me a bit to get used to. What about you?"

The two stood from their seats and began walking toward the elevator. "I just went to polygraph school out in Columbus. Really liked it out there. Had a northeast vibe, but the people were country. Just nice people. Not fast paced like here. Everyone's always so angry around here. You say 'hi' to a stranger and they look at you funny."

"Definitely different. I grew up on a farm. Been riding horses since I was eight years old. It was difficult to find that type of life here. I'm raising three kids now on half an acre. Not something I envisioned." Nelson replied as they stepped into the elevator.

"Well, you clearly love your job, then. We sacrifice a lot to do this stuff. The good ones do, at least."

The doors opened, and they walked into a hallway with concrete floors and a foul smell, even worse than the one outside, smacked James in the face. He looked up and saw a sign that read *Autopsy Room* over a pair of double doors that each had a small window which was covered, not allowing a visual of what lay behind them. Slightly further down was a small water fountain, and a lavatory located along the same wall as the double doors.

"Detective James, give me a quick rundown of what you have so far on this case. I read the patrol reports but doesn't look like you guys generated much paperwork in the bureau yet."

"Call me Richie," James said with a nod. "No need for titles when we play on the same team. So, I'm still kinda new to the unit. Getting my feet wet and trying to follow the leads. Just had a second one, pretty similar. We've been bouncing back and forth, so paperwork has been on hold."

"Oh?" Nelson said, but the complete lack of surprise on her face indicated that she knew more than she wanted to admit.

"As far as the first one goes, the neighbor hadn't heard from the family in a bit. Called for a wellness check and patrol found them all dead on the floor next to each other. Now, seeing the new case, I'm sure they were posed that way. We've tossed 'serial killer' around, but those words are a little taboo around here. Trying to collect facts before really throwing out something like that."

"Well, you seem to be an intelligent guy. We don't show up to all homicides. So, something about these cases caught our interest. Anything else of note?"

"Yup." James said, looking up to recall the important details. "We found a single pearl at each scene. Like it was planted there. The first one could've been random. The second one confirms it was placed. Hard to say it isn't related based on that."

Nelson's eyes widened and the way her eyebrows raised seem to say *'yeah, I know.'*

He pushed the door open with his palm and the large room behind it slowly opened like a Broadway show curtain. James just stood and looked at the wild scene in front of him. Approximately thirteen bodies lay on stretchers scattered around the room. There was very little space to maneuver. As he scanned, he observed all the workers dressed in scrubs from head to toe. A long clear mask covered their faces, and music from the 1980s assaulted his ears. A surreal scene, to say the least.

The bodies ranged in age. To the far right, against the furthest wall, he saw a body slightly curled up and stiff. Completely black and charred, it was clear the unrecognizable human had died in a fire. The face mask he was wearing did little to block the unbearable smell permeating the room.

"We'll be in the back. You two can follow me. We're going to start with the father," Clark said, exiting a back room and walking past them.

Like a game of Asteroids, James maneuvered around the stretchers with his eyes fixated on the bodies around him. He'd thought he was prepared for this moment, but it was shocking to see up close. As he reached the corner of the room, he stepped behind the table that Keith Daigle lay on and leaned against the wall. Wasting no time, Clark began her procedure.

James watched as she slit an X through the chest and abdomen. After pulling the skin open, Clark grabbed a large lopper tool and began cutting all the ribs as if they were tree branches. The crunch of each rib would now be etched into his memory forever.

"Agent Nelson, I haven't seen you in a while. How are the kids doing?" Clark asked.

"They're nearly grown. Crazy how fast it happens. Gretchen just started college this year."

"Wow, has it been that long?" Clark asked while pulling on the ribs to access the vital organs.

The women talking about such mundane topics added to the surrealness of the moment. James tilted his head back at the wild scene unfolding in front of him. He began thinking that the body looked like a costume. It looked fake. *How was this a person mere days prior?*

Clark removed interior organs that James could not identify and weighed them. She then cut a small piece off and bagged the rest.

"Can I ask what you are doing, or looking for?" James asked.

"Oh, I forgot you've never been to one of these. I'm first looking at the overall health of the organs and checking their weight. I take a small sample of each so we can send it to the toxicology lab."

James nodded as Clark finished removing all of Mr. Daigle's insides. Moving to the head and neck area, Clark continued. "Looks like you have a fracture of the hyoid bone. You have clear marks on the exterior of the neck, petechiae under the eyes, and the fracture. Clearly a strangulation case, but I'll wait to write everything up."

James lifted his camera and took photos of the fracture that looked more like what you'd see in a butcher's kitchen. Between the smell and just the overall visual, James was struggling to stick around. He felt trapped behind the table, pushed up against the wall. After snapping a few shots, James took a deep breath and noticed Nelson looking him up and down.

"Why don't you go in the hallway and call your boss? I'm sure he'd like an update," Nelson slapped his back with a grin, rescuing James from what was occurring.

A sense of relief came over him as he bumped into the stretcher and bee-lined for the hallway at the front of the room. Bursting through the doors, he leaned down, pressing his sweaty palms onto his thighs. After taking a few deep breaths, he straightened back up and looked around. He spotted the water fountain, dashed over to it, and began to relieve the cotton mouth he was experiencing. He took a last messy swallow, feeling the cold water trickle down his face and onto his shirt, stepped back and leaned against the wall for a few minutes, waiting for Nelson. His brain seemed scattered; something he was not used to.

"You okay, big fella?" Nelson said, laughing as she emerged from the room a few minutes later. "Everyone deals with their first one differently. You'll get numb to it, I promise."

James felt a weak smile tug at his lips as he shook his head and stood up. "Wow. That was something else. Didn't feel real, ya know?"

"Well, you popped your first cherry, my friend. You know what to expect now."

"I guess so. Anything else come up?"

"Sure did. We'll still have to wait on some of the tox results like

Michelle said, but they found a little puncture about half an inch deep on the back of his neck. Shape of a cross."

James didn't see the connection. "Okay. And?"

"Well, remember we mentioned my office working cases that intrigue us? This one had serial killer vibes. I think it's time to go talk to your boss. I think we found our connection."

James was locked back in. What a massive case this was turning into, and he was right on the front line. "Say no more. Let's go."

SIXTEEN

ON HIS WAY TO EDWARDS' office, Webb's mind was running through all the information he had taken in over the past few days. He was starting to feel himself sinking mentally, as he had done just a couple of short years ago.

The urge for the truth, no matter the cost.

Squeezing the shifter while sliding it forward, he backed his vehicle into the small lot. He sat briefly while rubbing his hands up and down his face. Taking a deep breath, he refocused his thoughts and tugged at the door handle. Webb walked toward the front door of the office, converted from an old Victorian home, and entered. He pulled on the handle and made his way in.

"Morning, sunshine." The secretary said with a smile.

"Well, hello, Ariana. How are you today?" Webb responded with a grin.

"Living the dream Mr. Webb."

"Question is, whose dream is it, Ariana?"

"Definitely not mine!" Ariana let out a loud, obnoxious laugh. "The coffee should be done brewing. Mr. Edwards asked to see you once you got in."

Webb nodded and made his way to the small kitchenette down the hall. He pulled at the cabinet handle and reached in, removing his South Lake PD mug that he used daily. Sliding his fingers behind the handle of the full pot of coffee, he poured the liquid fuel to the brim. No sugar. No cream. Mug in hand, he made his way toward his boss's office.

"Whoa, good morning sunshine," Edwards said with a big smile as Webb crossed the threshold of his office.

Webb snorted. "Do you and Ariana rehearse together or something?"

Edwards looked back at Webb in confusion.

"Never mind. What's up, boss? Heard you needed to talk." With one hand in his pocket and the other holding his coffee, he entered the movie scene office. No expense spared while furnishing. Leather furniture, hardwood floors and lighting fixtures that cost more than Webb's car. The dimly lit room gave a rich feeling to the space.

Edwards nodded his chin toward the door and pointed in that direction and Webb knew his morning was about to take a turn. He shut the door and plopped himself down on the leather loveseat. He brought the mug to his lips, endeavoring to brace himself.

Edwards sat in his high-end chair, crossed his legs, and placed his fingertips together in front of his face. With squinted eyes and no movement, Webb waited for the news.

"I got a call from Carmine Tarascio."

Webb slumped back on the couch, looked toward the ceiling, and closed his eyes.

"Will you just listen, Carter? Let me explain what's going on."

"Jonny, I can't deal with these guys. It just doesn't feel right man. Getting Gordo off was the right thing, but this is going to get out of hand quickly if we keep entertaining this stuff."

"Can I finish?"

Webb leaned forward again, resting his elbows on his knees with his coffee mug dangling from two fingers. Raising the mug, he signaled for Edwards to continue.

"Carmine couldn't make it today but wants to set up a meeting. Just the three of us. One of his higher ups has a trial coming up. They're looking to dump their current attorney and slide over to us."

Webb just sat, slowly shaking his head. "Listen, getting an innocent guy off is one thing. But I'm not defending true murderers. That's not what I do. That's not what you do!"

Edwards bobbed his head side to side while teetering his hands like a scale. "True, but this is endless money, man. Jonny needs to upgrade his Yankees season tickets."

Webb rolled his eyes in disgust.

"I'm kidding, Carter. Relax," Edwards said, sitting up with a more serious tone. "But for real. He does want to meet. Normally I'd dismiss it, but there's a problem."

Webb sat waiting, but Edwards didn't continue. Webb raised his eyebrows and widened his eyes, pushing his boss to continue.

"Pam's the prosecutor."

Webb's heart instantly sank. "Shit." Cupping his hand around his eyes, Webb attempted to squeeze the stress from his head. "It's clearly a conflict of interest for me. Not a good idea."

"Obviously. But they don't know that, Carter. After she changed her name back, I don't think many people made the connection when she moved over to this jurisdiction."

The stress was rapidly mounting for Webb. The nicotine sticks in his pocket were burning a hole in his thigh, begging to help calm him. "You aren't going to beat her in a case, Jonny. Won't happen. She's an animal in there. So meticulous."

"I know. That's the problem," Edwards said with a slight quiver in his voice. "Carter, if they can't beat her, they'll take her out. This isn't a low-level player on his team. It's one of his right-hand men."

Edwards was right. Tarascio was a loose cannon who felt untouchable. He needed time to sort this out.

"Let me think," Webb said, using the thumb of his free hand to crack the rest of his fingers. "I'm sure he's waiting to hear back. Just buy me a little time. I'll come up with something."

"I know. You always do."

Webb stood and left the office, downing the last gulp of his coffee. He proceeded back to the kitchenette for a refill, needing to slow down and create a plan. He poured another cup of coffee, and leaned his back against the counter, staring through the wall in front of him. The silence was peaceful.

The quiet was interrupted by the sound of Michael Jackson's '*PYT*' blasting from his phone. Shocked his ringer was on and embarrassed by the music, he quickly reached for his phone to end the awkwardness. One person was assigned to that ringtone, so he already knew who it was.

"What? Are you stalking me?" Webb said jokingly.

He initially only heard slow breathing into the phone, so he waited for a response. "Carter, are you around?" Pam's voice quavered.

The urgency in her voice caused him to push himself off the counter to stand up straight. "Yeah, are you okay? What's going on?"

"I don't want to talk on the phone about it. Can we meet up? Like, right now?"

His mug clattered across the counter as he bolted to the door. "Yup. Mozzicato's in ten minutes?"

"Thank you, Carter."

The line disconnected.

THE SMELL of coffee grinds accosted him as he walked through the restaurant door, the bell above it tinkling. Webb made his way to a rear booth, away from the other patrons. Sliding into the old, ripped leather seat, with the doorway in view, he waved a waiter over. "Let me get a couple Espresso shots when you get a chance. Thank you."

The waiter nodded and headed behind the counter.

His thumb tapped on the table while his knee bounced up and

down rapidly. Webb waited. Webb's eyes snapped to the doorway as the café door struck the metal bell again when it was pushed open.

Pam walked in.

She stood still while frantically scanning the room. Wearing a long red wool coat, her straight brown hair fell to the middle of her back. Sliding her glasses up to the top of her head revealed her gorgeous emerald eyes. Webb raised his hand to grab her attention. She locked eyes, put her head down, and walked over.

As she arrived at the table, the waiter placed the drinks in front of them.

"What? Are we redoing our first date here? Espressos at Mozzicato's?" There was a hitch to Pam's usual easy-going laugh.

"You obviously sounded stressed on the phone. Figured a familiar place with a happy past might be appropriate," Webb watched Pam continuously looking toward the door and windows. "What the hell's going on?"

"Ahhh, just needed a break, that's all," Pam said without making eye contact. Webb watched as her eyelids tensed, and eyes continuously widened. The facial expressions made Webb nervous, as her fear was obvious. She couldn't get comfortable in the seat, keeping her purse clasped in front of her and not removing her coat.

"Pam, I know you. You called for a reason. I don't want to go all interview mode on you and start calling things out. Just talk to me." This was not like her. Almost nothing fazed her.

She took a sip of her espresso while still eyeballing the door. "So, how're things?" Pam asked, ignoring his prodding.

"You remember back in 2015, we went to the show in the city." Pam looked away from the door and locked eyes with him. "You remember leaving, what happened?"

Pam nodded her head. "Of course, I remember."

"A Glock .45 pointed right at us. Tried to rob us," Webb paused briefly and leaned up to the table. "Pam, that's the only other time in my life I've seen this look on your face. Don't play me for an idiot. I can't help if you don't tell me what's going on. You called for a reason."

A single tear slid down her cheek and rested on her top lip. "Something's off Carter. I had a meeting set up yesterday with Sandy, my informant. He didn't show up. I called, texted, but nothing. Tried again today and his phone's off. He's never missed a thing with me in five years. Something is not right. I feel like someone's after him, or me. I'm just scared."

"Ok. I'll look into it. Can you send me all the info you have on him? I'll get started right away. Don't worry about it. Probably just off on a bender or got robbed by a hooker," Webb offered a smile, trying to lighten the mood.

The left side of her mouth slightly curled, attempting to crack a smile. "I don't think so. I know this guy well. Not his thing." Pam slowly shook her head while fiddling with her purse.

"Well, I guess I should tell you something too, then," Webb said, thinking of the information he just received prior to her phone call. "Jonny got a call from Carmine Tarascio."

Pam looked up in shock.

"Yeah, I know," Webb said, exhaling. "He wants to meet up with Jonny and me to discuss a case."

"Please don't, Carter. Don't get involved with them at all," she pleaded.

Webb placed both hands on the table and looked into her eyes. "I'm not. Calm down. You know me better than that. I just have to figure out how to navigate this."

Wiping the almost dried tear from her face, Pam attempted to gather herself. "I was worried about my CI, now I have to worry about you. Carter, Carmine's an idiot. He just doesn't care about anything. He's a real dangerous guy."

Webb nodded and pursed his lips. "I know. I can handle it. Just do me a favor and keep me in the loop with your guy. I'll start doing some digging." Reaching into his pocket, he tossed a twenty on the table. "Let's get out of here. I'd rather not be seen together for now."

Pam agreed and stood, leaving her barely touched espresso on the table. As they reached the door, Webb pulled on the handle, allowing Pam to exit first.

"Do you think this is all connected to your old case?" She asked as she walked past him.

Webb kept his face neutral. "I don't know. I guess we're going to find out."

SEVENTEEN

WITH HIS JACKET zipped to the top, he tucked his chin under the collar to keep warm while in the brisk night. His nose hovered over the metal of the zipper with his hands tucked in the fur lined pockets. He retrieved an old gold pocket watch and popped the latch. The small hand past the five, while the larger one sat on the nine. They should be leaving any minute.

Hidden approximately fifteen feet into the woods of the backyard, he watched through the large glass sliding door that allowed a perfect view into the kitchen area.

He watched as the middle-aged woman came into the room. Swiping two water bottles off the counter, she yelled something to the rear of the home. Moments later, three young children ran into view, two of whom were dressed in their team uniforms. They walked out of view and the garage light flashed on, signaling their imminent departure. Right on time.

Without moving at all, his eyes tracked as the rear fog lights brightened the driveway as the vehicle reversed from the garage. He stood rigid as the garage door closed, and the motion light turned off.

He waited for a few minutes, knowing a child could have forgotten something, but the vehicle did not return.

Each step slowly and softly hit the grass as he approached the rear of the home. Careful not to activate the floodlight, he looped to the side of the house and then moved flush across the rear siding. He reached one of the three rear doors just outside the laundry room; this would be his entry point. A door he had not seen the family use, but a door with no deadbolt.

With his pocketknife in hand, he used his thumb to push on the flipper, exposing the blade. Pressing his body against the door to create a slight opening by the handle, he pushed his knife inward against the striker plate. Feeling the blade maneuvering the latch bolt, he pressed in, releasing the door from its frame. He was in.

Quietly stepping into the home, he gently closed the door just in case anyone was left behind. With each step, his foot touched the hardwood as if he was walking on a cloud. Coming around the corner, he observed the living room and kitchen. An open floor plan. The gas fireplace lit up the high ceiling living room and empty food wrappers were lying on the end tables. Stopped, he briefly listened. Quiet.

He stepped into the sunken living room and approached the fire. Crouching in front, he raised his hands and rubbed them together to warm up. As the friction warmed him up, he stood, walked to the couch, and sat down.

With an eerie grin on his face, he twisted his head from left to right, observing the inside of the home. There were photos of the "happy" family everywhere. Locking in on the mantle, several frames were standing there. Tilting his head to the side, a photo piqued his interest.

With his hands on his thighs, he pushed up from the deeply cushioned couch. Locked in on the photo, he approached the mantle.

The family of five was dressed in suits portraying a mobster family from the 1920s. Pinstriped suits and fedoras on the men, and the mom decked out in a sequined dress. The father held a prop gun in his right hand, with his left hand grasping the lapel of his jacket. He exhaled with a slight chuckle.

"Such a beautiful family. I'm sure you're just perfect." He whispered to himself.

Flipping the frame around, he tugged at the clips to release the backing board. Tucking it in between his fingers, he pushed the glass upward to gain access to the photo. Taking it out, he replaced the backing board and sealed the frame back up. Reaching upward, he placed the empty frame back onto the mantle and walked toward the laundry room. His feet shuffled along the floor with the picture held in front of his eyes.

He reached for the doorknob and opened it, feeling the cold air flood toward his face while he stood for a moment with his eyes closed. Before exiting, he stopped and looked back into the home. "Make sure you all do your homework," he murmured.

As he emerged through the doorway into the backyard, he softly closed the door, confirming it was again locked. Slowly walking through the backyard, he disappeared into the night.

EIGHTEEN

THE GATE ARM rose as James pulled the police Taurus through the parking garage. The sound of the tires screeching echoed throughout. He approached the area for detective vehicles and found an empty space. He swung the door open as the black SUV that had been following him pulled alongside. Standing in between the vehicles, he waited as Agent Nelson gathered her belongings.

"Damn James, you drive like Andretti. I almost couldn't keep up, and that's saying something."

James threw his hands up. "Life's short. Gotta take chances," he smirked. "Let's go in so I can introduce you to everyone and get you caught up."

They walked down the concrete ramp as Nelson looked around the area. "Looks like a pretty nice PD you guys got here. Newer too, no?"

"It is. I've only been here a few years, but from what I'm told the last one was covered in asbestos. Had it been a school, it would have been condemned ten years earlier. But we're only cops," James joked.

"Hey, life's short, gotta take chances, right? A wise man once told me that," Nelson replied while tucking a loose strand of hair behind her ear and smiling.

As they made their way into the building, James got a call from Dealto. "Hey, you going to be back soon?"

James smirked again. "Maybe, what's up?"

"The FBI is involved. Been going back and forth with them all day. They're sending an agent over now, I guess. I didn't get a ton of details but wanted to give you a heads up."

James smiled at Nelson, wanting to surprise his boss with their arrival. "I can't hear you; you're breaking up boss. You there?"

"Can you hear me now? Richie ...."

James pulled on the metal handle to the Deception Unit office door, swinging it open to see Dealto with his head tucked by the window trying to access better cellular service. Turning around, he noticed his new detective. Hanging his phone up, he slid it back into his pocket. "You're an asshole." Dealto said, his face deadpan.

"Please, not in front of the agent, boss," James said sarcastically. "Sir, this is Agent Brigette Nelson with the FBI. We were just hanging out with some dead people and got to talking. Thought I'd bring her over to meet everyone."

A flustered Dealto walked over and shook Nelson's hand. "Sergeant Dealto, nice to meet you, ma'am. You can call me Dom. I see you met my newest headache here."

"Doesn't sound like that headache will be around long if he keeps up his antics," Nelson raised an eyebrow at James, a small smile playing at the corners of her mouth.

"I like her already," Dealto responded with a smile and nod of the head.

"Listen, Sarge, I'm not here to step on anyone's toes. I don't know what you heard from my office, but I'm merely here to assist. Whatever you need."

"I appreciate that. This thing is starting to spiral a little. Want to get out in front of it, ASAP. Having the feds at our disposal always makes things easier. Did George Carlin here catch you up to speed?"

"For the most part, yes. But I wanted to go over something we caught at the tail end of the autopsy." Nelson placed her folders on James' desk and shuffled through them, pulling out a piece of paper with an anatomical drawing. "While checking the body for wounds, the examiner observed strangulation marks around the neck as well as the petechiae. However, there was also a very small puncture on the back of the victim's neck."

Dealto sighed and rested his elbows on the countertop. Placing his hands on the side of his face, he rubbed them up and down. "Great. I was worried about that. But didn't want to disturb the body at the scene. Was just hoping it wouldn't be there if I didn't look."

"Yeah, we had some suspicions, but the killings were a little different than in the past. We wanted to confirm." Nelson responded.

"So, it is a serial killer? I heard some of the old timers talking about it at the main desk." James looked between Dealto and Nelson.

"Sure looks that way," Nelson replied. "Or you have a copycat on hand. Does he know about this case, sarge?"

"Not really," Dealto shook his head.

James looked on like Gaylord Focker, waiting to be let into the circle of trust.

"Webb. He was working on this before the whole termination thing went down." Dealto said finally, straightening and standing akimbo.

"Obviously those weren't solved. I assume we have a bunch of case files we can study and try to pick up some clues." James rubbed his hands together, feeling his face flush with excitement.

"Yeah, we do," Dealto said contemptuously. "Listen, kid, you have to understand something. Being up here, you're going to be privy to a lot of information. That information has to stay here. Understand?"

"Of course, boss."

"After Webb got let go, we did a lot of digging on him. There were people that thought he was the actual killer and was throwing these cases intentionally. It really makes a lot of sense."

James rolled his eyes and crossed his arms. "Really?"

Dealto simply nodded his head.

James looked over at Nelson, seeing if his boss just had it out for Webb, or there was some real truth to this.

"It's definitely a possibility, from what I've been told." Nelson agreed.

James spun around, walking toward the window. Knowing that he was having beers with a possible serial killer just a day prior made him sick. He replayed the conversation in his head, just now realizing that Webb was working him over for information. How could he possibly have fallen for it?

"I know it's a shock, kid, but it looks like you just lost your best friend. What's up?" Dealto's brow furrowed.

James turned back around and reapproached the two. Not wanting them to know of his meeting with Webb, he pushed the conversation along. "No, it's just crazy, that's all. Where do we go from here?"

"Why don't you two head out and try to get eyes on him? Can't hurt to see what he's up to."

Nelson raised her keys in the air in front of James. "I'll drive. I don't trust my life in your hands after your last driving display. My kids need mom to make it home at some point."

James threw hands up to surrender, grinning. Looking over, he saw Dealto was scribbling something down on a small notepad.

"Here, this is the last address I knew he was staying at," Dealto said, handing over the notepad. "Saw him at court recently. He's still driving that dark, beat-up Honda Accord."

"I don't have a lot of details on this guy, Sarge. Just read his name in the files. Anything I should be aware of about him?" James asked.

Dealto took a deep breath and leaned back against the wall, folding his arms. "He's smart. Best cop I've ever worked with or been around. It pains me to say that too because he seems to have become such an asshole."

"I can work with that," James said, feeling confident in his abilities and now overly cautious of everyone.

Dealto let out a small exhaling laugh. "Can you? That's what everyone says. Carter is always steps ahead of everyone here. Sees things we don't see. Just an unbelievably savvy guy. I'm not saying you're not smart, but just remember, if you think you understand him or think you know what he's going to do, that's when you're in trouble."

The words struck James hard because it's exactly what he just went through with Webb. Wishing he had heard this a few days earlier, he made his way to the door and motioned Nelson to follow. "Let's do this."

While walking down the hallway, Nelson was still holding her files and flipping through pages. "You got some test answers in there or something?" James prodded.

"I'm just an over-preparer. Like to have my details in line, that's all."

"Anything else you want to tell me about this case? Seems you have more information than I do," James said, a slight edge to his voice.

Nelson rolled her eyes. "Oh, stop it. You're just like all the guys in my office. Knowing you were newer in that unit; I wasn't sure what you had been briefed with so didn't want to bring it up. I figured you wouldn't have much knowledge of it."

"Fair enough."

They exited the building and made their way back to Nelson's Ford. As Nelson got onto the main road, James slid his phone from his pocket and called his wife. "Hey hun, just checking in on you guys."

"Hey, I just finished a run and am getting the boys off the bus now. How's work?" Marie said, short of breath, while greeting her children.

"Interesting to say the least."

"I don't want to know. You know that's not my cup of tea. Don't know how you can handle that stuff."

"I never tell, you know that."

"Hey, meant to ask this morning. Did you take the family picture out of the frame on the mantel?" Marie said with sheer confusion.

"Take it? What do you mean?"

"I don't know, the frame's empty for some reason. Kids must be messing around. Not a big deal."

"Hey, I think that's him right there at the gas pump," Nelson pointed across James' face.

"Who's that?" Marie snapped inquisitively. "I thought you said Shaw was off today?"

James looked over at the gas station. "Yup, that's definitely him. Great eyes, can't believe you saw that."

Nelson smirked and pulled across the street to keep eyes on their target.

"Do you hear me?" Marie asked.

James was locked in on Webb but could vaguely hear Marie in the background. "Yeah, yeah. I hear you. I gotta go. Something just popped up."

"Richie!"

James ended the call, sliding his phone back into his pocket. "Looks like he's about to take off. Keep a little distance."

Nelson tilted her head down and looked up with a slight smirk. "Thanks for the advice. It's my first time doing surveillance. Not sure how I'd survive without you."

The vehicle exited the adjacent lot and Nelson maintained a safe distance from Webb, leaving a vehicle in between them. Keeping their distance, they were able to follow seemingly unnoticed. As they approached a four-way intersection, Webb's vehicle pulled up to the stop sign and held momentarily. The vehicle in front of them stopped behind Webb, as they approached directly behind. Too close for comfort while tailing someone.

James flipped his visor down in an attempt to hide his face in an attempt to stay unnoticed.

Nelson was peeking past the vehicle in front of them at Webb's. The Honda then proceeded forward. "Looks like he glanced back here, but I don't think he noticed us."

The Chevy in front of them turned right, leaving no one between them and Webb. Nelson stalled at the stop sign, then slowly continued. With his eyes locked on Webb's vehicle, James watched as his right blinker illuminated, signaling a turn onto Sefton Drive.

"Safe to follow down there?" Nelson asked.

"Yeah, it's a cut through. Won't get stuck, just pull up slow in case he pulled over."

As they approached the turn, Nelson slowed down and turned on to Sefton Drive. James looked out his window but did not see Webb's vehicle. "Shit, speed it up."

Nelson accelerated down the street as James checked each driveway in case he'd tried to tuck behind a house. "I got nothing."

They scanned all the side streets as they passed, but Webb's vehicle was gone. Coming up to another stop sign, they stopped and looked in both directions.

"You gotta be kidding me." Nelson leaned back in her seat, running her hands through her hair. "Is there any way he could've seen us?"

"I'd find it hard to believe, but who knows? I'm sure tailing someone in this obvious fed car didn't help. Even still, that'd be impressive."

"Yeah, no way he saw us. That was barely a couple of minutes. If he did see us, he's clearly up to something. Why else would he be looking?"

James bit his bottom lip and gazed out the windshield.

"I don't know, but something's not right."

NINETEEN

AS HE PULLED his Honda into the lot across from the Stadium Market restaurant, Webb flicked his headlights off and parked. His mind was racing as he became increasingly worried about Pam.

Webb needed to keep a close eye on Tarascio and his crew. He reached for the binoculars on the passenger seat and focused them across the street. It seemed to be a slower night for the eatery, as the parking lot was less than half full. The light from the restaurant's neon sign slowly blinked, bouncing off the windshield of the Honda.

Looking to the rear of the establishment, he saw Carmine Tarascio sitting by himself, drinking a draft beer. His men a short distance away, leaned against the bar while talking to a group of females. Webb decided against entering the restaurant and continued to watch.

Tarascio lifted the glass to his mouth and inhaled the remains of his beer. He stood from his small table and made his way toward the entrance, momentarily disappearing from sight.

Webb dropped the binoculars to his lap, watching as the door swung open, revealing Tarascio by himself. He milled around on the sidewalk, talking on his cell phone. His hair was slicked back, and with the top button of his shirt undone his gold chain gleamed in the streetlight.

Just his appearance sickened Webb.

As he reached the end of the brick building, Tarascio slowly moved toward the side, out of sight. Webb knew this was his opportunity to approach without being seen by anyone.

Webb exited his vehicle and reached for a Camel Crush. He struck a match, inhaling the nicotine into his lungs. With the cigarette in hand, he zipped his jacket and made his way toward the building with his head down and eyes looking up. The full moon lit up the dark clear sky and streetlights illuminated the sidewalks, making it easy to navigate. He could see Tarascio on the side of the building with one foot against the wall, leaning back, still talking on the phone. Not wanting to approach from the front, he made his way to the far side and around the building. Scanning the back of the building, he observed a cook throwing a trash bag into a dumpster. Hidden behind the corner, he waited as the employee reentered the restaurant, leaving no one but Tarascio in sight.

Webb slipped across the rear alley and leaned his head to the far side, seeing Tarascio in the same spot. Revealing himself to Tarascio, he made eye contact and waved him over. "Carmine, we need to talk."

Tarascio looked up with a confused yet concerned look. "Hey, lemme call you back," he said into the phone as he ended the call. "We got a problem, pal?"

Webb rolled his eyes at the fake tough-guy persona Tarascio portrayed. "It's Carter Webb," he replied as Tarascio moved closer with his hand tucked behind his back.

"Damn, Carter. You almost caught a bullet to the ol capo, you mameluke," Tarascio replied with an annoying cackle.

Webb's blood pressure rose just being in the presence of the obnoxious mob boss. He breathed in through his nose to calm himself. He needed answers to secure Pam's safety. "I spoke to Jonny about your meeting. I need some information before I decide to help out."

"Ohh," Tarascio said, throwing his hands up. "There's only so much I can tell you, Carter. I just need you to get my guy off, that's it. I promise it'll be financially rewarding for you."

Webb stood still, staring back at the middle-aged prick. "Your father was a hell of a guy. Regardless of his business dealings, he was genuinely a good man. Kept all his business in house. I can't say you've been operating the same way."

"You're right, you can't, but," Tarascio shrugged his shoulders. "I get things done, Carter. That's all that matters to me."

"See, that's the problem, Carmine. You drag too much of your dirty laundry into the streets."

"Listen, if you came here to tell me how to run my business, you can bounce. I don't got time for some has been cop trying to tell me what's right and wrong."

Webb ignored the jab and continued to stare motionless at the man. "What if I don't think I can help? Then what?"

"Then I need to handle things my way. I actually called Jonny, trying to do it the *right* way. Keep things quiet. You're the only one I can see capable of beating this bitch prosecutor."

That one stung, and Webb could feel the intensity of his heartbeat as he exhaled. "Who's the prosecutor?" Webb asked, trying to see if the connection was made.

"Some hot shot trying to make a name for herself. Mazur or something like that. My people on the inside say she's a real killer. Impossible to beat." Tarascio took a cigarette out of his breast pocket and put it between his lips.

Webb took in the information, knowing where the conversation was heading, but needing to hear it before deciding what to do. "And if I say no?"

Tarascio slid a cigarette from the box in his jacket chest pocket and placed it between his lips. As it dangled around, he flicked his thumb across the rigid metal of the lighter, firing it up. He looked up and exhaled the smoke into the cold air. "Then we do what we have to do to get her off the case."

Webb's nostrils flared as the words left his lips. "You'd risk killing a prosecutor to get your guy off?"

Tarascio threw his hands up. "Whoa! I ain't killin nobody," he exclaimed, taking another pull off his cigarette. "I got people for that, Carter." He laughed and slapped Webb's shoulder.

Webb turned and ran his hand through his hair. "That'd be a mistake. You don't want to do that." He turned back around and looked Tarascio in the eyes. "I know I can beat the case. I can't have innocent people getting dragged into this."

"What makes you so sure you can beat her? Rumor has it, she don't lose."

"Just give me some time to look into it all," Webb said, trying to buy himself some time to create a plan. "No one's beating me, Carmine. I don't lose."

Tarascio smirked as he sucked at the remains of his cigarette and threw it down. Blowing the smoke in Webb's direction, he twisted his foot over the butt. "I like you, Carter. We can make some real money together, ya know."

Webb raised his hand in front of Tarascio. "Just this one time. Let me go through the details and we'll see what we can do."

Tarascio draped his arm around Webb as they walked to the front of the building, squeezing his shoulder. "Well, you think about it, my friend. That offer won't be hanging out there forever. It's quite the opportunity."

Webb rolled his shoulder to remove Tarascio's hand as he stepped away to create a little distance as they walked. "I'll keep it in mind."

Webb allowed Tarascio to walk in front of him as they made their way to the front of the restaurant. Staying back in the small alleyway, Webb watched Tarascio turn the corner toward the front door. As he watched, a vehicle parked a block away pulled out from the side of the road. The vehicle's headlights remained off as it inched toward them. Webb narrowed his eyes and felt as if he could see the situation unfolding in slow motion. The window of the vehicle lowered, and the front passenger was holding a firearm. The driver's head was tucked low, staring at Tarascio as he walked.

"Shit." Webb mumbled under his breath.

Without a second thought, Webb sprung from the side of the building, sprinting toward Tarascio. Tarascio turned at the sound of Webb running. Tarascio walked backward to avoid Webb, reaching for the small of his back.

With his arms extended, Webb leaped toward Tarascio as he attempted to grab his firearm. As his right shoulder crashed into Tarascio's gut, several shots were fired at them. The bullets ricocheted off the brick and small pieces of dust flung through the air. Webb and Tarascio slammed to the ground, and the squeal of tires echoed as the vehicle sped off.

The front door of the restaurant flung open as several members of the crew came running out with guns drawn. Webb looked up as the men began screaming, pointing their guns at his torso. Webb simply rolled onto his back and raised his hands. Taking a moment to breathe, he didn't feel any pain and knew he had not been struck. At least not yet.

Tarascio jerked up into a kneeling position. "Easy, easy! He's all right!" He yelled. With one knee propped up and his arm resting on it, Tarascio looked over at Webb. "You son of a bitch. I thought you were coming at me. Come to find out, you were protecting me."

Webb hopped to his feet and dusted himself off. Extending his hand, he grabbed Tarascio's and pulled him up. "Eh, I just reacted. Can't help myself. Bad habit, I guess."

"That looked like one of Romano's guys. What the hell's that all about?" one of Tarascio's goons exclaimed.

Tarascio's eyes darkened as he shook his head, looking down the street in the direction of the vehicle. "I don't know. Seems like we got ourselves a problem." Tarascio combed his fingers through his hair. "Carter, I owe you for this. You let me know what you need."

This was not the plan to be in even deeper with the Tarascio family. He looked up as they all heard sirens in the distance getting closer.

"Go ahead," Tarascio said. "Get outta here. We'll take care of this."

Webb simply nodded and jogged across the street toward his vehicle.

TWENTY

JAMES SHOVED the last bite of his meatball grinder into his mouth, got up from the booth, and tossed his wrapper in the receptacle. "You ready to head back?"

Chewing the final mouthful of her BLT, Nelson stood and nodded her head.

James grabbed his radio off the table with a scowl on his face. As the two of them walked towards the exit, a loud tone screamed from his radio, which was tuned to the patrol channel. James knew from the familiar tone he had heard many times before that a serious incident had just occurred.

"All units, multiple calls for shots fired in the area of the Stadium Market. Complainant reports a dark colored vehicle was seen fleeing southbound from the scene."

James grinned, tilting his head, and raising his eyebrows at Nelson. "Well, guess this night ain't over. Let's roll."

They sprinted out to Nelson's SUV, and she tossed her keys to James. "You drive, I don't know this area well."

James caught the keys, his grin broadening. "I knew you loved my driving."

They jumped in the vehicle, and with James' foot pressing down on the accelerator, the two sped off out of the parking lot, still several blocks from the scene. Almost immediately, James saw a vehicle speeding toward them. Slowing down, he noticed Webb's Honda fly past them on the left. "You gotta be kidding me?"

"Yup, I saw it. Flip it around," Nelson replied.

James spun the wheel to the left, quickly pulled into a driveway and reversed. They heard the tires underneath them squealing as he accelerated the SUV to the limits in the endeavor to catch up with Webb.

"He's really moving," Nelson said.

"I'll get up there, don't worry."

The Honda became closer and closer as James sped through the main artery streets of the city. The traffic light blinked yellow and low traffic allowed for a quick tail. As they got closer, James was able to make out the license plate he has already memorized, confirming it was, in fact, Webb. Once confirmed, he backed off slightly to create a buffer. If Webb was leaving the scene, then he would be on high alert for a tail.

"I think I should just call it in and get him stopped. What do we have to lose? Let's take our shot." Nelson said, pointing to James' radio.

"No, don't. He might be leaving the scene, but he shouldn't have any idea it's us following him. We have to keep this close to our chest while we figure it all out." James said, shaking his head.

Nelson tsked as she exhaled while focusing on James's driving. "I guess," she expressed in a monotone voice.

They approached the downtown area and Webb was closing in on the entrance to the highway. Without signaling, his vehicle sped off onto the interstate. Trying to close the distance, James turned into the on ramp, but Webb was already too far ahead. Not wanting to alert Webb any more than he may have already, James pulled to the side of the ramp and parked. James slammed his hands against the wheel, frustrated that they had now lost Webb twice within a few hours.

"It's fine. If he was involved, he's not going to go anywhere that'll cause issues for him. He'll likely just drive for a bit and let the dust settle."

"I don't know how you remain calm like this. I don't operate at that pace. My brain won't shut off until I've got what I'm looking for."

Nelson looked out the window and bit her bottom lip. James noticed and guessed her brain was also spinning with something. He stared directly at her, waiting for her to notice his eyes burning through her. After several seconds, she turned from the window and focused her eyes straight ahead.

"I see you looking," she murmured. "I promised myself I wouldn't get all wrapped around the axle on this one. You and I are one and the same. I've always had trouble pacing myself. But I've gotten really good at it over the years. The agents I work with don't have that mentality."

The side of James' mouth slowly curled upward. "Talk to me, girl."

The air released from Nelson's lungs in defeat. She repositioned herself in the seat to face James. "I've spent a lot of time looking at these cases, formulating a profile for this killer. Carter fits the description really well, but ... something just doesn't add up to me for him."

"Well, it's starting to add up to me."

"Yeah, but you have to understand the psychology of a serial killer. There's a reason. I just can't make the connection with him."

"Guy's an oddball. I know he's smart and was great at what he did, but he ain't all there, Nelson."

"A lot of people said he went crazy over this case though. I know you don't know a lot because it was so hush hush, but he was taking time off and working the case on his personal time."

"Working the case or covering his tracks."

Nelson slowly shook her head. "You all look at it through that lens. You have to step back and put all the pieces together. Can't force the pieces in where they don't fit."

"What you're trying to tell me is that Webb planted evidence on some guy to take the fall for the killings, but that was just coincidence? Had nothing to do with Webb being the real killer, right?"

"Listen, I don't know. I'm not ruling him out, I just need it to make sense to me."

"Well, it does to me. So, what's our move here?"

Nelson rolled her neck around, face scrunched in thought. She stopped rolling her head, and slowly nodded, turning back toward James. "Jimmy Zaniewski."

James had no idea who that was or what she was talking about. He shook his head in confusion.

"Jimmy was the guy Webb tried to frame. He wouldn't talk to the local police or feds at the time. It's only 9 o'clock. Let's go pay him a visit."

James slid the vehicle into drive and accelerated onto the highway. "Address?"

Nelson began flipping through her files, muttering to herself. "Jimmy, Jimmy, Jimmy. Ahh, here we go. 20 Taunton Street, third floor."

"It's right off this exit, about a block down. See," James chuckled. "Can't always give up and be patient. Sometimes you have to go get it."

Lightly pressing on the brake to slow the vehicle down as they exited the highway, James rolled toward the red light. Not seeing anyone coming their way, he sped through the intersection and approached the street on his left.

"Just like that," James made the turn and pulled up to the three-family home.

"Damn. Place is a dump. For a decent neighborhood, this house looks totally out of place," Nelson replied with a breathy, almost whistling tone while rolling her eyes.

"Welcome to South Lake, young lady. The armpit of America."

James and Nelson exited the vehicle, stopping to look over the home. James made eye contact with Nelson, motioning toward the exposed badge on her hip. "Let's cover up to start, don't want to spook him early." Nelson nodded and pulled her jacket to the front and buttoned the bottom to hide her credentials. James followed suit.

James stepped up the old wooden stairs to the front door. The old home's foundation had settled unevenly, causing the porch to slope downward. He cupped the side of his hand to the thin window next to the door and peeked inside.

"Looks like a foyer." He gripped the handle and swung the door open, holding it for Nelson to follow him. As he stepped inside, he looked over the metal mailboxes affixed to the wall. The only one that was labeled was the first floor, which read "landlord."

"Might as well start here."

James rapped the wooden door multiple times with his middle knuckle, trying to stay away from the hard "cop knock." He leaned in and pressed his ear to the door in an attempt to hear movement from within. The sound of slippers sliding across a linoleum floor grew louder as they moved closer. James backed away, throwing a thumbs up to Nelson.

The deadbolt smacked back, and the door was pulled inward. A tall, older white male in his sixties stood in front of them. Wearing flannel pants and an old Ralph Lauren robe, he looked up at them, confused.

"Can I help you?" he spewed with his eyebrows lowered and pulled close together.

James glanced at Nelson, knowing it might be easier for the attractive agent to get the information they needed. She made eye contact and appeared to be on the same page.

"I am sorry to bother you, sir. I know it's a little late, but we were hoping you can help us out?" Nelson unbuttoned her jacket and pulled the side back to expose her badge.

James rolled his eyes and loudly exhaled through his nose. "So much for not trying to spook him," he whispered.

The man leaned in, squinting his eyes while trying to make out the letters on the gold badge on her hip. "FBI? Again? It's been a few years since that all went down. What the hell happened now?"

James and Nelson again made eye contact at the comment.

"Oh, no, nothing wrong Mister ... what was it?"

"Hinkson. You can call me Dennis though, dear." Awkwardly wiggling his eyebrows up and down.

James quickly tilted his head downward, covering his smile at the old man's attempt.

"Nice to meet you, Dennis. I'm Brigette and this is my partner, Richie. We're looking to talk to Jimmy. Have you seen him today?"

The thin Irish looking man tilted his head, looking at them like they were stupid. "Jimmy? I haven't seen Jimmy in years. He moved out shortly after all that stuff with the case."

"Any idea where he moved to?" James questioned with a pen and notepad now in hand.

"Beats me," Hinkson raised his shoulders. "He just up and left. I mean, I felt kind of bad. Everyone thought he was odd, and the neighbors were uneasy around him. But killer? I don't know. I think you have a better chance of finding kiddie porn on his computer before a dead body in his closet." Hinkson rubbed the back of his neck and let out an awkward laugh.

James continued to prod. "Did he say anything before he left? Give any indication where he was going?"

"Nope. The whole thing was kinda odd. The guy was a loner, but he'd talk to me a little. Not like him just to leave. He even left most of his stuff behind."

James turned away frustrated, rubbing his hand through his hair.

Nelson threw James a look that was both placating and suppressive before continuing. "What about his stuff? Did you get rid of all of it?"

"Most of it, the junk, anyways. I boxed up a few things and threw them in the basement," Hinkson said, pointing to the door next to them.

"If it's not too much trouble, we'd love to take a look at some of that stuff. Seems as if it's been abandoned after all this time."

"Sure thing, dear. Gotta warn you though, it ain't the nicest down there."

"That's all right, Dennis. I'm not judging you." Nelson batted her eyes and smiled. Hinkson grabbed the keys from the inside of his apartment and held them in front of his face, attempting to find the one he needed. There had to be fifty keys on the ring, none of which were labeled.

"Ah, here we go," Hinkson said as he exited his apartment into the hallway where the basement door was. He opened the door and reached his hand to pull the dangling string from a bulb above and light up the stairway. "There's no handrail here, so be careful."

An eerie feeling slithered over James as he peered down the stairway. He stepped through the doorway and made his way down, his hand on the wall for support. Hinkson led the way as he slowly took one step at a time. Nelson followed, with her hand on the shoulder of James for support. The stone and brick walls were not smooth; they were jagged as if the foundation was built by hand. Reaching the bottom, James heard a loose crunch under his shoes and looked down to see the floor was all dirt. The ceiling was no more than seven feet high. James felt his claustrophobia creeping in but tried to ignore it.

Hinkson pulled on two more hanging strings to give a small bit of light to the area. James looked around at the cluttered space. With only two lights to illuminate the room, James eyes squinted to gain focus. A thick layer of dust covered all the boxes and random items, indicating no one had stepped foot down here in quite some time.

"His stuff is back there in the corner. Some of his things may be a mite damp; I've had a little problem with water leakage in recent years. Can't seem to find the problem, not that I've really looked," his grin was lopsided. "I'm gonna head up to get back to my program.

You folks just give me a holler if you need something. I'll leave you to it."

James bent down and pulled open one of the boxes, exposing its contents. He pulled a flashlight from his rear pocket to inspect things more thoroughly. He compressed the rubber on switch as he began to shift its contents around. "Guy was a big Detroit Lions fan. Pretty much all memorabilia in here."

Nelson was across from him, going through a large plastic tote. Holding up a stuffed lion, she pressed at its paw, releasing a roar. "Not much in this one either."

They ripped through the last few boxes, scouring the contents, but finding nothing of interest. James dropped an item back in the box and then sat down on the floor. "Nothing. All junk. Not even sure why he kept this stuff-oh, what the hell!" James jumped right back up, reaching his hand back and brushing it along the back of his pants. "This dirt is moist. My ass is all wet," he said.

Nelson let out a halfhearted chuckle before her smile melted into a harsh line of defeat while kneeling in front of a box of her own. "I'm sure the guy was just trying to be nice."

James brushed his hands together, feeling the moistness of his hands mix with the dust, leaving a grimy texture. He let out a huff of disgust and frustration. He began walking toward the stairs. "Let's get out of here."

James made it halfway up the stairs before realizing that Nelson hadn't followed. He turned and saw her still crouched down, rubbing her hand in a circle on the floor. James threw his hands up before thumping back down the stairs. "What now?"

Nelson didn't respond but continued to rub her hand on the floor, almost as if she was attempting to follow some sort of trail. James watched in silence as she reached the wall to his left. She looked up at him. "Look at these bricks."

James flashed his light on them, not understanding what was happening. "I, again, feel like an idiot. What?"

Nelson tapped at them with her fingers. "They're newer. Have a redder color." Nelson then began picking at the mortar between each brick. A small amount of water seeped through the area she manipulated. Pulling a folding knife from her waistband, she scraped at more of the mortar. James moved closer.

Exposing the edges of one of the bricks, Nelson pulled at the deteriorated mortar, releasing it from the wall and exposing a small hole. James bent down and shined his light through. The beam of light bounced off a wall on the other side of a small hollowed out storage space. He could make out what looked like clothing and human flesh. An awful odor poured through the air, as insects escaped. The smell caused flashing memories of his recent visit to the morgue.

James turned to look at Nelson at the same time she looked at him. He saw confusion and distaste written on her face in the raising of her eyebrows as her head tilted to the side. James looked back at the hole. He pressed the button on his flashlight, darkening the area. Standing up, he pulled his phone from his pocket. "Guess I should probably call my boss."

TWENTY-ONE

WEBB SPED DOWN INTERSTATE 84, pushing the old Honda to its limit.

The case against Tarascio's man was going to be hard to beat. He knew Pam worked too hard, and they'd have no chance to win. She always fell asleep early, and if Tarascio's men were to make a move, that would likely be the time. Webb's eyes were immersed on the road and twitched thinking of the troubling situation.

He exited off the interstate on the exit to Pam's neighborhood and made his way to the drive-thru of the twenty-four seven Dunkin Donuts. The drive-thru was empty as he turned into the parking lot. The young employee mumbled something inaudible, but Webb assumed she was requesting his order.

"Yeah, let me get a large black. That'll be it, thanks."

Webb released his foot off the brake and rolled toward the window, reaching for his wallet in his back pocket as he did so. He reached to his other pocket. Nothing.

"Shit." He said out loud. Webb hoped he left it at home, but feared it was left behind during the commotion at the Stadium. He used his emergency twenty a week earlier and never replaced it.

Webb brushed off his brief worry as he continued forward and stopped at the drive-thru window. He looked in at the only visible employee, a girl in her late teens. As she made her way toward the computer right by the window with a hot cup in hand, Webb noticed that her eyes were rimmed red, and her mascara was smudging. She placed the cup down by the register, about to ring up his coffee so Webb waved his hand at the girl. His movement caught her attention as she turned and pulled open the window.

"Hi, what's up? Did you want to add something to your order?" She endeavored to make her voice professional, but it caught a couple times and Webb noticed that her nose was red.

"I'm sorry, I just wanted to make sure I asked for my coffee black. It's been a long freaking night, you have no idea," Webb said, trying to buy time.

The teenager blinked. "Oh, I have an idea," she mumbled as a tear rolled down her cheek.

"Geez, I'm sorry." Webb glanced at her nametag. "Emily, is it? I wasn't trying to compare here." Webb shifted his car into park and turned his body to face the girl. "Talk to me, Emily. What's going on? I'm nobody special, but I am old, so I've probably been through something similar."

Sniffling, she wiped her hand across her cheeks, using her fingers to remove the falling tears. "It's nothing, my boyfriend broke up with me tonight. That's all."

Jackpot, Webb thought as he pursed his lips and slowly shook his head. "Ah, I'm sorry, Emily." Webb said, continuing to use her name to establish a quicker connection with her. "If you don't mind me asking, how old are you?"

"Seventeen."

"Seventeen. Let me tell you something. I'm not going to give you some annoying advice and tell you, 'Oh who cares, you'll find someone else'. 'You're so young', yada, yada. That doesn't make it any easier. It hurts. It's gonna hurt. That's just part of the process."

Emily looked up, finally making eye contact with Webb as he

smiled at her. "All I'm going to tell you is, just give it time. Little by little, it'll get easier. The best thing you can do is keep yourself busy. Don't let your mind dwell on it."

A slight smile came to the corners of her mouth. "I know ... it's just hard. He was my first real boyfriend."

"I've been there," Webb nodded his head. "And it is going to be hard. Don't let anyone tell you otherwise. I say, pick up all the shifts here you can, and just sink your mind into work. Exhaust yourself and stay busy. When you get home, you'll pass out. While you're here, you'll be busy. Worst case scenario, it still hurts, but you made some extra money while being busy, right?"

Emily's smile grew. "Yeah, makes sense." Looking at him for a heartbeat before reaching behind her and grabbing the coffee, she handed it to Webb. "What about you? Why such a bad night?"

Webb waved his hand in her direction. "Nah. It's nothing. I'll be okay. Just have to take my own advice," He winked at her. Digging his hand into his pocket as if he was going for money, he continued, "What's the damage?"

"You're all set. I appreciate the advice. Thank you."

Webb bowed his head in thanks and raised his coffee. "Have a good night, dear. Be sure to work too hard," he winked again and drove off. While he knew using verbal judo to get what he wanted was wrong, he enjoyed practicing his skills.

Free coffee in hand as he continued towards Pam's house, he popped the top and sipped the steaming hot java. The hot liquid traveled down his throat, and he felt the warmth as it hit his chest, calming some of his nerves. Driving down Pam's street, he stopped four houses down on the opposite side of the street. Several vehicles were parked on the same side of the street, making it easy to blend in. Turning the vehicle off, he sat in silence as he sipped his coffee.

An hour had gone by before Webb took down the sixteenth ounce of his coffee. Pulling the release on the center console, he reached in and grabbed his cigarettes before exiting his vehicle.

He leaned against the car and slid a filter from the box. Looking at Pam's house, he kept hearing her voice telling him to quit as he rested the stick on his lips while holding the lighter in his other hand. Pausing, he then flicked at the metal and lit the nicotine stick.

Inhaling the smoke deep into his lungs, he looked up, blowing the remains into the cold sky. Flicking his thumb at the filter to drop the loose ash, he gazed toward Pam's front yard. Lifting his hand back to his mouth, he took another drag.

He squinted at the front of the home.

Movement.

Webb tossed the cigarette, ducked down, and jogged toward the home. Tapping the back of his hand against the small of his back, he made sure his firearm was with him as he silently moved along the sidewalk.

Webb slowed down as he darted toward a tree in between Pam's and her neighbor's yard. Webb couldn't make out who the figure was, but they appeared to be alone. Webb watched as he crept down the driveway, along the side of the home. No exterior lights were on, making it hard for anyone to see him approaching. Webb snuck up behind the figure, a man judging by the way the dark clothes contoured to the broad shoulders and thighs. Just as the man was about to approach a doorway on the side of the home, Webb pounced.

Leaping through the air, Webb grabbed the man's shoulders and allowed all his body weight to make them both crash to the ground. The man thrashed around as Webb pushed down at the man's arms to stabilize him. He straddled his legs around the man's waist and pulled at his shoulders to flip him over. The man was flipped toward Webb as they became face to face. Webb clenched his fist and raised it upward, ready to rocket the closed fist into the man's nose.

Just then, the light above the door flashed on. The man blocked his eyes from the glare while covering his face from the balled fist. Webb looked up, squinting, and saw Pam rushing out of the house.

"Carter! What are you doing?"

Webb froze as she ran toward him, pulling at his raised fist to get him off the man. "Are you okay, Paul?" she asked, turning to the man on the ground, whose face was scuffed up from the fall.

"Yeah, I'm fine."

Webb stood back, saying nothing while watching the situation unfold in slow motion. He opened his palm in front of him, in the direction of the man. "What the hell's going on, Pam? You know this guy?"

Pam sighed. She crossed her arms, took a deep breath before saying, "Yes, Carter. Paul and I have been dating for a few months. I meant to tell you."

A confused Paul looked back and forth at Webb and Pam, not saying a word.

Webb looked through Pam as he listened to her explanation and felt his face fall into an expressionless mask. He tossed his hands up in surrender. "No, no. I'm sorry. I just, I don't know. I'm gonna take off." Heart thumping, Webb turned and started jogging back down the driveway.

"I'm sorry, Carter!"

Webb didn't look back.

TWENTY-TWO

JAMES TWISTED his wrist to check his watch. 9:03 am. He had spent the past twelve hours in the basement as a search warrant was secured, followed by the rest of the detectives making their way out to process the scene. With Agent Nelson assisting, the State Police allowed the FBI to control the scene without intervening.

Exhausted from holding the scene for the night, James sat on a chair watching co-workers collect evidence and take photographs. They had knocked down a six-by-six section of the wall, which revealed a small room on the other side. The room was no bigger than a walk-in closet. The body was tied to a wooden chair, but impossible to identify. Maggots had gnawed away at the flesh, making the deceased unrecognizable. Bones of the deceased were visible through the half-eaten body.

"How long you think it's been there, boss?"

Dealto's cheeks filled with air as he blew out through his mouth. "Hard to tell. I'm going for at least a year or two, though. There's nothing left of it. I can't even tell if it's male or female. The smell must have just been trapped in here all these years."

James stood up and approached the opening in the wall, body

turned more towards Dealto than the crime scene. "Has to be a male."

Dealto came up next to him, looking in at the skeleton. "Why's that?"

"I'm no expert, just took a couple of college classes back in the day. I know males have thicker bones and smaller hips. Hips also sit a little higher. I mean there's still a little meat on this guy, but that's my two cents."

Dealto looked over the body, seeming too non-verbally agree with James' assessment. "The ME will be here soon. We'll have them make this a high priority. Michaels, you got enough DNA samples?"

"Oh yeah. I took a bunch of swabs and hair strands. I'll take the clothing after the autopsy's done. I'll get this stuff to the lab this afternoon and have them expedite it."

"Good, I'll call Jessica and see if we can get some of those results back today or tomorrow at the latest. We need some answers before the media gets ahold of this."

James turned to the opening and stared again at the crime scene. Michaels was still swabbing dried, soiled areas in the dirt, while Shaw continued to take photos. James locked in on the decaying body. Slumped over and lifeless, it looked fake. The things he had seen over the past week or so, he couldn't believe were real. He swept away into thoughts of life and death.

Someone smacked his back, the sound echoing slightly in the basement, snapping out of it, he turned to the side to see Dealto looking him in the eyes. "Are you okay, kid?"

"Yeah. Yeah, I'm fine." James said, turning and walking back to his seat. "Been a long freaking night, that's all."

"If it makes you feel any better, this is one of the crazier weeks I've ever been a part of myself. Just getting up here and seeing all this must have your head spinning."

James slouched into his chair and reached up, running his hands through his hair. "Not really. I don't think it's all hit me yet. Information overload at this point. My brain feels like scrambled eggs."

James stretched backward, releasing a loud yawn. His ringtone started playing and his jacket pocket started vibrating. He knew immediately it had to be his wife, who he had forgotten to call while so immersed in his investigation. "Hey, hun. I'm still alive," he yawned with hope she wouldn't be upset.

"Richie! Are you free? I think someone was in the house!"

James popped up from his chair, now laser focused on his wife's voice. "Whoa, slow down. What are you talking about?"

He could only hear shaky breathing into the phone, and he knew that she was crying. Marie never cried.

"I don't know, what am I supposed to do?" She said through her tears.

"Get out of the house now! If any of the boys stayed home from school, grab them and go to the Lalla's house. I'm on my way!" James hung up and stared at his phone, trying to compute.

"What's going on, James, you good?" Michaels questioned, peering through the opening.

"I think someone broke into my house. I-I gotta run?"

"Get out of here!" Dealto ordered, pointing his arm in the direction of the staircase.

James flew up the rickety staircase, skipping several steps. Exploding through the front door, he sprinted to his vehicle like Al Bundy taking a pitch in the backfield for Polk High. He fired his car up and sped out of the area. No longer did he feel the exhaustion from the long night holding the scene. His chest felt heavy with anxiety, his brain thinking the worst. The cell phone rang again, this time from his neighbor, Adam.

"Adam, is Marie there?"

"Yeah, she just got here, she's okay."

"Have you called the police yet?"

"Yeah, all set. They're on their way. She's okay, and the kids are in school."

"Thank goodness. I'll be there in a minute. I'm about two miles out."

James hung up the phone and tossed it onto the passenger's seat. Pressing his foot harder on the gas, he accelerated through the upcoming yellow traffic light that turned red as he went through, receiving not so nice hand gestures as he passed.

He flew around the corner to his street on two wheels. As he approached the home, he saw several police cruisers parked out front. Pulling up behind one of them, he jumped out of the vehicle almost before coming to a complete stop. Sprinting down his driveway, he saw four officers outside the home with their firearms in the low ready position covering the exterior. Officer Burrus, one of his field training officers before he transferred, was among them. James ran up to him.

"Marcus, what do you got?" James gasped, leaning down and resting his hands on his knees.

"Calm down, bud. House seems clear, they're just checking the basement right quick. Your wife good?"

"She's next door."

"What the hell happened, anyway? Call came out like a home invasion. I almost crashed getting here as fast as I did."

James's head sunk and chest felt heavy as the words came out of Burrus's mouth. The brotherhood in law enforcement was something James loved about the job. They always took care of their own. "That's why I love you, man. Appreciate it," he softly said. James began to open his mouth to explain what happened but was interrupted by the radio.

"We're clear inside," the officer signaled to those holding the perimeter.

James ran to the front door and went inside. Seeing five officers coming up the stairs from the basement, he approached them.

"Find anything?"

"Nothing seemed out of the ordinary, but we'll have you check it all out to be sure. We haven't spoken to Marie yet."

"She's next door. Let me check on her and see what's going on. I didn't get much from her, she was a mess on the phone. I'll grab her and be right back."

"Sounds good. We'll help ourselves to your fridge in the meantime."

James shook his head and shot the officer a grin. Turning around and jogging out of the house, he made his way next door, where he saw Marie standing in the driveway. Her head was on Adam's shoulder as he rubbed her back, consoling her. Looking up as he approached, she threw her arms around him and cried into his chest.

"It's okay," he comforted her. "House was clear. No one's inside."

She pulled her head off James' chest. He looked at her beet red face with tears rolling down her cheeks. "Someone was. Someone broke in."

Looking her in the eyes, he wrapped his hands around her shoulder. "What do you mean? Why do you say that?"

She wiped the tears off her face and attempted to gather her emotions. "The picture, Richie. It's back."

James just stared at her. "What picture? What are you talking about?"

"The photo of us and the kids on the mantel. It's back in the frame."

James then recalled their phone conversation that he had only been half paying attention to when she told him. "So, the kids were messing around. I don't get it."

Marie took a step back away from James and wiped her nose. She shook her head in fear. "No. It wasn't them. I asked them after we got off the phone. They were clueless. The picture has something written on it too. The glass is shattered. Someone was *in... the... house*!"

James raced back into the house and ran directly to the fireplace passing officers standing in his kitchen. He scanned over the eight photos Pam had on the mantel, his eyes landing on the one in the middle. The glass had been smashed, but the photo was still inside. He grabbed the thick wood frame and pulled it down. There was something written on the photo, but he couldn't make it out.

Turning it over, he pulled at the spring tension clips and pulled off the backing. Glass fell to the floor and bounced off the gray brick hearth. James slid the photo out and placed the frame down. He read the words written in red marker.

Such a beautiful family. Or are you? Lucky for you, you haven't been chosen. The gods have elected to let you live.

James's blood boiled as he read the message. Still looking at the photo, he saw a small cross drawn underneath the message. The same cross that was carved into the neck of the first victim. Dropping the photo to his side, he paced around, rubbing his hand up and down the stubble of his cheeks.

"Are you good, James?" an officer yelled from the kitchen.

"No. Not really. I have to make a call. Be right back."

James walked out the front door and saw Marie standing in the driveway with fear written all over her face. "Did you find it?" She yelled to him.

James didn't stop walking or even look in her direction. He simply said "Yup."

Making his way to his vehicle, he opened the passenger side door and retrieved his cell phone from the seat. He pulled up Dealto's number and made the call.

"Hey, what's up? Everything okay over there?"

James paused and took a deep breath to calm the rage forming inside. His teeth were tightly biting down as he grunted out words. "He came to my house."

"What? Who did?"

"That psychopath, Webb! He was in here, scoping out my family." James squeezed the steering wheel with white-knuckled intensity.

"Slow down, kid. What do you mean Webb was there?"

James ground his teeth, restraining himself from hopping in his car to hunt Webb down. "You have to get over here. I'll explain. It's all involved with the case we're working on."

"This thing won't stop building," Dealto said, followed by a deep exhale into the phone. "I'll head right over, but we found something over here."

"What?"

"When Michelle got here from the ME's office, she went through our dead guy's pockets. Had a wallet on him."

James's head shot up. "Let me guess, Jimmy Zaniewski."

"That's unfortunately correct. I guess Webb, or whoever, didn't let him get far. Guy's been living right underneath his landlord the whole time."

The confirmation didn't surprise James at all. "Just head over here ASAP if you can."

After pressing the end button for the call, James plopped into the passenger seat of his vehicle.

Staring out his windshield, his mind was a whirlwind, but a singular thought grounded him: find Webb.

How could an ex-officer go after another officer's family? The thought made him sick to his stomach. Wanting to be left alone in a locked room with this man for an hour was all he wanted. He felt a manic grin form at the corners of his mouth. Exhaling with a slight audible laugh, he knew what he needed to do.

James got back out of his car and looked up at his home. It was surrounded by police officers. Marie was crying again, now sitting in the middle of the driveway while an officer tried to console her. The sight of his wife in front of him poured gasoline on the fire inside.

If Webb thinks he can intimidate me by frightening my family, then I guess we have to turn up the heat.

TWENTY-THREE

JAMES'S LEGS bounced rapidly up and down while he tapped his finger on the desk. His chest rose and collapsed just as quick as his finger tapped. Locked in on the files in front of him, he sifted through the past murders investigated by Webb. There had to be a connection. James's family had now been victimized, though not yet hurt. It couldn't get to that point; he wouldn't allow it to.

The snap of the door handle pulled him from his trance. He looked up to see Dealto entering the room. Twisting his wrist, he checked the time. 6:46 a.m. He'd thought he would have at least another hour to research before the rest of his team would be in.

Dealto walked up behind him and squeezed his shoulder. "Figured you'd be here already. What time did you get in?"

The room fell silent momentarily as James finished reading a paragraph. "I don't even know."

Dealto rolled a chair up beside him and placed his coffee on James's desk. "You doing okay?"

James' head sank. The anxiety and fear finally all hit him at once. "I'm just trying to keep my emotions in check. I take every case seriously, but this one is obviously different. I have to stay focused and figure out this puzzle.

"James, I'm not typically the kind to pull people off cases. But like everything lately, this is different."

"Absolutely not," James spun in his chair to glower at his boss. "There is no chance in hell I'm sitting this one out. This is personal."

Dealto clenched his jaw and sat back. "That's the problem. It's personal. I can't have..."

"No. I respect you and I know I'm new up here, but regardless of what you say, there is no way I'm sitting this one out."

Dealto's face softened as he looked into James's eyes. "You're not going to like hearing this, but you sound just like Webb. This is what happened to him. He couldn't let things go and started running cases by himself. Alone, on his own time. I can appreciate the passion, but you have to see the problem here."

James began gnawing on his thumbnail and stared at the floor.

Being compared to Webb just a short time ago would have been an honor; now it disgusted James. Removing his finger from his mouth, he leaned in toward Dealto. "I'm not Carter Webb; I'm Richie James, and *that's* who I want to be. Enough with taking me off the case. Won't. Happen." Leaning back, he crossed his legs and steepled his fingers. "Tell me more about Webb. I need to know everything about this guy."

Dealto squinted his eyes and took a deep breath while leaning his head backward. He rocked back and forth in his chair for a long moment. Then his chair came back forward. Dealto crossed his right leg over his left in an L, resting both hands on his calf. "The guy did eighteen years here. He was only two years from retirement, although, I don't think he ever would have left. He did a year or two in patrol and his talent was obvious to everyone in the building. Webb was a worker. Smart. Charming. We knew if he showed up to a call where a crime had been committed, he would make an arrest. Whether he had to dig into every detail to find evidence, or just managed to get anyone and everyone to confess, he made every detective's life so much easier. Their caseloads shrunk in half."

James listened, beginning to again chomp away on his fingernails. "So a short stint in patrol. Then what?"

"Pat Dresko was the sergeant in narcotics at the time, he pulled him in pretty quick. Tried for a month before they would even allow it because of manpower issues."

Dealto reached over and grabbed his gas station coffee that sat on James's desk. After taking a slow sip, he continued. "Want to say he was with Dresko and his guys for about three years. As soon as he went down there, that unit exploded with success. Massive gun seizures, money, tons of drugs. You name it. I think that's where his obsession started. I know you never worked in that unit, but you learn a lot there. Doesn't matter how many people you arrest or how many drugs you get off the streets. There's always more product and always another guy waiting in the wings to take the empty spot. Drove Webb crazy. I remember talking to him and he was saying how he felt like he couldn't make a dent in the drug game, no matter how hard he tried. It only made him push harder. And literally, whoever took over, he was able to get to 'em. Carter was always one or two steps ahead."

The words increased the fear in James' soul. This wasn't going to be easy, but James knew he could be better. He was never one to back down and always believed in himself. The fear quickly dissipated as he refocused on Dealto. "That's all I've heard about the guy. His obsession with solving every case and his intelligence. Guys used to tell me he was so good, it almost seemed like he was planting things on people just to solve the cases."

Dealto cocked his head to the side and raised his eyebrows. "Well, we'll get to that. After just a few years in narcotics, the guy flipped everyone he arrested and took down half the city. Everything we thought about how good he was seemed true. Chief Cardona was in charge at the time. He loved Webb. Decided to create this whole Deception Unit because of him. It was perfect. We had a group of detectives that were just on another level. Putting them together to work on the most complex crimes was smart. Why waste all their talents working on petty crimes?"

James ran his hands up and down his face, followed up by smacking his cheeks to try to help himself focus after another restless night. Dealto had paused, so James nodded for him to continue.

"Then, they put me in charge of the unit. Been running it for almost sixteen years. We've been unbelievably successful at closing cases. Webb was a huge part of that. They sent us all to polygraph school pretty much right away. Wanted to build our skillset even further. Webb was already an amazing interrogator, but learning everything he did there, then having the opportunity to interview people almost on a daily basis - I've never seen or heard of anyone on this guy's level."

James silently chewed his bottom lip. The fear and anxiety began to sneak their way back into his thoughts. He took a deep breath, exhaling slowly to calm himself and refocus. "Tell me about the murders you guys investigated. How did all that lead up to him being fired?"

Dealto took another swig from his coffee, wiping the residue from his mouth before continuing. "Those killings went on for about six months. We had eight bodies turn up. Two families of three and one couple. They didn't turn up as fast as the ones we're currently seeing. The first of the victims was a couple. Middle aged with kids grown and out of the home. They weren't staged like these cases have been. However, they did all have the cross carved in their necks."

"What did you guys make of the cross? Any idea of its significance?"

"None." Dealto let out a large exhale. "No DNA hits. No fingerprints. No real reason why these families were killed. We couldn't come up with any motives that made sense. State Police, FBI, all assisted at some point. It baffled everyone. After the third one is when Webb got weird."

James furrowed his brow. "Explain weird. What was he doing?"

"He was always here. Ruined his marriage. He was just obsessed with figuring it out. He didn't want to work on anything else. Refused applicant polygraph tests, got kind of insubordinate by not wanting any other cases. I'd assign something and it would just sit. He'd read the initial report just to see if there was any tie to the killings, but there never was. So every case would just sit unattended. The inability to solve it just consumed him."

"Why though? The guy obviously had cases he couldn't solve in the past."

Dealto chuckled without humor. "No. He *never* couldn't solve a crime. That's where all the 'Webb plants evidence on people' jokes came from."

James's knee bounced like a massage gun, trying to release the stress. He tasted blood and realized his fingernails were half-gone.

"Finally, we get a call from Webb who's out on Taunton Street. Says he had a good lead on the case and was about to make contact with someone at the home." Dealto continued, his own knee starting to bounce.

"He was alone out there at the time?"

"Of course. Guy just did his own thing. I was his boss and all, but Cardona told me to leave him be. Let him do his thing. When he called us, we flew over there. Long story short, we find him out back talking to this guy Jimmy Zaniewski. There's a tool back by the shed where they're standing. Looked kind of like a screwdriver, but the end of the metal rod was in a cross shape and the top of it was scorched. Looked like a branding tool of some sort."

"So that would explain the sign left on all the victims." James concluded.

"Right. So, obviously, it seemed like Webb got a big find. How he figured that out or found a link to Zaniewski, I still don't know."

"You guys must have dug deep into this Zaniewski guy. No connections to any of it I assume."

Dealto shook his head. "Nothing. Anyway, we walk up and

Webb's trying to calm this guy down but he's yelling, like, *really* pissed off. He's telling Webb it's not his, and he has no idea where it came from. Starts accusing Webb of planting it there. I tell Webb to take a walk and cool off. Try to find out what the hell's going on. Same thing though: he says Webb showed up and walked with him to the back. Starts asking all these questions about this tool. Zaniewski said it wasn't his. He had a little burglary in his past and felt like Webb was trying to pin something on him. Didn't seem like he knew anything about the murders."

"Do you believe that?"

"Honestly, I have no clue, kid." Dealto rubbed his hand through his hair. "So, I have Michaels talk to the neighbor, who says they saw Webb milling around the backyard. Almost called police, but then noticed his badge. Neighbor said it looked like Webb threw something in the grassy area. So, whether I believe it or not at the time, I have a potential problem. Had to notify the captain, who hated Webb by the way. And in turn, he informed the chief."

"Just curious, why'd he hate Webb?" James asked.

"Because of how good Webb was. He kind of made us all look bad. You know how the egos are in this job, some guys can't stand other people's success," Dealto threw his hands up and pointed at himself. "But I was his superior, so he made me look good."

James rubbed his fingers across the stubble on his chin, still not putting the pieces together.

"I tell Webb what's going on and, of course, he gets pissed at me like this was my doing. I let him know he has to get up to the chief's office ASAP. He gets up there and it's just him, Chief Cardona, and Captain Miller."

"Oh, it was Captain Miller? That guy's such a dick. Did an interview with him when I was coming over and had a few shitty run-ins with him after. Heard he was a pencil pusher his whole career. Never did real police work. Luckily, he retired shortly after I started." James shook his head in disgust.

"You ain't lying about that, so you'll probably like this next part,"

In spite of everything, Dealto grinned. "From what I'm told, he walks in and it's the chief and Miller in there. Miller just starts laying into him about being a corrupt cop, finally catching him planting his evidence. Cardona, who was never one for confrontation, just sat and let them two go at it. I guess Miller tells him to turn in his badge and gun because he was going to be on leave while a full internal investigation would be conducted."

"So how long was he out before they let him go?"

"Not long, because it got much worse. Miller, being the prick he is, was just taunting Webb the whole time, right in his face. Almost antagonizing him. You know what happens when you poke a bear." Dealto said while raising his brow.

"He hit him!?"

"Knocked the crap out of him. Completely unconscious. Broke his jaw. Miller had it wired shut for like six weeks. I think most of the force loved it." Dealto laughed. "About a day or two later, Webb was arrested. They terminated him within the week. He didn't fight back. Didn't want union representation. Just took it and walked away. I think Webb was so upset with the way he was treated, he wanted nothing to do with the PD."

"Why do you hate the guy now? Sounds like you guys were cool." James asked.

Dealto sighed and shook his head while rocking the foot draped over his knee. "I don't hate the guy, but ... I reached out for weeks. He picked up a few times and just blasted me for throwing him under the bus. Called me every name in the book. It got old pretty quickly. I just started laying it back on him. Then, when the FBI got involved and started throwing his name around as a suspect, I just couldn't look at the guy the same. Just the thought of it possibly being him changed everything."

James tried taking in all the information to complete the puzzle. "What about his personal life? Kids? Family? I know you mentioned his marriage."

"Oh yeah, Pam was great. They were perfect together. Think they lasted about five years, but the deeper he got into this job, and particularly once these cases started, she just couldn't do it anymore. She was getting older and wanted kids. Webb was so wrapped up in this job that she couldn't see herself with him anymore. They got divorced after the second murder."

James sat up. "Is she still around? Maybe I can meet up with her, get some deeper inside info from her."

"She'd never. Pam ripped me a new one for even bringing up that he might be involved. I have a good working relationship with her now, but I'd steer clear of that conversation. You've probably met her. It's Pam Mazur over at court."

"No shit. She's a hell of a prosecutor I'm told too."

"Damn straight she is. Probably the best. Same mentality as Webb. Tarascio's got one of his top men fighting a case right now she's working on. No way she'll lose it. That'll help us a lot to have that goon off the streets."

The words cracked James's brain like a rocket hit off the bat of Aaron Judge. He felt like he just placed his first puzzle piece. He let out a slight laugh and placed it on the table. "Remember I said we saw Webb leaving the area of Tarascio's after those shots were fired? What if Webb's working with him now?"

Dealto's face scrunched while he scratched at the side of his neck. "Why? I don't see the connection there."

"Neither do I boss, but this is obviously no coincidence. You got Patsy, head of one mob family whose daughter just got murdered. Then, Tarascio is shot at outside his restaurant where Webb was likely fleeing from. Webb's ex-wife is in charge of trying to put away one of Tarascio's top guys. Not to mention, he just helped get one of Tarascio's guys off on murder. It all connects, and Webb's definitely involved. The guys gone rogue."

Dealto took a deep breath while looking up, seemingly thinking. Rocking the chair forward, he stood. "I don't know, kid. But I know I've only had two detectives since Webb left. Finally having another brain in this office is definitely welcome." Dealto rested his hand on

James' shoulder and gave a weak squeeze. "But listen, I know you're going through a lot, so if you ever need to take some time away from this to be with the family, just ask. Family comes first. I'm going to check in with Lieutenant Mocarsky. We have a meeting with all the brass once Michaels and Shaw get in."

Dealto turned and made his way to his office. James spun his chair back toward his computer and smiled. He had a thought on what could be Webb's motive. Now he needed to find a way to catch him.

TWENTY-FOUR

THE ELEVATOR DOORS opened to the third floor of the South Lake Police Department as members of the Deception Unit along with Nelson exited. It was quiet in the hallway as the song of their shoes could be heard shuffling across the carpet. The secretary in the Chief's office was ensconced behind a large mahogany desk on a leather chair that must have cost the taxpayers a fortune. The desk sat behind the double doors in the center of the room, facing those that enter. Directly behind the secretary was a hallway and two offices to each side. With the phone to her ear, she made eye contact with the detectives, smiling and signaling" One minute." Finishing her call, she hung up the phone and sighed.

"I can't go five minutes without someone calling to inquire about these cases you all are working on." Looking over the top of her glasses while she shook her head.

"Well, it won't last much longer, Kristen. I promise," James gave her a tightlipped smile.

"I sure hope so. I'm not used to getting calls about unsolved cases. They're all in the conference room. You can head in."

James took control of the situation and led the team toward the rear office. He had only been in the chief's conference room once before, during his initial interview. As they approached the double doors with frosted glass, thick black lettering above the door read "Briefing Room" and just under it read "Do not disturb." When he pulled on the handle, the door was locked. Swiping his fob to the reader, nothing happened.

"Still too low on the pole for this room, kid," Dealto said while brushing past him and using his fob. Tugging the silver metal handle again, the doors opened. Dealto, Michaels, Shaw, James and Agent Nelson entered the room.

James stood still briefly, looking at the room. With a large table surrounded by approximately twenty chairs, he observed his chief along with seven high ranking members with brass. A hundred-inch screen sat behind the chief along with several other monitors displaying surveillance cameras throughout the city. The large screen showed an aerial shot of James' home, detailing multiple officers posted around the property. The sight of his own home in an ops plan sent chills to his core.

The administration all stood at everyone's arrival, but every one of them came up to James to conciliatorily pat his shoulder or shake his hand.

"How you doing, James?" Chief Elijah Quick himself, gripping his hand firmly.

"Been better, obviously." James gave the chief a halfhearted smile.

"How's Marie and the family?" The chief let go of James's hand and gave him a hearty thump on his back.

"A mess, but as good as they can be. Kids don't really know what happened and, hopefully, we can keep it that way. The Feds got them a house for the time being with round-the-clock security."

"We'll get to the bottom of it. Don't you worry," Chief Quick squeezed his shoulder. He then stepped back and looked James over. "You don't look good, James. You know, you can take some time if you need."

James looked down, just now realizing his appearance. His navy blue Van Heusen slacks were wrinkled and dirty from the night in the basement. The light blue button up shirt was untucked, with the top buttons undone, and the tie that was there just two days earlier was missing. He surreptitiously leaned his nose to his shoulder and grimaced; it was obvious he hadn't showered in days. Rubbing his hands across his now thick facial hair, James could not believe he was standing in front of the brass looking like this. Turning to his partners, he threw his hands up.

They all sheepishly looked away, clearly not wanting to kick James while he was down. Turning back to Quick, he combed his fingers through his now greasy hair and tucked in his shirt. "I'm sorry sir, it's just been a long-"

"James. It's okay," The Chief smacked his shoulder again. "Dealto said you're insistent on continuing with this. If you think you can handle it, let's get to work."

The whole team sat around the oval table. They all rested large case jackets on the table and opened them up. Quick nodded to Mocarsky, the lead in the Detective Bureau, to start the meeting.

"Why don't you just start from the beginning on all this Sergeant Dealto and get everyone up to speed."

Before Dealto could speak, James quickly took control of the meeting, not worrying about being out of line. This was his family and his fight. "I got it, boss. Just chime in if needed," James said while flipping to a page plastered with notes. "I know you've all been here much longer than me. So, I apologize for taking control, but this is personal." He looked up and stared his chief in the eyes with determination. "Now, as far as the past cases, I'll give a quick overview."

The room was completely quiet. The command staff, all dressed in their white uniformed shirts, equipped with gold pin bars on their collars, gave James their full attention.

"Roughly four years ago you guys worked on a serial case. Going through all the reports, the Deception Unit handled all of them, with Detective Webb running point. Through the investigation and talking with Sergeant Dealto, it looks as if no link could be found between the victims. Seems totally random, if I'm correct?" He looked around the room.

"Correct," Dealto nodded. "Dozens of interviews with all the victim's families and friends, not to mention all the checks through social media and in-house records."

"No connection, but all with the same branding we're seeing on our current victims I'm told," newly promoted Captain Dresko of the Patrol Division replied.

"Yes sir. All victims had a small cross like symbol branded on the back of their necks just below the shirt line."

"What about the current victims? Any connection to each other?" Quick asked, with his hands folded under his chin and elbows resting on the table.

"Not that I've found yet. I've read through the past and current case files a couple of times, but only had an hour or so to try to find a link with them." James released a sigh of exhaustion. "We all know Detective Webb thought he had a suspect, but we all know where that suspicion ended up. Before I continue, is everyone good with the past cases?"

"I believe we are," Quick said while scanning the room as everyone nodded.

James flipped through his disorganized hieroglyphics and found the one he was looking for. "The first case popped up about a week ago. Family of three who were found staged on their living room floor. Lying next to one another, branding on their necks and a pearl found in the mother's hand. The second was a family of four staged at their dining room table. Odd scene, but all were sitting upright as if they were preparing to have dinner together. All appear to be strangled. In this instance the branding matched the previous case, the difference in the second being that the pearl was not in the mother's hand but instead was found lodged in a bowl of corn. We're still waiting for the official ME report, but suffocation seems clear with all of them. Waiting to find out if there was branding on the second family. Were there any pearls found in the past investigations?"

Dealto raised his finger up to chime in. "I remember finding something near one of the bodies on the second murder. I don't think we ended up seizing it, though. I just thought it was just lying in the area. But after these murders, I jogged my memory from the past investigations. I can't confirm it was a pearl, but I'm fairly certain it was. Obviously should have tagged it, but hindsight is twenty-twenty."

"Glad you said that. I flipped through the photos of the third case, and I'm also not positive, but I think I see one on the floor. Checking the reports, no pearls were seized in any of those cases."

James looked over as Dealto released an audible sigh and rubbed his index finger and thumb over his eyes.

"I had the two pearls sent to Jessica over at the lab and asked her to rush them. She already ran a bunch of the DNA found on scene, and nothing was found. I assume the results will come back today on the pearls. This guy is clearly clean, so I'm not optimistic about getting anything on it. Just trying to cross and dot everything."

James caught the eye of Michaels who was nodding with a calculated look on his face. For the first time, James saw the look of a man that seemed to be accepting him as a co-worker.

"To me, I feel we're dealing with the same suspect, or even a copycat. I'd venture to say it's the same guy. Why the delay in killings is the interesting part." Dealto observed as he leaned back in his chair and looked around the table.

"That's what I'm trying to figure out," one of the captains chimed in while throwing his hands up.

"What are you thinking for next moves? Any ideas?" Chief Quick asked.

James squirmed in his chair a little and sat back. He knew his next comments were going to be met with pushback. Not wanting to beat around the bush, he was direct with his ideas. "I want to bring Webb in. I need to interview him."

Multiple members of the table sighed and threw their hands up while leaning back in their chairs. James looked at Dealto. His eyes were closed, clearly knowing how the brass was going to respond to the statement of Webb possibly being a killer.

Chief Quick didn't respond immediately as he sat motionless with a blank stare on his face. He inhaled deeply, looked over at James, and calmly spoke. "Ok. Tell how you plan to go about that, Richie?"

"Thank you, Chief. I know it's bold but hear me out." James sat up in his chair, resting his elbows on the table. "You first asked why the delay in murders. Well, again, I'm not telling you I have one hundred percent figured this out, but once Webb left, the killings stopped. These were all cases he specifically was running point on."

"You're going to have to do better than that kid," another Captain vocalized while shaking his head.

Several groans filled the room, as multiple people began complaining, tossing out reasons why this was a bad idea. While rumors had floated over the years that Webb could be involved, no one truly believed it. It was merely said in jest amongst officers during "locker room" talk.

"Okay, okay!" Chief Quick's voice drowned everyone else's. "Everyone just stop talking for a minute and let James explain. While I know we all worked with Carter and know him personally, James can maybe offer an outside view," Chief Quick turned to James. "What else you have?"

"Two more things. I just found this out, but I know that Webb's ex-wife is working over at the DA's office now as a prosecutor. I don't know her, but I'm told she's the best."

"She's an animal. Girl don't stop working till she gets her conviction," Michaels nodded with a serious look.

"Right. And apparently, she's now handling one of Carmine Tarascio's top guy's case." James said with his palms up and eyebrows raised.

"We talked about that earlier. How's that connect though?" Dealto asked.

"After we spoke earlier boss, it hit me. Webb just got one of Carmine's guys off while working with Attorney Edwards. Edwards is now defending this case as well. In addition to that, Pasquale Romano's daughter is one of our last victims. It's possible the mob has some role in this and there could be some kind of turf war." Sitting back, James let the information settle in for a moment as he began to rapidly tap the table with his finger. "Additionally, Agent Nelson and I were heading to the shooting at Tarascio's place, and we saw Webb speeding away from the area. I really think he's working with them."

"Shit." Chief Quick muttered with pursed lips while rubbing at his chin. The connection James made had clearly shocked his chief. "I knew Webb had gone off the deep end, but working with criminals just seemed a little far for him,"

"Maybe. But tying it all back to me, I was speaking to Sergeant Dealto earlier. Webb lived for this job and hated losing. I know it wasn't solved, but there were strong suspicions he planted evidence on his last victim before being terminated. Maybe covering his tracks. Maybe he didn't lay out enough evidence for him to solve the case he was investigating, that he had committed. Needed to get that piece in place to seal it up?"

"Webb's too smart for that kid. On the off chance he's our guy, he would've been steps ahead," a captain said while pointing at James and rolling his eyes.

"Again, maybe. But everyone makes mistakes. Things could've gone wrong during the last killing and he had to get out of there." James shot back. "Finally, I couldn't figure out where I came into play and why he would come after my family. However, I feel like Dealto opened my eyes this morning. Webb lived for his investigations. Lost his wife and job over it. This unit meant everything to him. The whole time he's been gone, his desk has remained unfilled."

Dealto nodded his head, his eyebrows raising to his hairline. "Until now. You 'took' Webb's spot."

"Exactly. An interview can potentially put all these cases to rest." He looked over the room as everyone was silently nodding their heads. No one responded, as each one of them appeared to be contemplating the dangers of bringing in a man like Webb for questioning. Everyone knew how intelligent he was. If he was in fact a killer, sniffing around him could go sideways quick.

James looked towards the chief, but his eyes landed on his home sitting on the monitor's screen behind Quick. The view once again threw a chill down his spine. The reality of his family being in danger was one he never imagined he'd find himself in. He had to put an end to it.

Everyone looked at the Chief.

While rubbing his right hand up and down his face, the Chief sat staring out at nothing. The room was completely silent. James could hear the air exhaling through his nose as he waited. His knee bounced uncontrollably under the table, hoping to get a shot at Webb.

"Okay," Chief Quick said while bellying back up to the table. "Webb is a very savvy guy, and this can cause a lot of pushback on multiple levels. I don't want to meet anywhere in public, and I want to keep it quiet for now. Dealto, how do you want to go about this?"

Dealto sat quietly while looking at his team. "Well, first off, I agree with James. As we all know, Webb's no dummy. He knows he has all the constitutional rights to tell us to piss off and decline an interview. I'd rather James and Nelson stay away from making contact with him. If he sees a federal agent, he'll sniff that right out. If he is, in fact our guy, I don't want James out there since that could also spook him."

James stood and leaned over the table, pressing his palms into the table. "Boss, I want this interview. There's no one in this damn room more determined to get a confession from this guy. I'm ready,"

Dealto threw both hands out flat, slowly raising them up and down. James knew Dealto was trying to settle him down, but he *needed* this interview. There was no way he was being pushed out of it.

"Calm down. I believe in you. I do." Dealto looked at James directly. "You've laid out more in the past twenty minutes and were able to put together more than we did in the past four years. As you said, you have more of a reason than any of us to get to the bottom of it. I truly empathize with that and can't imagine being in your shoes."

James's breathing slowed as his heart rate sped up. There was no way failure was an option for him. He sat back down.

Dealto pulled at a notebook on the table toward himself, looking around the room as he began to put together a plan. "I want Michaels and Shaw to meet up with Webb. He's clearly savvy to a tail, but I think you two can play it off. Follow him and approach when he parks. When the placement is right. Just pop out and shoot the shit with him. He left on good terms with both of you and you can just say you saw him. Just poke fun that you were tailing him and wanted to run up on him. Exchange your pleasantries and keep it very light at first. He mentored you when you came up, right, Shaw?"

"Yes sir. Taught me everything I know." Shaw nodded slowly, with a sense of disappointment on her face.

"Talk about a couple of cases you solved and how his coaching was the reason why you did. Really lay on that positive reinforcement to try to catch him off guard. He'll likely see right through it. But my guess is he's cocky enough to come in, just to see what we have."

"Not a problem sarge."

"Michaels, you and Webb started at about the same time in the unit, right?"

"Yeah, but he taught me almost everything too," Michaels said with a surprisingly unconcealed grin.

"I know, but you're an asshole and would never tell him that,"

Dealto said, which received several chuckles throughout the room. "I want you to work in the cases we're working on now. The complexities, the similarities, all that. Tell him you want to run some things by him and see if he's willing to come down and take a look. Again, put your ego aside, and ask for help. He should eat that up."

"I don't see him stepping foot in this building. Especially if he knows you're here." Michaels said as he tossed his pen on the desk.

"I know, tell him I'm off for the day. You'll sneak him up the back stairwell, out of camera view. It'll be hard to convince him, but I think his cockiness at having another crack at the case, or an insight to what we have, will bring him in." Dealto said.

James was biting his lip as his knee bounced a million miles an hour under the table. "Boss. I want the interview."

Dealto again signaled for his young detective to stop pulling at his leash. "Once he's in the building, show him a little of what we have, but don't get too in depth. Then, walk him right to an interview room. James, you'll be waiting inside. I want you to conduct the interview."

James sat stoic, staring at his boss like he was holding a piece of meat. "Thank you, sir."

"I like it," Chief Quick smacked at the table. "Let's get going on this immediately."

The group all nodded in agreement.

"I appreciate everyone's help on this," James said while looking over the group in front of him. "Let's get back to the office and get this son of a bitch in here."

TWENTY-FIVE

RICHIE JAMES HAD GROWN up in White Plains, New York, and later attended Pace University. Growing up with a father in law enforcement, his lifelong dream was to follow in his footsteps. After losing him to lung cancer in his senior year of college, his determination was even stronger. Wanting to get started immediately, he began applying to police departments weeks before his graduation. Always wanting to be a detective, he only applied to larger agencies so he could focus on his dream.

Just one month after graduation, James found himself in the academy of the NYPD. After a brief stint in the patrol division, he quickly found himself in the street crime unit. Not quite meeting his goal, he spent almost four years taking down low level criminals. Pushing his cases to the limit, James interrogated all his arrestees, searching for bigger crimes. Always successful, his interviews led to information that would solve several of the city's homicides. Once Marie received her promotion, he knew he had to do what was best for his family. If four years of solid police work wasn't going to propel his career forward, a change of scenery was necessary for him as well. South Lake Police Department was smaller in size, but offered all the opportunities he needed. He knew he would have to start from the bottom, but hard work was something he never shied away from.

He leaned back in his chair and turned to his right, pulling the desk drawer out. Retrieving his binder from polygraph school, he flipped to the interrogation class slides. Webb attended the same school he had and would be aware of all the tactics he would be employing. Webb had steamrolled him at the bar just days before, so he would need to use that to his advantage. He knew his best approach would be to play into his naïve encounter. Attempt to rope Webb into giving up information, without him knowing too early that he was a suspect and potentially giving up damaging information.

James sat at his desk, death gripping the radio, waiting for the call that Webb was coming in. Glancing at the clock on the wall, he saw it was only 10:24 in the morning. The day was still young. The hum of the water cooler was all that could be heard as his eyes burned a hole through his radio.

"We have eyes on Webb's vehicle at his office," Shaw said over the radio.

"Copy. Keep me updated," Dealto responded while sitting behind his office desk.

James placed his radio back in the charging dock, refocusing his attention on the case reports and photographs, combing through every detail.

"Hey Sarge, I think we've been spotted," Shaw said over the radio a few minutes later.

James's heart raced and dropped into his stomach.

"What happened?" Dealto responded.

"Well, he just waved to us across the street and is walking over as we speak."

Dealto didn't respond to the comment. James stared at his radio, feeling sweat form on his brow as complete silence stretched on for several minutes. He had confidence in Shaw and Michaels, but if this didn't work, he would have to draw up a new plan everyone could be on board with.

After what seemed like hours of staring at the black Motorola, James finally heard the crackle from the speaker as Shaw keyed up.

"We're good. He's heading back to his car and following us in. If you two can lay low, we'll be in shortly."

James released an enormous sigh of relief.

He had been in countless interviews, but never one of this magnitude. Nevertheless, he willed himself to be calm and steady. Grabbing two bottles of water, his cell phone, and a notepad, he made his way to the interview room to await his opportunity.

James entered the room, placing a water bottle in front of each chair. Sitting in the chair to the right, his back would be to the camera and Webb's face in clear view. The table was pushed to the far wall, allowing only two sides to sit on. This would eliminate barriers, allowing him to move in close when needed. With no windows, no clock, and bare walls, distractions were limited.

After waiting for what felt like another two hours, James could hear Webb's voice just outside the doorway, talking to Michaels and Shaw. He paced around the room and anxiously waited. The steps hitting the thin carpet of the office grew louder, as the voices came closer. The slightly cracked door swung outward, and James found himself standing in front of Webb and Shaw.

"James really wanted to talk to you privately about this, if you don't mind? I'll have him fill you in on what else is going on." Shaw smiled at Webb, holding the door open for him.

Webb looked over at James, with a slightly confused expression. "That's not a problem. Haven't seen this kid since his polygraph," he pointed at him and laughed.

Webb entered the room, and Shaw shut the door behind him. James extended his hand, shaking Webb's, trying to show gratitude. "I appreciate it, Carter. This will make sense shortly. Cameras aren't on of course, so this is all off the record." James knew, however, that Shaw would be flicking the switch to record once

Webb entered the room. A confession on video is a confession hard to defend.

James sat down and motioned for Webb to sit across from him. "Man, I'm not used to sitting on this side of the table. Feel like I'm about to be interrogated," Webb joked.

All the basic interrogation skills were going to be thrown out the window. James knew he would have to use advanced skills on his end, in order to reel Webb in. A tall task for anyone.

"Thanks for meeting with me the other day. This whole thing has been a lot for me. I handled some pretty crazy things in New York, but this thing is just unreal."

"This is definitely a wild one." Webb sat back in his chair and crossed his leg. James picked up on the physical barrier Webb was exhibiting by crossing his leg. While maybe done subconsciously, he would still need to remove it before moving forward.

"How's everything going with Jonny Edwards over at the practice?" James asked in a weak attempt to build rapport. A short silence fell over the room, as Webb paused while staring at James.

"It's been good." A weak answer. Webb seemed to already know he was beating around the bush. No need to play the game if it wouldn't get him anywhere. Barely a minute in and it was time to change his approach already.

"Listen, I'm not going to play you for an idiot. You're a smart guy. Likely the smartest I know, from what I've heard," James said, tossing out some positive reinforcement. "Shaw and Michaels already laid out what we have going on with these cases. So first of all, thank you for coming into this room, and not telling them we met just recently. Shows I can trust you." More false positive reinforcement.

"Yeah, no problem. I get it. Worked up here not long ago. I know how Dealto can be."

"We had another attempt by this lunatic." James said, tossing out a small lure.

Webb uncrossed his legs, leaned forward and rested his elbows on the table. He locked his hands in front of his face and stared directly at James. He appeared intrigued.

"Wow, so fast? That'd be three in a matter of weeks. This is not how he operated back when I was looking into him."

James listened to the words, being sure to dissect everything, not wanting to miss something important. Clearly, Webb knew this was likely the same suspect. But without all the new case facts, how could he? Michaels and Shaw were specifically told not to give up certain details. He'd bank this for later, rather than calling it out now.

"Yeah, this thing's going crazy." James took a deep breath, looking down while rubbing his hands up and down his thighs. "He came after my family, Carter."

James watched Webb's body language closely as he provided this detail. Webb's eyebrows raised and eyes widened. He leaned back in his chair, shoving both hands through his hair. "What! Are you kidding me? Is everyone okay?"

James remained calm. "Yeah. They're fine."

The room again fell silent. James allowed the silence to fill the room, hopefully creating anxiety. Webb leaned forward, rubbing his chin and staring down at the table briefly before his eyes popped back up toward James, re-engaging in the conversation. "So, what the hell happened?"

James's head slowly shook back and forth. He bit his bottom lip, trying to suppress his emotions from leaking out into the interview. "He broke in when we weren't home. Left us a note written on a blank Polaroid photo,"

"How did he get in? When did this happen? And a note on a Polaroid? What did it say?"

Webb was clearly trying to control the interview. James had hoped Webb would be chattier, slipping up on certain things he said. His body language was one of calm concern.

"I don't know, Carter," James murmured, keeping his face blank.

Webb tilted his head and shook it. He then slowly sat back in his chair while maintaining eye contact. "Is your family okay?"

"You know they are, Carter."

Webb stilled. He looked James in the eye then shook his head, gritting his teeth. "Didn't take long for these assholes to pollute your brain, did it? I'm not going to go through some sabotage interrogation. Let's save the *I and I* games. I knew you were talented the day you walked into the polygraph suite. You're going about this interview the same way I would have. But your emotions are giving away too much. I get that. Now let me in on what they're feeding you."

James wasn't at all thrown off by the comment. He had confidence in his interviewing skill and received great training at polygraph school, but Webb was better. While he had hoped he could use his earlier naiveness to his advantage, it wasn't going to work. Going right at him was the only move.

"I respect you as an investigator and know you're the best interrogator out there. So, I agree: let's skip the BS and just come clean. I know what you've done, and I know you went after my family."

Webb let out a loud laugh and shook his head. "Good lord. I always thought I had intelligent people working around me while I was here. To be honest, I spent the last year of my time here trying to add you to this office."

James did not believe the words rolling off Webb's tongue, but he nodded his head slowly, remaining composed. "Is that why you came after my family? All because I took your place?"

Webb's cheeks blew out on a large exhale. He sat for a moment in silence, while bellied up to the table. "As I'm sure you've heard, I'm not the most touchy-feely guy out there. Trying to put myself in your shoes, I'd lose it. So, I get that. But this unit meant everything to me. I put it ahead of the only person in the world that understood me. Badge or not doesn't matter to me. I'm still out there doing what I love doing. Trying to stop bad people from doing bad things. I'm glad it was you that took my spot. After everything went down, I don't trust Dealto anymore."

James watched and listened as Webb spoke. His body was square to him, strong eye contact and void of all barriers. He exhibited no negative micro gestures and his words felt straightforward. No signs of physiological body leakage that would indicate deception were observed. Was he this good of a liar? Or was there truth behind his words? James was cautious.

"Ok. Say I bite on that. Explain the day you got put on leave? Branding tool in hand."

Webb rubbed at the corners of his mouth, looking around. His body language revealed that he was contemplating his next move.

"Let me start with this. I'm not the type to say I gave everything to this PD, and they bagged me. I didn't give anything to this PD. Didn't do any of my work for them. I work hard for myself. It's what drives me in life. It's my fuel. I can't stop until I've got what I need. Maybe I'm not the nicest person in the world, but I'll be dammed if I let rapists and murderers victimize the few good people left in this world. I'll search this whole country until they're eliminated."

Hearing the word eliminated stuck in James' head. An odd choice of words. He wanted to hear more. "I get that. Go on."

"Let me ask you. What's the connection between all your victims?"

"Don't have one," James acknowledged, knowing this was not an intimate detail of the crimes.

Webb tightened his lips and looked away briefly. Looking back at James, he continued. "I never gave all my information out to this office. Some things I needed to keep close and confirm before exposing. So, let's talk about your victims."

Webb shifted around in his seat, laying both hands upside down on the table as if he was making a peace offering. James's elbow rested on the table, while his hand was under his chin, holding his head up. He stared into the eyes of Webb as his heartrate slowed and the room began to feel warm. James couldn't help but start believing Webb and was open to learning what information he was speaking about.

"All the victims fit a common theme. I'm sure you've gone through all the social media on them and read any reports they may have been in from here and surrounding PDs. Anything catch your eye?" Webb was calm and cool in his questioning, as his eyes widened.

"No. All typical happy families. Their social media were plastered with family photos, vacations, and holidays. Normal good people content."

"Well, I'm not saying they're not good people. They didn't deserve what happened to them. However, tell me about the criminal checks on them. Tell me about the reports you read."

"Just some domestic stuff. Nothing outlandish. But there's not domestics in my family, I can tell you that."

"You're better than that. Dig deeper," Webb said as he leaned in toward James. "How's your marriage been the past few months since poly school?"

James pulled on his ear, knowing things were far from perfect. "Not great. I mean, we're okay, but things have just been tough. A lot of arguing, but nothing out of control."

"Okay, so let's go further. If you pull up your wife's social media. How's it looking? I'll actually answer that. It probably looks great. Everything's normal and you guys are the poster for the all-American family. Am I right?"

James nodded.

"Now, if you go through those families, like I did, they're all the same. Husbands have all been arrested for beating their wives. Children have been in the middle, and DCF has been involved. In all of them. Even the first couple. It's not easy to get ahold of DCF records, but you'll see they had their only child taken away after a pretty nasty altercation."

"Again, how does that involve me?" James tossed his hands up.

"I can't answer that. What did the note say?"

James wrestled with the idea of giving up the information, but his internal Spidey sense told him Webb was being genuine. If Webb wasn't the killer, he needed all the information he could pull. Cooperating was the only way to get it. James couldn't risk pushing Webb away and being confrontational. "It just said we weren't chosen. Something about the gods letting us live or something."

Webb sat back and folded his arms across his chest. "So, no arrest between you guys and no DCF ever involved?"

"No. Never."

"I can only assume that's why you guys were spared."

"Tell me about the day you were let go," James said, trying to force Webb to answer the question.

"Jimmy Zaniewski. Guy was a piece of work. Incarcerated for a few years, beating his ex-wife of course, and lost all parental rights to his only kid. When I started putting together the dots, I just went crazy running names and looking for his possible next target. Most were dead ends. But when I went to Jimmy's house, I found the branding tool out back. Called the team and told them to get there quick."

"So, you didn't plant that there? Neighbors said they saw you throw it down."

Webb looked annoyed at the accusation. "No. I picked it up to look at the end. Should've been more careful but wasn't expecting it to be anything. I had been to dozens of houses before that. So yeah, they probably did see me toss it back on the ground. Then I went and spoke to Jimmy, trying to just get info on whether it was his or not. Guy freaked out, thinking I was trying to frame him for a burglary. From what I heard, he took off and disappeared after that day."

"Yeah, well, we found him. He's dead."

A slight micro gesture of surprise shot through the Webb's eyebrows. He didn't know.

James cleared his throat. "So why do you think the tool was there?"

"I think our boy got spooked one night and beat feet. Dropped it behind. Next thing I know, I'm being accused of planting it. I was never even asked to explain. Not even Dealto. He and I were close, man. Guy just threw me under the bus. I was done at that point. Didn't want to say nothin' to nobody."

It all made sense to James.

Webb wasn't his guy.

"Listen, I got to get the hell out of here. Use your head. Whenever you think you've reached the end of your digging, go deeper. Everyone leaves clues."

"What about the branding? How's that tie in? And what about Carmine? Why are you helping those guys?"

Webb stood up. "Pam's trying to put his top guy away. She doesn't lose. I lost her once, can't lose her again," he said, ignoring the branding question. Extending his hand, he shook James's. "Dig, kid. Keep digging."

Webb walked to the door and was halfway out before turning around and saying "And no hard feelings. Glad the fam's okay." Webb exited the room. Passing Shaw and Michaels who were waiting in the hall he added "And fuck you guys too,"

James walked out of the interrogation room and wandered back into the main office, feeling oddly blank. Michaels and Shaw followed him.

Dealto came out of his office, as his three detectives stood looking at him. "Well, that threw me for a loop. Should've known he'd have some answers. You believe him?" Dealto asked.

"I do. We're looking in the wrong direction. Our guy is doing it on purpose, trying to throw us off."

"So, what's the move?" Michaels asked.

James took a deep breath and exhaled. "Time to take out the shovels."

TWENTY-SIX

PLACING his hands on the door of the Deception Unit, he flung it open. Webb was once again furious his integrity was being questioned by his old team. The thought brought back the old feelings of when he left the department. The idea that Dealto could see him as a serial killer drove him crazy. He liked James but couldn't assist the PD after they crossed him this way. *Again.*

The elevator doors opened, and he walked through the lobby toward the exit. Two patrolmen taking a complaint looked at him with surprise. He ignored them and made his way out the electronic sliding doors. Seeing the road clear of oncoming traffic, he jogged across the street toward his Honda. As he gathered his thoughts, he replayed the conversation with James. He had just gotten more information that could steer him in a new direction. Zaniewski was dead, and James' family was spared. More dots to connect.

When his phone vibrated, he fully expected it to be a member of his old team calling to patch things up. Fishing the phone from his pocket, he was surprised to see who it was.

"Pam, everything okay?"

"It's not, Carter. I'm starting to freak out a little."

From one bad conversation to another. "What's going on?"

"It's Carmine's guys, they're everywhere. I'm not being paranoid. His guys are constantly tailing me."

Her words were shaky and slightly unclear. Webb knew she was scared. Saving Carmine from a bullet didn't seem to do the trick. Time was running out. Keeping his tone calm, he tried to alleviate some of her anxiety. "You've dealt with this before. I know it's scary, but they're just keeping an eye on you, hoping to find an out in the case."

"That's not going to happen, and this isn't the same. Carmine will do whatever he has to, to get this guy off. I'm scared Carter."

Her words rang true. "Let me look into it. In the meantime, you have to stay away from your house. You're welcome to stay with me or go stay with your boyfriend for a bit. Grab a rental car to buy yourself some time."

"We're not together anymore," Pam quickly blurted out. "I'm heading home now to park the car. Was going to sneak out and have my mom meet me somewhere. I'll stop to get a rental in the meantime. Please do what you can. I'm sure they took my CI out. He's still MIA. This whole thing has me shaken."

"I'm on it. I'll let you know if I get any information. Just please be careful. Maybe take a few days off."

"I'm scared, but I won't let them win. There's no way I'm letting this guy off that easy."

Webb sighed. "Figured as much. I'll be in touch."

Pam's determination and dedication to her job is something he'd always loved about her. They were one and the same. Hanging up the phone, he held his phone up to his head, thinking. He could never live with himself if he let her down again. While they were no longer together, he still loved her. Pulling up Carmine's number, he pressed call.

"Ohhh, if ain't my guardian angel," Tarascio said in a smug tone.

"What's going on, Carmine?" Webb said, trying to keep the conversation light. "I think I got a good plan for your guy. Just need a week or so to button up some details." Webb hadn't even looked at the case, but he needed to pry at the mindset of the boss. A risky move, but the only one he had.

"Eh. Likely no need," Tarascio said as the sound of him sucking a cigarette came through the speaker. "I can't wait that long. Things are going sideways over here without him. That piece a shit Patsy's after me, and money's not flowing right. Gotta put a stop to this thing now. Once this prosecutor's gone, it shouldn't be a problem."

Webb's body temperature rose as he heard the comment. He was out of time and needed a plan immediately. "She's beatable, Carmine. Don't do anything stupid and make things muddier for yourself. Give me the night. I'll call you in the morning."

"Can't make you any promises, but you call me back." The phone disconnected.

Webb threw his phone down in frustration and flipped the center console open. The urge for nicotine was strong. Webb flicked at the Camel Crush box with his finger, retrieving a smoke. Lighting it up, a deep inhale refocused his mind. He started making his way back to the office; he needed to go through the files Edwards had gotten on the case.

As the tires came to a halt outside Edward's office, he killed the ignition and exited. Dropping the Camel to the pavement, the cinders flew off the tip with an orange hue. His right foot stomped out the butt and he headed inside.

Entering through a side door, he skipped turning on the lights in an attempt to stay unnoticed. Sliding his thumb down the top of his iPhone, he clicked the flashlight to illuminate the room. Entering Edwards' office, he sat behind the desk and began sifting through the drawers.

Got it.

With the large three ring binder sitting on the mahogany top, he pulled on the chain of the desk lamp. Webb was locked into every word he read, storing each in his memory. The police had to have a misstep somewhere that could blow this whole case up. Knowing the goon was guilty didn't sit well with him, but he had to protect Pam.

The case reports were well written. Detective Jeffrey Michaels, a seasoned veteran, had made the arrest. Michaels was always meticulous with his investigations, and this one was no different. If there were a misstep, it would have to be from someone other than him.

Webb went through the chain of custody procedures. Officer Jim Froberg was the property officer and also a firearms instructor. Webb had gone to the academy with Froberg in the early 2000s. He was a good guy, but always looked for the easy way out. This was going to be Webb's way in, he just had to find it.

His fingers flipped back through the supplemental reports, and pulled Froberg's out. There were three in total. One showed him receiving the firearm used in the crime, and one stated the firearm was sent to the lab for analysis.

The third was the one.

Webb knew that when a firearm was used in a crime, it was typically taken to the range to be fired, showing it was in working order to commit the crime. The report, however, had very few details included. Reading the narrative, Froberg noted the wrong caliber of the firearm. But more importantly, the gun was never properly signed out of evidence. The gun was also fired by another firearm instructor. This showed a massive break in the chain of custody and a huge break for Webb.

If he could have the firearm suppressed as evidence, the state would have no case.

WEBB WAS STILL SIFTING through every word in an attempt to find a backup plan if his suppression of evidence didn't work. Eyelids growing heavy, his breathing slowed.

The sound of the doorknob being twisted echoed in the office, and Edwards walked in. "Damn Carter, you scared the hell out of me!

What are you doing here already? And why are you at my desk?" Edwards held his hand on his chest but smiled at Webb.

Webb leaned back in the chair and slapped at his cheeks, trying to wake himself up. "Sorry, bud. We got a problem though, need to talk about Carmine."

Edwards tossed his briefcase onto the leather couch and sat down, crossing his hands behind his head. "Well, this seems important, so what do you got?"

"I got a call from Pam last night. Carmine's guys are all over her. Tailing her everywhere she goes. I made a call to him, trying to feel him out." Webb paused, rocking forward in the chair. "He's gonna kill her, Jonny. We need to get this case tossed, like yesterday."

Edwards rolled his eyes and exhaled. "Holy shit. I'd like to say no way that would happen, but that guy's a lunatic," he shook his head. "What the hell are we supposed to do? That case is freaking tight. No way Pam loses that thing."

Webb adjusted himself in the chair, sliding his fingers through pages toward the evidence. "Right. Michaels had the case and did a bang-up job. Can't find a thing on his end. However, there's a problem with the gun. Froberg broke the chain of custody and also had another officer test fire it. It's kind of a long shot, but I think we can get the gun suppressed from the case."

Edwards sat for a moment, staring off into the room. He softly rubbed his fingers across his lips, as he began nodding his head. "I think that can work. The serial number was scratched off the firearm, wasn't it?"

"It was." Webb nodded.

"That's good. I'll check out the photos taken and see what I can come up with. Maybe we can get a suppression hearing granted and get in there in a few weeks."

"We don't have weeks, Jonny. I'm not sure we have hours. This needs to happen ASAP. I'm not waiting around, hoping her body doesn't show up somewhere."

"You're right. I'm going to put a call in to Judge Alexander. She owes me a favor. Sounds like no better time to use it. I'll get it put on for tomorrow if possible. Super short notice, but the state will have to accept it, seeing as he's still locked up. Why don't you go grab us Starbucks? When you get back, we'll work on a plan." Edwards reached into his pocket and handed Webb a twenty-dollar bill.

Webb noticed his hand shaking as he gripped the cash. He took a deep breath to steady his nerves as he made his way out. Sleep would be minimal over the next few days, so a heavy dose of caffeine was in order. Webb needed to get this case thrown out so he could refocus his attention.

But until Pam was safe, that had to wait.

TWENTY-SEVEN

WEBB'S KNEE bounced up and down while he slowly swiveled in the courtroom chair. Edwards had managed to get a speedy suppression hearing in place, but that was only half the battle.

The real test was right before him.

The sound of the wood door behind him slapping closed rang through the courtroom. Pam walked in holding her files with the inspector by her side. She made eye contact with Webb for a split second before looking away.

"Damn, she looks pissed," Edwards said under his breath, leaning in toward Webb.

"I didn't explain anything to her yet. Even if I did, she wouldn't have been happy. Let's just win this thing and I'll explain later."

Webb turned toward the courtroom as a small crowd was gathered in the seats. Tucked in the corner, Tarascio sat with his arms folded across his chest. Looking in Webb's direction, he winked at him. Knowing his ex-partners had questioned his integrity for something he didn't do, he felt the irony, as he was now fully immersed in going against what he believed. He knew this was the only way to save Pam, but the thought of letting a true criminal out of jail would haunt him.

"All rise."

The room stood as Judge Alexander entered the courtroom. Settling in behind the bench and sliding her glasses on, she opened her files.

Tony Valentine leaned over toward Edwards and whispered into his ear. "Ahh, this bitch hates me. Put me away a few times. If she let me slip the ol bracjole in just one time, she'd be singin' a different tune," he let out a smug chuckle. Webb's blood boiled as he once again questioned his decision.

"Good morning everyone. The defense has called for an immediate suppression hearing due to some new information regarding this case, State vs Valentine. Is that correct Mr. Edwards?"

"That is correct, your honor."

Pam immediately stood, interjecting. "Yes, Ms. Mazur."

"Your honor, the state has only had a day to look over this new information. We are requesting two weeks to review all the facts to be properly prepared."

"Overruled. Unfortunately, Mr. Valentine is still incarcerated without bail, and this new information could potentially be critical to his release." A defeated Mazur slowly sat while shooting a dirty look in Webb's direction.

"Mr. Edwards, are your witnesses in the courtroom?"

"Yes, your honor."

"You may proceed."

"Your honor, the defense calls Officer James Froberg to the stand."

Unshaven, with a faded uniform full of stain, Froberg stood from the crowd, making his way down the aisle. He passed through the low double doors and approached the bench to be sworn in.

"Good morning, Officer Froberg." Edwards said with a big smile.

Sighing, Froberg nodded and rolled his eyes, not saying a word, Edwards rested his elbow on the witness stand, sliding his free hand into his pocket. "Officer Froberg, can you say for the record, what your current position is with South Lake PD and how long you've been an officer?"

"Yes, I started in 2005. I'm currently the property officer."

"And can you explain your role as the property officer?"

"I'm responsible for receiving all evidence, investigative holds, and found property. After they're tagged, I place them in our evidence room. I also transport evidence to the forensic lab for testing, destroy evidence once requested by the court, and return property to the owner."

Edwards nodded his head while looking at Froberg from the corner of his eye. "And how does this evidence get to you? Is it left at the main desk? Does an officer hand it to you? How does it work?"

"Once an officer seizes something, they tag it with a label. The label describes the property, lists a case number, time seized, officer's name, and a brief description of what it is. The property is then placed in an evidence locker. That locker is locked and there is access from the rear. That rear door is locked, and I am the only one with the key to unlock it." Froberg calmly answered without hesitation.

"Interesting. And why is it that only you have a key to those lockers?"

"We need to maintain a proper chain of custody."

"Chain of custody? And what exactly does that mean?"

Froberg rolled his eyes at the question. "You know what it means."

Edwards walked closer to the witness stand. "I have an idea. But can you explain it, please?"

Froberg sighed. "When anything is seized, we need to keep track of every hand that touches that piece of evidence. We need to ensure that it is not tampered with in any way."

"That makes sense," James responded, followed by a short pause. "And when evidence is transferred to you, do you complete a supplement report? Or any documentation showing the evidence was moved?"

"Yes. My report will document when I took ownership of it. If it's ever needed for court, or sent to the lab, it also has to be checked out and checked back in."

Edwards slowly walked around the front of the witness box with a confident swag. "Man, seems like a lot of work. And you always do this?"

Webb watched closely, following Edwards' question. Froberg's eyebrows quickly drew up, causing tension in his forehead. His eyes flashed wide, just prior to answering. The fear was setting in. "Yup. I mean, yes." Froberg responded with a crack in his voice.

"Are you familiar with this case and my client?"

"I am, that's Fatts right over there," Froberg said, pointing at Valentine with a cocky grin.

Edwards stopped walking, tilted his head, and turned back towards Froberg. "Fatts?"

"I'm sorry. Tony Valentine."

"Right. Can you explain your process of handling the evidence in this case?"

"There was a firearm seized for the shooting. It was tagged by Detective Michaels, then I removed it from the locker and placed it in the evidence room."

"After you took ownership, did it stay in the evidence room the whole time?"

Froberg looked up, appearing to recall the steps he took during the investigation. Edwards stepped up to the witness stand, placing Froberg's supplemental reports in front of him. "You can refresh your memory."

Froberg flipped through the pages. "Yes, thank you. The firearm was sent to the lab for testing, then brought to the range to be test fired."

"Did the lab results show any DNA?"

"They did not."

"And how did the gun fire? Everything in working order?"

"Yes sir. Officer Pergolizzi took it down to the range. Everything came back functional."

"Good, good. And what caliber gun was it?"

Froberg looked down at his report, sliding his finger across the paper. "It was a forty caliber."

Edwards made a dumbfounded look while staring back at Froberg. "Forty caliber? I'm sorry, I thought your narrative said nine millimeter."

Panic rushed over Froberg, as his eyes went side to side while looking at his report. "Yeah, I must have written that wrong on page one of my report."

Edwards waved his hand toward the witness, dismissing the mistake. "Eh. Mistakes happen. I assume it was just a typo, right?"

"Yeah, definitely a mistake on my part."

"Oh, and you said an Officer Pergolizzi test fired the gun, correct?"

"Yes sir."

"Can you tell me what time Pergolizzi checked the firearm out of evidence?" Edwards slid the tracking log over to Froberg. Looking through the document, his face began to change colors. Pinching two fingers around the top of his nose, the muscles under his ears flexed.

"Doesn't look like he did."

"Isn't that a chain of custody issue? Are you sure he took the right gun out? Do we even know how long it was out for?"

Froberg gawked at Edwards. Webb watched with his leg crossed and gnawing at his fingernails. His anxious gestures came through in similar fashion as James'. Froberg was floundering, just like Webb hoped he would.

Froberg shook his head and exhaled. "I'm not sure."

"You're not sure?" Edwards said, while tapping at the report in front of Froberg. "I assume this was just another mistake on your part?"

"Yes. I must have forgotten to complete the paperwork."

"Do you make mistakes often, Officer Froberg? Seems like quite a few mistakes for just one case."

Froberg was silent, not answering the question.

Edwards cocked his head. "I'll take that as a 'yes'."

"Objection. The defense is making an assumption." Judge Alexander looked over at Froberg.

"No. I don't think I make mistakes often."

"You don't think? That's interesting." Edwards laid it on thicker. "So, we have no idea how long this gun was checked out for, and we have no idea who else could've been handling it. I thought the whole point of chain of custody was to know, without a doubt, where the evidence is at all times?"

"It is," Froberg said quietly as his head sunk into his chest.

"Well, seems like we have a problem here," Edwards began walking around. "Can you read me the serial number of the firearm seized?"

"I can't."

"And why is that?"

"There were no identifying marks on the gun. They were all removed prior to us seizing it."

"What about any marks on the firearm? Anything in photos that were unique?" Edwards slid over photocopies of the pictures taken at the scene. Froberg looked through them.

"No. Gun looked new."

Webb knew this was a pivotal moment in the testimony. Edwards and Webb had discussed showing the court that there was no way to prove the firearm in evidence was, in fact, the one they seized. With a kink in the chain of custody, the firearm could've been changed.

"So, we have the wrong caliber listed, the gun was not checked out, and we have no clue how long it was out. And, we have no way of even saying for sure that the firearm in evidence is, in fact, the gun you seized. Is that correct?"

Webb looked over at Pam, whose eyes were closed as she shook her head. Webb knew their argument was setting in.

"I know it's the gun!" Froberg said while leaning forward and grabbing at the wood around the witness box with both hands.

Edwards sauntered back toward his prey. "Well, Officer Froberg. I'm sure you think it is. But you seem to have made quite a few big mistakes in this case. Not sure I can take your word for it. Based on the break in chain of custody, I don't think you can prove that." Edwards rested both palms on the witness stand, peering at the defeated Froberg.

Froberg shook his head.

Turning to his left, Webb watched as Valentine smirked.

"Your honor, there's no way this firearm can be admitted as evidence. It was not found on my client at the time, and only one witness was able to identify him in possession of what they thought was a gun. Based on Officer Froberg's proficiency in mistakes, lord only knows what happened when this gun was out. I have nothing further." Edwards walked back, slapped Webb on the shoulder, and sat down. "That went better than expected."

"Ms. Mazur, do you have anything?"

Pam was whispering into the ear of her inspector. Webb attempted to listen but couldn't make out what she was saying. She did, however, seem to be panicking.

"Ms. Mazur?"

She finished her conversation and stood. "I don't your honor."

Webb felt an odd sense of relief flow through his body.

"Based on the facts presented, I have to suppress the firearm in this case. The state will have to prove its case without using that piece of evidence. Is that understood, Ms. Mazur?"

"Yes, your honor."

"Additionally, based on the circumstances, I'm going to place a one-hundred-thousand-dollar bond for the defendant."

This was exactly what Webb had hoped for. The state's case was going to be weak, but a very manageable bond for Tarascio to get Valentine released.

"I'll schedule a hearing date for December 20th, at ten am. This court is adjourned."

The courtroom stood as the magistrate made her way out.

Valentine let out an obnoxious cackle. "I'll be out of here in a few hours. Time to get back to work." He slapped Edwards's thigh.

Webb felt two hands gently massaging the back of his neck. He turned and found Tarascio grinning at him. "Oh marone, I think I found myself an angel,"

Refocusing his attention to his right, he saw Pam with her head down, agonizing over her defeat.

Webb felt his heart twist, plagued by the moral dilemma born from the steps he had taken to protect his ex-wife. The line between right and wrong blurred as he reflected on the choices made. The future holds uncertain implications for his professional relationship with Pam and the trajectory of his career. He felt a profound sense of unease about the choices that brought him to this pivotal moment.

"Glad we could help. Just trust me moving forward," Webb said, hoping there would never be a next time.

He sprung from the chair and dashed out of the courtroom to remove himself from the emotions inside. As he pushed the doors open and entered the hallway, his brain instantly shifted gears. What was done was done.

Now there were bigger fish to fry.

Standing still, he looked around as the corner of his mouth curled upward. He had spent years tracking a serial killer, losing his career and the love of his life in the process.

It was time to end this journey, and nothing was going to stop him.

TWENTY-EIGHT

THE SOUND of Webb's feet echoed through the parking garage as he jogged to his Honda. The killer was moving at a much faster pace than in the past, so it was time to grind before another family lost their lives. Having had so many of his cases fall flat by the inability to properly be prosecuted by the court, he needed to secure his suspect. Flinging the car door open, Webb knew this was more personal than it had ever been, and real justice was in order.

The tires screeched as he left the parking garage, nearly striking the gate as it lifted in front of him. For the past several years, he had kept every file related to this killer in his home as a constant reminder of his failure. The only case he hadn't been able to solve. His brain sunk back into the darkness of years prior, when his life fell apart because of it. This time, he wasn't going to try to suppress those feelings.

It was time he welcomed them.

And ended it.

With the new information he received from James, he could feel he was close to a resolution. Springing from his car, he dashed toward his apartment complex. Running past the people chatting, he threw out his arm to stop the closing elevator. He moved to the rear corner and scrolled through his phone to avoid conversation with the one elderly lady already inside. The bell dinged as he reached his floor. Nodding a smile to the woman, he made his way to his door. As he wrestled with his keys an odd sense of excitement flowed through his body. Webb felt a sense of purpose again.

He walked through the door and beelined toward the spare bedroom. His brain scrolled like a slide show of images of all the past crimes and the investigation notes he had taken. They were at the forefront, and nothing else mattered.

Reaching the doorway, he flicked on the light switch, illuminating the room. Pulling the chair out from the desk, he took a moment to look around. Flooded with crime scene photos, potential suspects, and newspaper articles, he soaked it all in. Everything hung from a corkboard, with yarn connecting various points. His brain finally refocused before the volcano erupted and he felt a sense of calm, knowing the answer was in front of him.

His hands grasped the screen of his laptop as he pulled it up and he began his search. Starting with the first homicide, he peeled apart every angle of the Daigle family. They fit the mold perfectly of the killer's MO. A home of chaos, but one to envy on social media. Littered with domestic abuse and a child who hung with the wrong crowd. Jotting notes on post-its as he went along, he slapped them on the desk, creating several columns.

The instance with Romano's daughter was very similar. However, this information was harder to find. His assumption was if Patsy had found out his daughter was being abused by her husband, the husband would quickly go missing. Still having access to several web pages he used as a detective gave Webb the ability to search records deeper than the average citizen, and, finally, he was able to dig it up.

His chair creaked as he leaned back, looking over his notes and the walls littered with photos. There had to be more of a connection than just dysfunctional families. For someone to go as far as to execute them, there had to be a deeper motivation in the mind of the killer. He sprung up from the chair, placing his hands over his face and paced around the room. "Think Carter, think!"

Frustrated but determined to put it all together, he stormed through the doorway and made his way to the balcony. He plopped down into his armchair and dug into his pocket in search for stress relief. He slid a Camel from the box, and after lighting it, took a drag. He watched the smoke drift into the dark sky while feeling the release of dopamine into his brain. The sky was lit up by the full moon shining in front of him. Very few clouds were above, but several stars twinkled as his head spun with thoughts.

"What would cause a person to be so enraged by an abuse-riddled and dysfunctional home?" he mumbled aloud.

Sucking in more nicotine, the endorphins relieved his stress, bringing more clarity to his thinking. He felt puzzle pieces aligning in his brain as the picture came into focus. Like a cartoon character with a good idea, the light bulb turned on.

The suspect must have been through similar trauma as a kid. A home filled with violence, but all smiles in public. This had to be an extreme case, so there had to be a trail of breadcrumbs he could follow.

Crushing the half-smoked cigarette into the ground with his shoe, he scurried back to his computer to follow the trail. Webb entered his four-digit code, 1028, Pam's birthday, and his computer powered back up from sleep mode. He opened a search engine and typed *national domestic abuse arrests*. This had to be a major case, or at least he hoped.

He clicked on several articles, but none of them seemed to fit the mold. Webb scrolled through the third page of results. A news article labeled "Son kills parents in gruesome attack" sent a chill through his body. Before even clicking on the article, he had an intuitive conviction this was the one. He could see the finish line.

He clicked the title and the article from The Indy Outlook written in March of 1991 opened up. Sixteen-year-old Robert Mitchard shot and killed his father during a physical altercation with his mother. When she tried to intervene and stop him, he killed her, too. Dismembering his father into twelve pieces, he stacked him up like firewood in the basement. When finished, he called the police and told them what he had done. Due to his age, court officials thought they could rehabilitate him, spending only thirty days incarcerated, followed by years of counseling.

Webb continued reading through the article and everything became clear to him. When police arrived on the scene, they found Mitchard's father placed in front of a backdrop, with a camera resting on a tripod pointed toward it. A single photo dangled from the slot at the front of the camera.

So many pieces were answered for Webb in this one article. Having taken place several states away from Connecticut and several years prior to his employment with the department, the dots couldn't be connected during his investigation. The case had not caught enough national attention to put it together.

With a new tab, he surfed to Accurint.com, the most used tool of law enforcement to locate and research persons of interest. He started with Mitchard, in an attempt to see if he had any local residences. Lo and behold, Mitchard had multiple Indiana homes up until 2017, when he moved to Connecticut. Since then, only one address was listed, and it was in South Lake. His mind still couldn't make a connection between Mitchard and South Lake. He went back to the search page and typed in Mitchard's father's name. The results showed several homes in Indiana, but, scrolling to the bottom, it finally made sense. Mitchard's father's first address was listed in South Lake, CT. The same home Mitchard was currently living in.

Webb leaned back in his chair and pressed his knuckles to his head in shock. He couldn't contain the emotions flowing through his body. Flipping his wrist, his watch read 3:12 a.m. While any normal human being would be exhausted from the mental strain he had endured over the past several days, Webb was wide awake.

    His jacket snapped as he pulled it from the back of the couch. He slid his arms through the sleeves and left his apartment. His eyelids were heavy, but a smile curved his lips as he walked, feeling purpose fueling his steps. The chase was on, and this time, he wasn't going to lose.

TWENTY-NINE

HIS 2008 HONDA ACCORD was tested to its limits as Webb pressed so hard on the gas pedal that the old car struggled to keep his foot from going through the floorboard. He slowed his speed and turned onto Rosemount Avenue, an older neighborhood with smaller ranch and Cape Cod style homes. He twisted the headlight switch, blacking out his car. Slowly rolling down the street, the home came into view. He slowed his car to rest on the side of the road so he could start his surveillance.

With his binoculars, he scanned the home for any movement or lights.

Nothing.

The home was completely dark. From experience, he knew deranged individuals tended to be night owls. The demons within wouldn't allow them much peace, causing severe insomnia.

An hour passed with no movement from the house. Headlights lit up the inside of his car as another vehicle turned down the street, traveling toward him. With squinted eyes he watched, not able to make out the make or model, as it slowly crept down the road with the headlights obstructing his view.

As it approached Mitchard's possible home, the left blinker flashed, and the car turned into the driveway. Very few people use a blinker when turning into their driveway. *Except those trying to follow the laws and keep a low profile*, Webb thought.

Webb watched as an older Ford station wagon with wood trim cruised up the driveway and came to rest. The dome light of the Ford glowed through the interior as the driver's door opened. Emerging from the car, the man's head came into view over the top of the vehicle as Webb peered through the magnified lenses of his binoculars. A white male approximately fifty years old, with a thick mustache and wearing a dark colored sweater, made his way to the front door. He swung his keys around his finger until he reached the door, placed the key in the lock and entered the home.

Webb tossed the binoculars to the passenger seat and stepped into the street. Making his way to the rear of the home three houses down from Mitchard's, he crept through the backyards. Staying far enough away from the homes to ensure he didn't set off a potential motion light, he reached his target location. Standing behind a tree in the back corner, he watched through an uncovered window. The cold air caused his breath to crystalize, and the moon lit a path for him.

Webb watched the man mull around the kitchen, appearing to make himself something to eat. Webb noticed the man's back turned away from the window, so he took the opportunity to sneak toward the home. His steps were void of any noise as he moved closer and pressed his body against the siding. Slowly, he turned his head and leaned toward the window as more of the kitchen came into view, little by little. He quickly peaked inside, then ducked back out of possible view. The sound of whistling could be heard inside as Webb's back was pressed against the home. A glass clink rang out, causing Webb to take another look inside. The man's back was directly in front of Webb as the man sat at the table eating. Two bowls sat in front of empty chairs at the table, both filled with food and utensils.

Odd.

The only thing that now separated Webb from his suspect were wooden studs and two thin layers of sheet rock. The thought caused Webb's heart rate to slowly increase from adrenaline.

He slid through the backyard to the other side of the home. Approaching two windows, he found the one toward the front of the ranch style home unlocked. He pushed his fingers under the base of the window and slowly pushed upward. With no curtains blocking his view, an empty room was in his sight.

With his palms pressing against the frame, Webb easily lifted himself upward and into the room. His feet hit the wooden floor, making no noise. Tiptoeing through the room, he quietly moved toward the door. He peeked around the door frame, which exposed the hallway. Old brown trim surrounded the doors with floral wallpaper covering each inch of the wall. The end of the hallway led to the kitchen. An old stained glass pendant hung above the wood rectangular table. Webb could see a bowl of food on the side of the table, but the man was just out of view.

Webb slid his hand across the small of his back and pulled out his firearm. With it tucked against his chest, he hugged the wall as he made his way toward the kitchen. His left foot pressed against the floor as he reached the corner of the hallway. He inhaled deep into his lungs and slowly released his breath. In one swift movement, Webb popped out from the hallway with his body bladed, and the barrel of his firearm pointed at the chest of the man.

"Don't move, Robert!" he yelled.

A spoon full of macaroni and cheese continued toward his mouth. Taking his bite, he began to chew as he placed the spoon back in the bowl. He swallowed the food, and with a chilling laugh, the man began clapping his hands together.

"Well. If it isn't Carter Webb. It's about time, my friend." Mitchard dabbed at his mouth with a napkin, after finishing his applause.

The unusual welcome did not surprise Webb.

"No need for the gun, my friend. I'm not going to hurt you."

Webb tilted his head while looking over the killer who had caused so much chaos in his life. With wiry glasses resting on the tip of his nose, the heavy set Mitchard looked back at Webb with a calmness only true psychopaths possess. The forest green sweater he wore looked like it was picked up at the local Goodwill and a silver watch from the 1980s poked out the bottom of the sleeve.

"Why don't you have a seat so we can chat, my friend?"

Webb closed the distance on Mitchard while sliding his Glock back to the rear of his back. He made his way around the table, and his anger took over as a closed fist flew at Mitchard's chin. Webb's knuckles made direct contact with his jaw, sending him flying off the chair. Moving around the chair, Webb attempted to grab the killer's wrists. While reaching down, he was met with a shoe to the groin that sent immediate nausea into his stomach. As he was trying to fight through the pain and blurred vision, Mitchard pulled at Webb's feet, toppling him to the floor. Springing back to his feet, Webb released another fist rocket at Mitchard's temple. This one left him unconscious.

With his legs pinned underneath the killer, Webb pulled them out and stood up. His legs now straddled Mitchard, pulling his limp weight onto the chair. While he lay motionless with his head flopped on the table, Webb headed toward the cabinets. Opening several, he eventually found a roll of duct tape. He walked back over to Mitchard and placed his hands behind the old wooden chair. Webb slid his fingertip across the tape to find the end and secured the man's hands.

After securing his feet to the legs of the chair, Webb sat across the table, gazing at the man that had caused his downfall. The man's mouth was wide open, soft snores hissing out. Wrapping his hand against the table, Webb woke the beast.

His eyes flickered open as his head wobbled. His glasses no longer attached, he looked across the table squinting, trying to focus in on Webb. A smile came across his face.

"Oh, Mr. Webb. I'm sorry. I must have taken a quick snooze." Blood dripped from his nose and his forehead glistened with perspiration as he sat up.

"Mr. Mitchard. I think we need to have a talk."

"Oh please, call me Bobby." Mitchard grinned, his teeth red from the blood flowing from his mouth.

The blasé attitude of the man fueled Webb's anger. It was time to find out the whole truth. "Ok, Bobby. Why'd you kill all those people?"

Mitchard cocked his head and clicked his tongue. "I don't know, Carter. What are you saying?"

Webb placed his elbow on the table and rubbed the insides of his eyes. He did not want a drawn-out interrogation, but he needed to take a step back in order to get what he wanted. Attacking the root of the issue would have to be his angle. "This must be your parent's house, right?

The smug twinkle in Mitchard's eye melted into rage.

Webb threw his hands up, shrugging. "Seemed like decent people. I read your dad worked at Pratt and Whitney back in the day. Tough job, but he clearly did what he had to, to provide for you and your mother."

Mitchard's chin moved downward as the level of intensity in which his breathing changed, as his chest slowly rose up and down. "My father was a piece of shit!"

Bingo.

A mad man can never control his emotions when faced with his own demons. Time to poke at his heart, to figure out his reasoning.

Webb leaned back, raising an eyebrow. "Really? The newspaper made it seem like you were just crazy."

Mitchard paused, his breathing growing more irregular. "That guy had no business on earth. I watched daily as he beat my mother. And when she was done taking her beating, I was next. *Every. Single. Day.*" he said through his gritted teeth.

"Ehhhh come on. It couldn't have been so bad that he had to die, right? I mean, the family photos they showed were great. You guys looked so happy together."

Mitchard sat motionless, but his intense gaze became more unfocused, as if he was looking right through Webb. Webb sat in silence, allowing the quietness of the room to feel loud in the head of his enemy. A tactic he often used in interrogations. The silence created an unsettling anxiety.

"That's all he cared about. His photos. All he wanted in life was to become a famous photographer. His Polaroid was his most prized possession." Mitchard turned his head toward the living room to his left, jerking his chin.

Webb looked over, seeing the camera resting on a coffee table. "He set up a studio in the basement. We spent hours posing for him. It was never good enough. That's when the beatings came."

Webb suppressed his surprise, trying to downplay the situation. "I don't know. Seems a bit extreme if you ask me."

Mitchard pressed his chest against the table, leaning toward Webb. "It wasn't," he whispered. "Mom would always defend him. When I killed him, she called me every name in the book. So, she had to go too. Besides, all she cared about was her damn pearl necklaces!"

"Damn. I guess I just don't get it then." Webb shook his head as he sat back and rested his hands on the table. "But all these innocent people. Why them? Why'd they deserve to die?"

Mitchard let out a cackle as he rocked back and forth. "Innocent!" he jeered through his laughter. "Please. Those families were just as messed up as mine. The gods don't want them here. They don't belong on this earth."

"How so, Bobby?"

His eyes glazed, and he broke eye contact with Webb, turning his gaze to the floor. Tilting his head, as if his brain went down memory lane, he took a deep breath before looking back into Webb's eyes. "They're all sinners, posing as worshippers. Domestic and drug abuse. Living a lie. This world has no place for those people, and I won't stop until they're all gone."

Webb listened intently. Mitchard was making insinuations, but the full confession was still lacking. He had to pry deeper.

"Well, I agree there are definitely a lot of fake people out there. Lots of bad people," Webb conceded. "But you know, that first one I investigated years back just didn't seem to fit to me. Just a young couple. Drug users." Webb softly conveyed, giving limited details to his investigation.

Mitchard leaned back in his chair and cackled, shaking his head back and forth like a mad man. The laugh was one clearly without remorse, one that chilled Webb to the core.

Mitchard shook his head, his laughter dying. "Oh, Carter, Carter. Those two were the biggest pieces of shit I took off this earth. You're making me question the detective skills I've heard so much about."

Not enough. Webb needed more. "I don't know. I looked into them a bit. Just seemed to fall into the trap of heroin. Not hurting anyone but themselves," he said.

The kitchen, still decorated from the 1980s gave Webb an unearthly view of the moment.

Mitchard's whole face was expressionless. "Oh, I guess I have mistaken you for a man good at investigations. You see, Carter, those miscreants mixed their heroin in their child's bottle."

The home was dead silent. The lack of remorse sent a shiver up Webb's spine. "They had a child?"

Mitchard's laugh was more like a bark, entirely devoid of humor. "Yes, they did at one point. That child was left alone in parks, at their home, and even found in a vehicle unattended. DCF wouldn't take the child. Oh no. They just kept giving them parenting lessons." Mitchard adjusted himself in his seat. "But eventually, that child was removed due to suffering a medical emergency after ingesting small amounts of heroin."

Webb's eye twitched at the thought of heinous crimes against children. Thoughts he had attempted to leave behind years ago.

"Again, Bobby, it doesn't make sense to me. They lost the child and were only harming themselves."

"Well, the child was set to return to their care. After spending a month in foster care, the state thought those bastards had learned from their lessons. I knew they hadn't. So before that child went through what I did, I had to do it."

Webb's mouth curled to the side as he rubbed his chin. "You know, the obituary said she had her master's degree. Seemed like a smart girl who could get back on the right track."

"No!" Spittle flew from Mitchard's mouth. "That dumb bitch screamed like a pig when I squeezed the life out of her." He sat back and calmed down. "Seeing the life drain from her eyes as she died left a feeling inside of me that I needed more of."

Webb felt a wave of excitement run through his body.

Mitchard had confessed to the crime.

One that would connect him to all of them.

Webb's mind raced as he faced his dilemma of what to do next. Pulling his phone out, he scrolled to the South Lake Police Department's dispatch center. His thumb hovered over the call button, but he paused. Looking up at Mitchard, his eyes were blank seeming to look through Webb. There was no soul inside. His nostrils flared, pulling his lip up exposing his blood stained teeth. The demon inside of him was obvious.

Webb had to make a choice.

Webb stood from his seat and walked to the rear of Mitchard. Tugging on the strings holding the curtains back from the window, he released the tie. Mitchard's brow furrowed as Webb moved back to his seat and sat back down.

Webb placed his phone on the table, clasping his hands together as he rested his chin on his knuckles. "Ya know, it's a tangled web we weave when first we practice to deceive."

THIRTY

JAMES SAT CROUCHED in his desk chair, with his back to the office behind him. The sound of Dealto and Nelson talking in the boss's office provided white noise. Shaw's Air Wick plug-in shot scents of brown sugar and vanilla through his nose while he pounded at his keyboard, trying to connect the dots to the new pieces he received from Webb. The connection was real between all the victims. Now he needed to figure out how to put it all together. There had to be a clue left behind by the killer.

The time was closing in on midnight, and he had no end in sight. He was relentless in trying to find the suspect before another family died.

Family. Marie. The kids.

Picking up his office phone, he punched in the number of the burner phone his wife had received from the Feds.

"Hey," Marie whispered as she picked up the phone.

"Hi, babe. Just wanted to check in on you guys. You alright?"

A small whimper could be heard as she started to speak. "I don't know. This whole thing has me shook."

"I know. Me too. But we're making progress on finding him. Got some good information that links our victims together."

"How?" Her voice perked up.

"Seems like that guy tends to go after dysfunctional families. Families that pose as perfect but are far from it."

The phone was silent. "Are you saying we're dysfunctional? What are you trying to say, Richie?" She asked quietly, with a shaky tone.

"No, no. Calm down. I'm not saying that. The other families had domestic abuse, drug abuse, infidelities, the whole nine yards." James said trying to dig himself from the hole he was building.

"We don't have any abuse in our home, so that only leaves infidelities."

James let out an annoyed exhale. Even in the situation they were in, she still managed to look at things cockeyed. "Marie, no. I don't even know why'd you'd say that."

"I heard that woman that was in the car with you the other night. The agent? She was at our house too when everything went down. She was gorgeous. Just seems to make sense based on what you're saying."

James dropped his head and scratched at his hair. He was too exhausted to argue, needing to focus on his task. "I'm not going to get into that with you. I just called to check in and say that I won't be home. Not leaving here until I figure this thing out."

"You're not answering the question about that agent."

"I love you, Marie. There's nothing to worry about. I promise. Hug the kids for me. I'll call you when I have an update."

"Richie-" she managed before he hung up the phone.

James felt the presence of someone standing over him. Swiveling in his chair, he saw Dealto standing over him.

"This job's a bitch sometimes. Not an easy life for the husbands and wives married to us."

"Marie's had a rough couple of weeks, but she's a trooper. She'll get over it," James said, brushing off the exchange. "What did the lab say?"

Dealto threw his hands up. "Gonna have to wait till tomorrow. Bridgeport had a triple homicide and they're finishing that up now, then calling it a night."

James couldn't believe they'd put this case on hold, knowing a cop's family was targeted. "I'll call down there myself and get them to handle it. Got to speak to the right person it seems?"

"Yeah. I spoke to Barbara Wright. I guess she just took over as the supervisor recently. She's from Texas and thinks us northeast folks get a little too wrapped up in our cases."

James pulled his chair up to his desk, which had accumulated a mountain of paperwork over the past few days. Sliding a stack to the side to expose his office phone, he punched in the number and made the call, hearing a familiar voice pick up. "Hey Jessica, it's Detective James over at SLPD. How are you?"

"Ugh, what a day. It's been nonstop over here. I'm finally walking to my car as we speak."

James needed to up the smooth talk to get what he needed. "Yeah, you don't even know."

"I heard a little. You guys found another body, right? Barbara was saying that psycho also came to one of y'all's houses too." Jessica said with an inquisitive tone.

James paused, contemplating telling her the truth. But honesty would likely earn him some sympathy and some quick results. "Yeah, it was mine."

"Oh man, I'm so sorry. Is everyone okay?"

"No one got hurt, but my family's not doing so well. Kids can't even sleep. This guy is still out there running around, and we have little to go on."

James could hear the hemming and hawing of Jessica after he spoke. "Is this your way of asking me to expedite that DNA sample right now?"

"Jessica, I know you have three kids at home. Put yourself in my shoes. I mean, that guy could end up in your house. I need to take this guy down now."

"You're right. I was actually going to stay but Barb told me to just take off, come in a little early and do it first thing in the morning. I'm walking back in. Give me about an hour."

James' head dipped, closing his eyes. "I really appreciate it. I owe you."

"No, you don't, it's only right. Let's hope we get something from this one."

James hung up the phone, with some hope that the results could help.

"Good job kid. Anything else come up in your searches?" Dealto shouted, causing James' head to snap up forgetting he was there.

"Well, Webb was definitely right about his victims. I can't put a link on why this guy would kill them, though, so it's making it hard to come up with a suspect."

"Well, you heard Webb. Keep digging."

Behind Dealto, James saw Agent Nelson walking from the rear of the office while placing her phone on the counter. "Geez, my kids wouldn't get off the phone. Feel like I'm missing so much this week being gone."

"Must be hard being away from them."

"Never gets easier," Nelson said, shaking her head.

"How's your husband feel when you leave?"

"Well, my wife, Sharon, is really cool about it. Knows how much this work means to me."

James smiled at the comment. This was information he could've used ten minutes ago to calm Marie down. He swiveled his chair and pointed his chin toward Dealto. "Hey boss, meant to ask you. Did Webb really try to get me up in this unit before leaving?"

"Yeah, he did," Dealto nodded. "Guy wouldn't shut up about it for months. To be honest, I was against it. It's such a tight-knit group, and I didn't know you well enough. Wanted to see more. But, as usual, I should've just listened to the guy. Proves me wrong time and time again, but I'm too hard-headed to listen." Dealto chuckled at his own ignorance.

James spun his chair around and buried himself back in his computer. Even though he had new information, trying to develop a suspect felt like trying to find a needle in a haystack. There were so many angles to try, all of which he was sure Webb had done in the past. He wanted to call Webb, but he decided against it.

A FEW HOURS had passed when James heard the door of the office being pulled open. Shaw and Michaels emerged through with coffees in hand.

"A little pick me up for you, James," Michaels winked and shot a smile. James couldn't help but think this was his way of saying *welcome to the team.*

As the sound of the cup hitting the desk echoed, James' phone began to ring. "Jessica, hey. Please tell me you have something."

"I do and sorry it took longer than expected." James' heart fluttered with excitement as his hand began to sweat on the phone handle. "Robert Mitchard. December 4, 1974."

"Holy shit, that's amazing. What was the DNA entered for?" James said, while jotting the information down.

"I don't have the details. But it was from a 1991 arrest for murder."

"Thank you so much. I gotta go, touch base soon!"

He hung up the phone and jumped out of his chair. "I got a DNA hit. A Robert Mitchard. He's about fifty years old. Ring any bells?"

The team shook their heads. James plopped back into his seat and ran the name through the National Collect system, looking for all arrests around the country on his suspect.

"Looks like he had a murder conviction in '91 in Indiana. Can someone reach out to them and see if they have a case report they can send over?"

"Already on it," Shaw shouted.

"I'll reach out to my office and see if we have anything," Nelson chimed in.

James pulled google up on his desktop and did a search on Mitchard. He ran Mitchard through the South Lake database, DMV files, and Accurint.

"Boss, I got it," he yelled without taking his eyes off the computer screen. Dealto, Shaw, Michaels, and Nelson all came over, surrounding him as they all looked at his computer screen. "This guy killed his parents when he was a kid. Claimed he was abused and pushed to the point of breakdown. Court seemed to take his side and tried to rehabilitate him."

"What's he doing coming to South Lake?" Michaels asked.

"I don't know, but I do know he's living here according to the last address in Accurint. I also found him listed in a report five months ago during a neighborhood canvass."

"I'll start typing the search warrant for the home now, if you want, James? This is your baby now I assume?" Michaels said while turning and making his way toward his desk.

"Definitely. And yes, a search warrant would be nice to have ready. We need to get out there ASAP and get eyes on the house."

"How do you want to handle this? You've been all over this from the start. Your call kid," Dealto agreed.

James pulled up the roster for patrol, checking who was currently on shift. "See if we can pull Grant, Rodriguez, and Hertzler. They're all SWAT guys who I trust. Nelson and I will take the eyes up front. Boss, if you and Shaw can park on the opposite side of the house from us?"

"It's going to take a couple of hours to get this warrant typed out and signed, but I'll move as quickly as I can," Michaels said.

James stood up, tossing his jacket on and sliding his radio in his back pocket. "That's fine. We ain't waiting long before we knock on this bastard's door."

THIRTY-ONE

HIS FEET RACED over the concrete as James and Nelson made their way to his car. Pride and anxiety coursed through him. A serial killer who had taken out several families and gone after his own. Staying focused and professional was going to be a tall task.

"Great job, James. This thing is coming together much quicker than expected." Nelson grinned at him as she put her seatbelt on.

"Don't mess with a man's family," James said with his eyes lasered on the road in front of him. Turning out of the parking garage, he sped toward the address. A short five minutes from the police department, he found himself on Rosemount Avenue.

"Which one is it?" Nelson squinted through the night.

James pointed. "Right there. 48. The white ranch."

Nelson leaned in to look in the direction of the home. "The one with the old wagon in the driveway?"

"That's the one. Looks like our boy is home." James pulled his radio from the cup holder, pressing his thumb against the side. "Hey boss, we got a visual. Cars in the driveway. Looks like a light is on inside, too."

"Copy. Shaw and I are about a minute out." Dealto confirmed.

"Just pull up behind me. Have the cruiser park over on Davis Drive and walk over. I'm not waiting out here."

"You sure? Don't you want to spot him first?" Nelson asked.

James took a deep breath and looked Nelson directly in the eyes. "I'm sure. I don't want this asshole having another minute laying around in his home enjoying his freedom."

Lights from behind lit up James' vehicle as Dealto stopped behind him. Exiting onto the sidewalk, the team huddled as they waited for the patrol officers.

"Why don't we hold off on an approach until Michaels is almost done with the search warrant? Once he's got the approval of the prosecutor and heading over to the judge's house, we'll move in." Dealto directed.

Nelson laughed at the comment. James looked over at her and smiled.

"No. Not happening. We're right on this guy. I'm not risking him slipping away on us."

Dealto breathed heavily through his nose, placing his hands on his hips. "I'll give you rope here. We have a right to hold the house until the warrant's done anyways. All legit." The whole party turned as the three patrol units walked up to them. "Appreciate the help, guys." Dealto nodded.

The Patrolmen were armed with their department issued AR-15s and wearing their external ballistic vests.

"I'm sure you don't have all the details yet, so I'll catch you guys up to speed: 48 Rosemount, the ranch down that way, is our target home. Suspect is a Robert Mitchard. We just got DNA back that links him to all the homicides over the past few years." Dealto explained.

"Is this the same shithead that broke into your house?" The young enthusiastic officer asked.

"Same one, buddy." James chimed in.

"Oh, hell yeah! I live for this kind of stuff."

James grinned, once again feeling the brotherly love within the field. "But listen, we have to be careful. This guy is dangerous. He's killed a lot of people. It's been years since he started this, and we haven't even had a sniff of who he was until now. I'm expecting him to be pretty savvy. Lord only knows what this guy could be capable of." James pulled sheets of paper from his back pocket that he printed before leaving the office and distributed one to each member of the team. "This is his DMV blowback photo. Nothing else on file, so I'm not sure if he looks the same or not."

"Dayyyum. Looks like Ned Flanders, man. You got me out here chasing a cartoon character," one of the officers replied as they all laughed.

Dealto shot a nasty look at the officer. "This isn't a game. This is a dangerous guy. Lock in. Now." The officer shut his mouth and stopped laughing.

"Agent Nelson and I will go around back in case he tries to dip out. Boss, you and Shaw stay by the front on the sidewalk, covering each corner." James stepped in closer to the SWAT boys, pointing his finger into the chest of the youngest officer. "You guys, go to the front. Knock on the door and look in there to see any movement. If he's playing any games, do what you have to." The three men nodded, and the whole group prepared for the approach.

The three officers along with Dealto and Michaels made their way down toward the house as James stayed behind with Nelson.

"Let's sneak through the backyard. I don't want him seeing us through the windows going to the back of the house. I'm really hoping he thinks he can run out. I'd love nothing more than to lay this guy out as he runs at me," James said, rubbing his fingers across his palms in anticipation.

"And I'd love nothing more than to see it." Nelson gave him a half smirk, her eyebrow raised.

The time was approaching six a.m., and the sun was just starting to peek over the horizon. The grass under their feet was wet, soaking their shoes as they moved through the yards. As they approached number 48, James observed windows, seeing that the drapes were drawn therefore not allowing a visual of the interior of the home.

They reached the corner of the house and James signaled to his team. "We're in position at the rear corner. Ready when you are," he whispered into the microphone.

"Copy. Any visual inside?" Dealto questioned.

"Negative." James replied.

James stood with Nelson, as he saw the officers making their way toward the front of the home. Shaw stood in the front corner with her firearm at the low ready. Dealto jogged down the sidewalk toward the opposite side. The officers disappeared as they approached the front door. James waited, as he heard knuckles banging the wooden door.

The anxiety of waiting made it feel like several minutes had passed. His eyes were focused on the home, looking for movement, or hopefully an attempted escape by Mitchard. James wanted to be on the entry team, but knew he had to allow the highly trained SWAT members to do what they do best.

"South Lake PD, open up!" James heard echoing through the cold night.

"Sounds like someone's gagging or coughing in there. No answer yet. What's your pleasure?" The patrol officer asked.

"Any visual?" Dealto asked.

"Negative, sir. But I hear someone in there."

"Knock again and then breach! I'm not letting him take the easy way out," James yelled into the microphone not wanting Mitchard to take his own life before he got his hands on him.

"Shit, I don't know. It'll be a stretch justifying a forced entry." Nelson said under her breath to James.

"Knock it off. There's a man clearly in distress in there. He's not answering. Exigent circumstances all day long. We're fine," James snarked, shooting a serious look at her.

The banging on the door echoed up the deserted street. "South Lake Police! If you don't open up, we're taking the door!"

The night was quiet.

The anticipation was building, and James needed this to move faster. He held his breath to eliminate any noise and then heard the beautiful sound of wood being smashed by a battering ram. Flashlights lit up inside as the officers moved through the house. James jogged toward the far, rear corner of the home, moving into the yard, facing the exit points. At her end, Nelson moved out into the yard and faced the same exit points. This way, if Mitchard came out, they would have him in a crossfire without shooting at each other. James held his firearm by his side, waiting for movement at the back door. The home became silent, as James could no longer hear the officers piling through the house. Was it possible he wasn't home?

A crackling from James' pocket could be heard, as someone was keying up on the microphone. He slid it from his back pocket and lifted it toward his ear, waiting for the transmission.

"House is clear."

Frustration filled James as failure set in. Moving too quickly on Mitchard may have just cost him the case.

Nerves and anger caused James to hit the house in frustration. "Clear? He's not in there?"

"Oh, he's in here, James. But he ain't alive. You have to come see this."

James shoved his radio into his pocket and sprinted to the front of the home. Leaping over the front step, he raced inside. He made his way through the small hallway toward the rear of the home. The corner of the wall became clearer as he came toward the rear of the home. All three officers' backs were toward him, staring at the wall in the kitchen. James slowed down and got a visual of Mitchard.

Suspended in the air by hooks in the framing, Mitchard was bound up by three strand white polypropylene rope. His head slumped down and his face was bloodied. Mitchard's arms and legs were spread eagled, bound at the wrists and ankles. His body hung in the middle of the four hooks, with rope surrounding him in a circular fashion.

Dealto joined them in the room. His face filled with shock as he looked up at the scene in front of them, his mouth dropping open. "What on god's green earth is that?"

The young patrolman turned and laughed. "Good," he said, walking by James. "Deserved it. Looks like a spider wound his ass up."

James returned his focus to Mitchard's body.

The odd scene brought even more questions than it did answers.

THIRTY-TWO

THE ROOM WAS QUIET, the only sound was the humming from the laptop computer. The thick curtains completely blocked the bright sunlight trying to creep through the window. The soft glow from the screen was the only source of light in the room. The leather chair squeaked while Webb slowly swiveled back and forth.

Squeak.

Squeak.

Squeak.

His finger tapped rapidly on the desk, while his right hand gripped the glass of a Miller Lite. There was a sense of calm inside of him, but he grappled with the ramifications of what he'd done, pondering the steps he'd taken to ensure he would go unnoticed.

Rising from the chair, he walked toward the balcony to get some fresh air.

Webb had thought of taking punishment into his own hands for years and always knew how he would do things. But walking into Mitchard's home that night, he was unsure if that would be the night. Squinting as the beaming sunlight struck his face when he walked outside, he reached into his pocket and slid a cigarette from the pack, placing it to his lips. With a flame to the tip, he pulled in a lungful of nicotine. Resting his elbows on the iron railing, he blew out the remains of smoke.

His vision blurred as his internal focus vividly replayed the events in his head. Webb could clearly see the face of Mitchard sitting in front of him. His eyes looked deep into the eyes of the killer, searching for any hope of a man who could change.

Mitchard's eyes were filled with emptiness. The man had no chance of rehabilitation.

It was at that moment he knew he was going to kill him to ensure no one else would suffer.

Webb exited the home, not saying a word to Mitchard, likely leaving him confused. The click of the latch unlocking on his trunk echoed in his head. Reaching in, he grabbed a backpack that had been stored in the corner for years, untouched. His hand snatched at the loop on top of the bag, and he slung it over his shoulder, quietly closing the trunk. Then he returned to his prey.

The musty smell of the home filled his nose as he could feel the rubber gloves snapping onto his hands. Webb grasped Mitchard's head, suffocating the life out of him. Mitchard struggled, trying to fight off Webb's strength, but it was too late. As his body went limp, an odd sense of accomplishment flowed through Webb's veins. Releasing the killer from the restraints, he sunk two small holes into the side of his neck. After eluding law enforcement for years, Mitchard had finally been bitten.

Suspending his body from the wall, he weaved the strand rope from anchors on the wall, capturing his prey in the middle. Using the Polaroid camera he found in the living room, Webb snapped a photo of the motionless offender. After placing the processed photo in Mitchard's pocket, he stared at his work. There would be several traces of himself inside the house, so clearing all of them was necessary before he could leave. A bottle of bleach was found in the bathroom. He wiped the place clean of all his DNA. Doorknobs, tables, countertops, and floors. This couldn't be foolproof, but the chances of locating his DNA would be slim.

While waiting for Mitchard to return home that night, he checked for surveillance cameras in the neighborhood and knew he was uncaptured. The photo left behind and the window where he'd entered unlocked, left his former team some clues to run on. He made his way to his car, taking all the cleaning supplies with him.

Webb blinked and refocused on the bright blue sky which seemed to tell him he had done the right thing.

His phone vibrated.

Sliding it from his pocket, he saw Pam's name. Seeing her name reminded him of the other challenges facing him. Flicking his half-finished cigarette to the ground, he stomped it out, as if she was watching him. He took a deep breath before answering. "Hey, what's going on?"

"I don't know, just frustrated, I guess. Needed to work through it, and you're the only one typically willing to listen." Pam said with a soft chuckle.

"Well, I'd be lying if I said I didn't know why. Losing isn't your strong suit."

"I just don't get it. How could officers be so reckless when handling evidence like that?"

Webb rolled his eyes. "Pam, when we were married, you met a lot of these people. You know damn well being really intelligent isn't a prerequisite to this job. We always have some low hanging fruit. Trying to find a place they can screw up the least is typically the hardest job of a department."

"Evidence Officer sure doesn't seem like the best choice to me."

"Everyone has friends in high places and gets taken care of. It's like that in every profession."

"I just have to figure out a way to make this right. I still have time to figure out how to rebuild this case."

This was a big concern of Webb's; Pam's relentlessness would not allow her to give up so easily on a case. The Tarascio family had backed off for now, but if Pam were to rebuild the case, she would find herself in the same situation, one she didn't truly understand the seriousness of. "Just take some time away from the job for a bit."

"We both know that won't happen, Carter," Pam snapped back. "I hate asking you specifically about work stuff, but I'm a little bothered about this whole thing."

Webb had known the question would come and that he would have to navigate his way around it. "How do you mean?"

"Carter, you sat next to me in the courtroom as your boss picked my case apart. Was this your doing?"

Webb remained silent for a few seconds, then took a deep breath, exhaling into the phone. He did not like lying to Pam, so answering the question without a real answer was his best way around it. "My job is just to assist Jonny with whatever he needs. He's the mastermind behind all the casework. I simply tie up loose ends when needed."

"I figured but had to ask. I know allowing bad people to run free is something that has always bothered you deeply."

The comment struck Webb hard. He still had such a deep love for Pam and did what he had to do to keep her safe. But by doing so, someone else would undoubtedly suffer at the hands of the mob. A sense of guilt came over him, leaving him wondering if there was another way he could've handled things. "Definitely something that bothers me. That's why I put my faith into people like you who make sure those people get put away for a long time."

How loaded that comment was.

"Listen, do you think we can meet up again? I just want to run this case by you one more time. I'm not asking you to give me any of your office's defenses or anything, but if I have something solid, I know you can help find it."

"Whoa, whoa, seems like a conflict of interest to me, young lady," Webb said, laughing. As Pam began to respond, he interjected. "I'm kidding, relax. Why don't we do the same spot tomorrow?"

"Thank you. I really appreciate it. I'll be there at 10 a.m."

"Sounds good, I'll see you then."

Webb hung up the phone with no intention of helping Pam with the case. Doing so could only reopen Pandora's box, bringing her into more danger.

But he wanted to see her.

Just her presence made him feel whole. His arms stretched upward, and he stood up on his tippy toes. Webb let out a yawn as his muscles pulled with relief. Turning, he went back into his dark apartment. His thoughts wandered as he struggled with the burden of his secrets. Something he was going to have to live with moving forward.

He leaned his shoulder against the door frame of his office. The room lit up as he reached in and flicked on the light switch. He scanned the walls that were now empty of any photos or mapping.

Focused on his desk, he glared at the old Polaroid camera sitting on top. The sight of the camera, once used by a crazed serial killer, gave a sense of accomplishment to Webb. He felt a smile form on his face.

No regrets.

THIRTY-THREE

JAMES STEPPED OUTSIDE and stood on the front steps. His shoulders were hunched up, trying to cover his face from the cold. The sun began to creep over the horizon in front of him, giving an orange tint to the sky. He slid his thumb up from the bottom of the screen and unlocked his phone. Searching through his contacts, he dialed the medical examiner's number. "Good morning Michelle, it's James. Sorry to wake you so early."

A yawn vibrated through the speaker of the phone. "Well, I assume it's worth waking if you call me this early. What's up?" The rasp in her voice made it clear he had woken her up.

"Yeah, unfortunately. I think we found our killer. He's dead. Weird scene here. I'm still trying to wrap my head around it," James rubbed his forehead. "We're about to process it. Think you guys can shoot over here in an hour or two to take the body?"

"Definitely. You know I love interesting cases. Let me grab some coffee and let the dog out. I'll get ahold of my partner, and we'll head over."

"Appreciate it. See you soon." James hung up the phone and slid it into his pocket. His brain was tangled with thoughts as he scanned the surrounding homes, looking for surveillance cameras. Just as he had put the pieces together, someone beat him to the punch. It didn't make sense.

James jogged to his vehicle and popped the trunk, retrieving the crime scene tote. With a slow walk back toward the home, his brain began dissecting everything that had unfolded. His thoughts refocused as he stood in front of the door, pushing it open with his elbow to avoid contamination. Nelson and Dealto were in the kitchen discussing the scene in low voices. He placed the tote on the floor and prepped for evidence collection.

"They coming out?" Dealto asked.

"Yeah, they'll be here in an hour or two," James said as he passed the two.

Tilting his head, he slowly walked toward the cold, lifeless body of Mitchard hanging in the middle of the wall. Placing his hands on his hips, James stood still, gazing into the face of the man that had broken into his home. Mitchard's head hung down and was pale from pallor mortis setting in.

Slowly turning his head, James nodded toward Dealto. "Hey boss, do you think we can have the patrol guys tape off the whole property? See if the OIC can send us a few more units to secure the exterior." James walked back to the tote and pulled two sets of latex gloves on his hands and passed the box to his partners.

"Have someone at the entrance with the log. I don't want anyone else entering the home unless I know about it. Nelson, let's split up and sift through this house. There have to be clues in here that connect this thing to someone."

Dealto stood still, staring at James with a smirk. "Geez James. Few days in and you're running the show already. But you are right. Just don't start looking to come after my job, hey." Dealto shot a wink in James' direction and walked out of the home to pass along the instructions of his new detective.

James pulled the camera from the tote and began taking photos of every room in the home, as well as the entire exterior.

He made his way back toward the body, taking several photos. Mitchard's face was battered. There had clearly been a struggle of some sort. Closely observing every part of the body, James noticed the white shiny corner of something sticking out of Mitchard's pocket. Carefully grabbing the tip, he maneuvered the item out.

It was a single Polaroid photo.

The photo was of Mitchard, hanging from the wall. No lividity yet on the skin, it must have been taken shortly after his death. The photograph puzzled James. He searched for any clue in the photo, but he was stumped. Slipping the Polaroid back into the pocket, he snapped more photos.

Working his way down the body, he lifted the pant legs. Mitchard's lower leg, just above the ankle, was red with hair missing. The sight made James believe that Mitchard was likely tied up at some point, but he couldn't figure out why. On the right, he noticed objects had fallen to the linoleum floor, more evidence of a struggle. Further right, he noticed the doorway to the living room. With one last look at Mitchard, he moved to the next room.

The whole home was clean and very vintage, and the living room was no exception. Floral wallpaper had been hung on the walls and a plastic slipcover over the green couch. A wood coffee table with drawers on all sides sat in the middle of the room with nothing on it. One of the middle drawers had been left slightly ajar, and it caught James's eye. Crouching down and pulling it open, he found a treasure trove of Polaroid photos. He quickly snapped photos of the pile, then pulled them together and flipped through, picture by picture.

Each photo was of a different family. All of them showed the families out in public. He recognized each of the victims from the past few years, as well as several others he could not identify. The victims' photographs all had the cross symbol etched in red marker on the film.

At the back of the pile, there was a photo of him and his family. Out for pizza at the local Uno's, completely oblivious to the man snapping their picture.

James looked up as his vision blurred, transformed into his thoughts. He recalled the night. How could he not have seen this happen? His hand scratched through his hair as his breaths became labored.

After tossing the photos into an evidence envelope, he stood up. James's instincts tingled, stirring a deep-seated suspicion that the killer's death was not as straightforward as it seemed. His mind wandered to a strange thought that sent a shiver down his spine. He couldn't help but think that Webb knew something about what had occurred in this house.

However, he had to stick with the facts.

James' thumb pressed against the back of his Streamlight, illuminating the room while he scanned for blood stains or odd signs. His light bounced off the shiny floor for clues, but it was spotless. No blood, no hair, nothing. His eyes shifted toward the fireplace; there were no photographs on the mantle. In fact, no photographs were displayed anywhere.

James walked back through the kitchen and down the hallway. As he passed the bathroom, he found Nelson collecting hair samples from the tub area. "Anything good?"

With her eyes focused on the tweezers gripping a strand of hair, she shook her head. "Nothing out of the ordinary. Just grabbing what I can just in case. What about you?"

"We'll talk when we're done. See what we can put together. Anything crazy though, give me a shout."

James continued down the hall, reaching the last room on the left. There was no furniture in what he assumed was a bedroom. Surveying the room, he saw a closet to his right, but after pulling at the knobs, he found nothing inside. The room had two windows. One facing the front of the home, the other facing the side. The curtains were pushed to the side. James found the front window locked, but the side one unlocked.

This could be a potential entry point. He again flashed his light on the glass, looking for fingerprints. Just below the center of the interior glass, he could vaguely make out a smudged print. A small flare of excitement went through him, and he went back to the tote for his dusting kit.

Twisting the cap off the white dust, he placed a piece of paper on the ground and poured a small amount out. Placing the handle in between his fingers, he brushed the bristles lightly over the dust and then swirled it around on the glass. As the print raised, he stopped spinning and placed the brush on the floor. With a lifter, he pulled the film back and placed it over the fingerprint. His fingers inched together from the corner all the way to the bottom, and he successfully removed the lifter from the glass.

James held the clear plastic to the light for inspection. It was subpar at best, meaning a database hit was far-fetched, but anything was possible. He scribbled the time, date, and initials on the lifter, finally dropping it in an evidence bag.

Going back to the hallway, he noticed a door with a chain lock near the top. A door he must have missed during his initial photo sweep. Shifting the chain to the left, he opened the door and found a basement. He turned his flashlight on. A creepy feeling came over him as he descended the steps to the concrete floor.

Shining his light around, he located a string hanging from the ceiling light. The sight in front of him sent chills through his body when he pulled the string. An empty tripod rested in the rear of the room, with a white backdrop hung against the wall. Spray painted across the drop were the words: *Is this good enough for you, DAD!* Scattered throughout the white backdrop were several derogatory comments about his father.

His chest tightened as he moved toward the makeshift studio. A leather briefcase leaning against the wall caught his eye. The snap of the metal cracked as the lock opened and struck the plastic case. His surroundings faded away as he lifted the top. Secured with straps, he found one side had more photographs and the other contained birthday cards. He was intrigued by the cards and removed those first. They were all addressed to *Bobby,* and all signed by *Mom and*

Dad. Each one was covered by black Sharpie writing. Written over the original message from his parents, were words like *alcoholic*, *devil*, *deviant*, *predator*, *abuser*, and *sicko*.

James' stomach twisted at the sight of the cards. Sliding them back into place, he removed the photographs next. These were all family photos of Mitchard with his parents. The backdrop was the same in each one, but it appeared to be in a different home. James assumed these were taken at the house Mitchard grew up in with his parents. Mitchard had a blank look on his face in every photograph. No smile. No expression. James could see the killer inside of him, just by staring at the pictures. The creepy feeling intensified.

"Nelson! Come down here!"

He could hear quick footsteps on the upper floor, and he turned to see Nelson stomping down the wooden staircase.

"Take a look at this."

Nelson came over and bent down beside James as he handed her the stack of cards. Her head shook as she flipped through and read them. "This guy was crazy. This whole house just gives me goosebumps. I never get like that."

James bit down on his bottom lip hard. The psychopath was dead, but it didn't seem to give him the closure he wanted. "Yeah, it's definitely weird, but I can't seem to find a clue that gives us any lead on who killed him."

"I grabbed a bunch of swabs and other items for analysis. We'll see what we can get from those."

James looked out of the corner of his eyes and rolled them, knowing that was unlikely.

"Hey, you guys down there?" Dealto yelled from above.

"Yeah. Just checking out our boy's shrine down here." James shouted back.

"Well, come on up and give me an update. ME just got here."

James stood and paused for a moment, mentally processing everything in front of him.

"Come on. We'll have Michaels and Shaw finish processing this room. You need a breather anyways," Nelson said, smacking James's back.

James took a deep breath and nodded. Walking to the stairs, they went back to the kitchen where Dealto was with the medical examiners.

"So, what'd you come up with?" Dealto asked.

James closed his eyes as he took another deep breath, exhaling with one cheek puffed out. He shook his head in frustration. "Well, we definitely have all those unsolved homicides cleared up. There's a ton of evidence here to say this is our guy."

"And what about this homicide, kid?" Dealto questioned.

James looked over at Nelson and raised his eyebrows. An odd feeling came over him. He had never come across any murder that he believed the victim should have died – until this one.

"Honestly, we have nothing, boss. We collected some evidence for analysis and took a shit load of photos. That's about it." James pointed over at Mitchard's body. "Found a polaroid in his pocket of him hanging on the wall. Apparently, the killer took a page from his book."

Dealto slid his hand down the back of his neck, rubbing up and down. "I'm getting too old for this shit."

"No camera anywhere either. The guy's got a studio in the basement. Tripod's empty. I don't know what to tell ya," James said, throwing up his hands in surrender. "Listen, boss. I just got this weird feeling Webb has some information on this. He knew more about this case than anyone else and-"

Dealto held his hands up, stopping James mid-sentence. "No. That's enough with Carter. We took a shot at him, and he wasn't our guy. In fact, he probably helped lead us here. Leave the guy alone. The more time that goes by, the more I feel like shit for how things went down. Leave him be."

James didn't put up a fight.

"You two can head out. You've been working on this case around the clock from the start. I got a couple more detectives coming down to help finish up the scene. I'll keep you updated with what we find."

"Yeah, I should probably go see my family anyways," James agreed.

Dealto extended his hand and shook both of theirs.

James and Nelson exited the home and walked back to the car. He was likely going to be able to close out some cold cases but having an unknown one added to the pile. None of the pieces added up. The house was clean and clear of any clues. The thought bothered him.

"We'll figure it out. We always do. Just go home, get some sleep, and spend some time with your family. That usually helps clear and refocus one's mind."

She was right. Dealto reminded him often to keep his family as a top priority, and it was time to do that.

James kicked his feet down the pavement, with his head down while sliding his hands into his pockets. About ten feet from the car, he spotted something on the corner between the street and the curb.

His eyes widened as the corner of his mouth curled up.

James's footsteps slowed, and then he looked down at a white cigarette filter on the ground. The blue camel logo beamed out, almost glowing from the filter. The top of the half-smoked cigarette still had ash at the end of it. It was fresh, and there weren't many people he knew who smoked a Camel Crush. James took a mental screen shot and left the cigarette where it was. He didn't alert Nelson to his findings. The door swung open as he hopped in his seat, feeling a devious smile on his face.

"You okay?" Nelson asked, her brows furrowed at seeing the look on his face.

"Yeah. I think I'm better now."

THIRTY-FOUR

THE FIREPLACE WAS LIT, and the flames flickered through the room, bouncing off the walls.

Sitting on the soft microfiber couch, James sat alone in silence, as his wife put the kids to bed. Knowing the man that had been in his home was now gone gave him a secure feeling. But having had his family as well as himself go through it gave him a new outlook. The last few weeks had weighed heavily on him. Trying to balance the intense cases he was working on had led to him neglecting his family.

The creak of the floor had him turning his eyes toward the hallway as Marie came walking down the step into the sunken living room. With her arms crossed, she flopped onto the couch next to James. She curled her legs up with her feet flat on the seat and leaned her head onto his shoulder.

James stretched his arm around her, holding her tight. "Thank you. I know this was a lot on you and the kids. You were amazing through it all."

Marie sighed, not saying anything.

James squeezed her tight, realizing how fortunate he was. She had kept their family intact, even in his absence. "What are your worries moving forward?"

"I'm scared now," she whispered. "Even being in our own home freaks me out."

James rubbed his hand up and down her back. "I know, I understand. But he's gone now. We don't have to worry about him coming back."

Marie sat up, wrapping her arms around her knees, resting her chin on top. "I know he is. But the security of being in your own home is shot now. I mean, I feel like I'm always looking around now."

James digested the reality of the comment. He had seen so many bad things happen to good people. This was the part of the job that gave officers a jaded view of life. They knew that anything could happen at any time. No one was untouchable. This led to a life of stress and alertness every moment. Trying to relay this to someone outside the field was always difficult. It was something officers never wanted to burden others with.

He pressed his head to hers. "It'll take some time, but we'll get things back to normal again. The kids are mostly unaffected by it. That's what matters most. And I'm sorry if it felt as if I was distant lately, or a little snappy. You and the boys mean the world to me."

Marie pulled her head back slightly away from James. A smile slowly curled up from the left side of her mouth. She leaned forward and kissed him softly on the lips. "I know. I'm sorry too." Turning, she placed her head back against his. "It's just still so real right now, I'm trying to work through it."

James placed his hand on her back and kissed her on the cheek. "I made a lot of mistakes and I'm sorry. I got too wrapped up in my work and feel like I stranded you guys. I failed you as a husband and father."

Marie sat in silence as James finished. His arms wrapped around his wife, squeezing her tightly. After a long embrace, he released his hug, placed his hands on her shoulders, and looked into her brown eyes. James simply smiled, remembering why he fell in love with her. She smiled back, laid down, and rested her head on a pillow. He rubbed his hand up and down her back, as she quickly fell asleep.

Standing from the couch, he walked to the kitchen and grabbed his bag. The zipper glided as he opened it, removed the case files and dropped them on the table. Bellying up to the edge, he carefully flipped through the most recent homicides. The gruesome details and photographs of crime scenes were a reminder to him that the victim's families finally had closure and justice had been served.

His brain shut off while he got lost in the image of the Daigle family posed on the living room floor. The case that started the roller coaster. A grotesque image that seemed only possible in movies. With a mix of nostalgia and determination, he removed the photo from the file and placed it in his bag. The visual reminder would serve as a restoration to order and justice.

The sound of sliding feet coming down the hallway caused James to turn. Wearing flannel pajamas covered with ninjas, he saw his youngest, Gianni, rubbing his eyes and yawning. "Hey buddy, why you up?"

"I don't know," Gianni said with a soft sleepy tone. "Can someone lay with me?" Looking at sheer cuteness and innocence, James smiled at his boy. This was all he needed to remind him of the little things in life.

James picked Gianni up, resting his son's chest against his. Gianni perched his chin on James' shoulder, while James tapped his butt lightly to soothe him. "Let's go tuck you back in, my little soccer man."

With his boy in his arms as he walked back to his son's room, everything felt right. James knew he couldn't protect his family from everything, but he would die trying. Placing his son on his bed, he pulled the Star Wars comforter over him, resting his head on the pillow. Laying behind his son, he ran his hand up and down his back.

"Daddy?"

"Yeah bud?"

Gianni turned his head toward James, with confusion in his eyes. "Are we going to have to leave our house again to sleep at that other place?"

A reminder that children realize more than parents give them credit for. "No. You don't have to ever worry about that again, little man. Now go to sleep," James smiled.

"Good. I like our house." Gianni rolled back over, tucking his stuffed koala bear in his arms. Within minutes, he was fast asleep.

The bed slightly creaked as James attempted to leave the room without waking up Gianni. Twisting the handle, he slowly closed the door behind him.

Walking back to the kitchen, he found Marie sitting at the table. With a rocks glass in her hand, it was tilted up to her lips as she took a swig of the bourbon. Swallowing down the remains, she placed the glass back on the table, looking up at James. James made eye contact and grinned. Walking over, he sat down next to her. He grabbed the bottle of Basil Haden, pouring a finger into the glass. Inhaling as he swallowed it down, and he exhaled to taste the flavors. James slid the glass back toward Marie and slowly nodded.

In a tender and unspoken understanding, James silently communicated that he had found the balance he sought. With his son tucked away in bed and his wife by his side, James savored the moment, recognizing clearly the words Dealto spoke and finding equilibrium between his demanding job and the needs of his family.

THIRTY-FIVE

THE BELL RUNG as Webb opened the wooden door to Mozzicato's café. Surveying the room, he noticed Pam sitting in a rear booth smiling at him. Her hair was pulled back, and she was dressed down, wearing a hoodie and jeans. No matter how she was dressed, though, her beauty was always evident to Webb. Her eyes sparkled and the smile he loved so much was upon her lips. Shifting between the tables, he slid into the seat across from her. "Wow, did you actually take a day off?"

"Kind of," she squinted her eyes and tilted her head. "I'm still working on the case, just took a day off from the office. Needed to be alone in my own space."

"Well, I can definitely relate to that. Feel like I get more done when I'm alone."

"Yeah, I'm aware of that, Mr. Webb. I had the pleasure of being your wife for a short time," she smirked at him.

"Hey now, take it easy," Webb leaned back and threw his hands up in surrender. "I know we've talked about this, but in all seriousness, our marriage falling apart was all on me. I'll never forgive myself for stranding you like I did back then."

"Oh stop it, you know I'm just messing with you. But ... yes, it *was* your fault," Pam laughed, slapping Webb's hand.

Webb grinned, his heart giving a small painful twist before changing the subject. "Hey, did you end up staying at your mom's the other night? How's she doing?"

"Yes, I did. Mom's good. Just needs to get out more. Feels like forever since she retired, she doesn't want to leave the house. She was asking about you, like always." Pam said, rolling her eyes in jest.

"She's great, I miss her. Can't believe I fooled her so bad that she actually thinks I'm a good person," Webb winked.

"Oh, you fooled her all right. Maybe you should give her a call, she'd love that." Pam tilted her head and smiled, staring into the heart of Webb.

"Yeah, I will. So, how's everything? Come up with anything in your case?"

Reaching toward the seat, Pam pulled up her briefcase and opened it. Pulling out some files, she placed them on the table. "Actually, I think I did."

Webb's heart sank, as he knew it would if she had. "Shocker."

"Thank you for your enthusiasm." She cocked an amused eyebrow at him. "So, while I lost the gun the other day in the wonderful suppression hearing, I realized I still have the bullet found in my victim. And, no shocker, your detective buddies never sent it in for analysis."

Webb nodded along. While he kept his facial expression calm and showing interest, internally, his fear was building. "That's great. I haven't sifted through all that case yet, just assumed it all came back clear." The lie rolled off his tongue with too much ease. He had noticed the lack of testing while reviewing the case and had hoped nobody else would realize it.

"I reached out to property today and asked them to expedite the processing, but I need your help."

"That's why I'm here. I aim to please, Miss Mazur."

"Do you still have a good relationship with anyone at the lab?

They're not my biggest fans and I don't think a request by me to speed up the processing will help much."

Webb felt his walls closing in, knowing the potential risk to Pam if the results came back showing a DNA hit. Not wanting to get too detailed, he thought it would be best to fill her in on some of the dangers. "I don't know Pam, there's more going on with this than you know."

Pam looked taken aback and stared at Webb, cocking her head to the side. "What do you mean?"

"Tarascio."

"Okay, what about Tarascio?"

"I got information recently that he was going to do whatever it took to get his guy off. He didn't care what it took." Webb made direct eye contact, raising his eyebrows in an attempt to get his point across.

"Are you saying he was coming after me?"

Webb nodded his head and tightly pursed his lips. "That's what I'm hearing. I'm worried that if you open this thing back up, and there's real potential of him going to jail, it could be a ... problem for you."

Pam was quiet, tapping her fingernail against the porcelain mug she was holding and gazing past Webb's face.

"Pam, your safety is the most important thing to me. I think this gun being dropped from the case may have inadvertently safeguarded your life. I understand it's important to you, and that there are certain implications if you don't get this guy locked up, but at what cost to you?"

Her eyes shifted around before responding. The comments seemed to have taken her by surprise, as if she really didn't realize the seriousness. She then locked eyes with Webb. "You really think he would go through with something like that?"

"Unfortunately, I do. Your job is dangerous. Your sole purpose is to make sure criminals pay for what they've done. Their job is to make sure you fail. Very few are willing to do what Carmine is. He's the exception, but I have no doubt he'd do it."

Pam sat up and took a deep breath, exhibiting bravery. "I'm a big girl, Carter, I told you that," she said seemingly refocusing and dismissing his comments. "What about you? How's this new job going, getting criminals off?" Pam sipped her coffee, completely shifting the conversation. Webb didn't pursue the situation.

"Good. It has its struggles and problems, but all jobs do, right? Still feel like I'm able to do the things I love doing, even though I don't have a badge anymore. How's your little boyfriend doing? Hope I didn't scare him too bad," Webb grinned again.

"Yeah, that's all over now. You may or may not have scared him off."

"Ehh, come on. If the guy can't handle a little tackle outside of his girlfriend's house, he doesn't deserve you anyway. I can't have you dating some pansy. I need to know you're all right."

Pam started laughing, gently placing her hand over her mouth and nose. "I have to say, Carter, I have never seen this sense of contentment in you. Something just seems different. It's a good look on you."

She was right. Webb had found a way to quell the inner demons that had haunted him during his time as a detective. Being able to lighten his burden by eliminating a notorious serial killer brought some closure to his unsolved cases. "I feel good. Just trying to weave through all the bad in the world."

"There's a lot of it, as you know, but I agree. Keep the negative out."

"That's the plan. Eliminate all the negative I can," Webb replied, raising his eyebrows and nodding. Knowing that Pam had noticed a change in him meant a lot. It meant he was on the right path. "Feel like I have a new purpose in life. Just trying to embrace it and keep pushing forward.

Pam's eyes softened as she smiled with her lips tight together. "That's awesome. I'm proud of you. You've come a long way. I like this new you." Pam put her hand over his and squeezed before grabbing her purse and slinging it over her shoulder. "I'm going to head out. If you change your mind about making that call for me, let me know. If not, I totally get it."

They both got up from the booth, coming together for a long hug. "I'll let you know what I can do. Just be careful and let me know if anything comes up."

"You know I will," Pam said, releasing Webb and sarcastically batting her eyes at him. "I see that cigarette box bulging in your pocket. Don't make me scold you as your mother would."

Webb smiled.

As Pam walked away, he sat back down and ordered a coffee. The conversation left him feeling even better about things than he had previously. Waiting for his coffee to arrive, his thoughts drifted into wondering what his next move was going to be.

THIRTY-SIX

SLOWLY OPENING HIS EYES, James focused on the sunlight creeping through the shades into his bedroom. With his head resting on his pillow and the comforter surrounding his body, he felt his wife's arm wrapped around his waist. Smiling at the calming moment, he took a minute to take it in.

He unplugged his phone from the charger and looked at the screen. A text message from Dealto had arrived late last night. Hoping for news about the case, he slid open his phone and checked the message.

'Come see me in the morning. Nothing urgent. But we had a break in the case. Very impressed with the work you've done on all this. Your determination and leadership are something to be proud of. Glad to have you on our team.'

A surge of gratitude welled up within James, reflecting on the respect his boss holds for the delicate balance between maintaining career and family. Seeing the silver lining in all the bad that had occurred was important to James. Knowing his boss appreciated all he had done was uncommon in law enforcement, but greatly rewarding.

James twisted his body to face Marie. Looking at her while she slept, he kissed her on the forehead, truly appreciating the woman he'd married. Leaving the bed, he found clothes for the new day and took a quick shower.

He could hear the sound of his boys talking in the living room as he made his way down the hallway. Webb peeked around the corner and saw they were all sitting on the floor playing a heated game of Candy Land. "Morning, monkeys. How'd everyone sleep?"

Without looking away from the board, they all simply responded with, "Good." Joey and Cole then started arguing about what space one of them had landed on, leading to a small wrestling match between the two. Webb just watched it unfold, saying nothing but relishing the simplicity of the moment. All was right again.

"I'll see you boys after work. Stop fighting and keep it down. Mom's still sleeping. Let her get a little more rest please, she needs it."

He grabbed the pot of coffee from the burner he set the night before, filling up a tall travel mug. Securing the cap to the top, he grabbed his keys and left the home.

James walked through the one-car garage to the driveway where he parked. He grasped at his coat to fight the cold winter day that fought through every crevice of his clothing. Winters had always caused depression, but James was using a new outlook to enjoy the weather. As he pulled out of the driveway with the radio tuned to sports talk, his mind was able to stay occupied during the drive to work. While lost in the broadcast, he found himself arriving at the station before he even registered where he was.

His car slowly rolled through the garage as the sounds of sirens echoed throughout. The first shift patrolman packed their cars and checked functionality. He waved at his co-workers as he passed by, giving a smile and nod to each. The sights and sounds had become normal, finally giving him a feeling of home in his new department.

He pulled into his assigned spot, killed the ignition, and walked toward the entrance. As he walked, he heard the ping of his cell phone signaling a text message. Checking it, he found a message from Marie that simply stated, *Have a great day at work. Love you.* James smiled at the gesture, returning a heart emoji.

The hallway on the second floor was quiet as James made his way toward his office. Michaels and Shaw were already at their desks, pounding away at their keyboards.

"Morning everyone."

Both detectives gave him a warm greeting, increasing his sense of belonging. Looking through the glass window into Dealto's office, he saw Dealto nod at him and was waved in.

Without putting his backpack down or taking his jacket off, James entered his boss's office and closed the door behind him. "Morning boss. Hey, I appreciate the text last night. Not used to getting a pat on the back."

Dealto grinned, cupping his hands behind the back of his head, leaning back in his old leather chair. "Eh, you caught me at a moment of weakness last night," he laughed. "We got some good news, and I was in a good mood for the first time in a while. Take a seat. I'll give you the rundown."

James swung the strap of his bag off his shoulder, dropping to the floor. He leaned it up against the desk and sat down. He leaned forward, elbows on his knees, rubbing his hands together and eyeing Dealto in anticipation.

"First of all, how's the family doing? They had a rough go at it these past few days," Dealto asked.

"They have, but they all handled it like champs. Really put a lot of things into perspective for me too. Thanks for asking."

"That's good. Well, I got a call last night from the medical examiner. We had this thing pretty tied up, and they told me they were able to link Mitchard's DNA to all the homicides. *All* of them."

James sat up. His mind raced as he realized that these cases were officially closed. With the DNA link and all they found in the home, there was no more work to do. The families of the deceased would finally have closure. He felt his chest welling with pride.

"You did good, kid. I really mean that. If you'd like to do the honors, you can write up the supplement for each, closing them out."

"That'd be great. Almost feels surreal." As he uttered the words, an odd feeling of confusion crept in. He contemplated the unresolved circumstances surrounding Mitchard's death. The few signs he had led to Webb, but he wanted to build facts before deciding what to do. He wrestled with the idea of leaving it alone, knowing the psychopath had it coming.

But James hated not having answers and needed to know.

The sound of his phone ringing snapped him back to the present. Taking it out of his pocket, he looked at his screen to see it was Michelle Clark calling from the Medical Examiners' office. "Good morning, Michelle. How are you?"

"Good, James. Hey, just wanted to give you a heads up that we expedited the autopsy for this Mitchard guy. We're going to be doing it at eleven. I assume you guys want to be here for it?"

"Yes, for sure. We'll be there. Thanks for the heads up." Ending the call, he looked up at Dealto. "Well, no rest for the wicked. That was Michelle, they're doing Mitchard's autopsy at eleven today."

A quick tap on the door caused both men to look up. Dealto waved his hand and Nelson opened the door. She was holding a steaming mug of coffee and smiled at both James and Dealto as she came in and closed the door behind her. "Geez, I'm just walking in, and you guys are already talking about an autopsy? Remind me to pass on South Lake cases from now on."

James laughed as Dealto smirked and pointed a finger at Nelson. "Oh, you love us, don't lie."

"This is true," Nelson said, placing her cup on the desk. "Are you ready to bring an end to this nightmare, James?"

James felt a spark of determination ignite within him as he met Nelson's gaze. "Absolutely. Let's finish what we started."

He walked out of Dealto's office and made his way back to his desk. James placed his hands on the back of his chair and looked around his working space. Covered with reports, folders and phone numbers scribbled everywhere, he smiled. The chaos in front of him was a reminder of his hard work and the place he would spend many years doing the same. He reached down and slid a desk drawer open to retrieve his gear. James slid his firearm and badge across his belt. Lifting his radio from the charger, he clipped it to his waist. Together, James and Nelson made their way to the Medical Examiner's office. Stepping into the unknown where the secrets of the new killer's mind might be revealed.

IN THE PARKING lot of the State of Connecticut's Medical Examiner's Office, James stepped out of his vehicle with his notebook in hand and camera slung around his shoulder. Looking towards the building, he felt a small wave of nerves roll over in his stomach, making him glad he hadn't eaten anything that morning. If Webb was, in fact, the killer, he expected the autopsy to be clean. Webb was a calculated person who would leave no trail.

James stepped onto the sidewalk and nodded as he saw Nelson pull up alongside his car and get out.

"You ready for this, big guy? Not going to pass out on me, are you?" Nelson gave his shoulder a playful punch.

"Yeah, my bad. Seeing sliced up dead people scattered around a room should be normal to me. We're not all as twisted as you," James returned with a faked right hook. "C'mon Mrs. Dahmer, let's go see your friends."

They entered the building and nodded, acknowledging the secretary behind the desk. She returned the greeting and pointed over to Michelle who was standing next to a cabinet against the right side wall. She appeared wide awake now, with a sense of urgency to get started when she looked over and saw them. "Oh perfect, I wanted to start a little early. Was hoping you two would get here before eleven."

"Oh, you know James. He just jumped out of his seat when he heard he had the chance to attend another autopsy," Nelson smirked at James.

James rolled his eyes, not engaging in the continuing attacks. "You got some booties and masks for us? I'm ready to knock this thing out."

Michelle opened a cabinet door, retrieving a box of each. She handed them over to James and Nelson, and they outfitted themselves.

"You two can follow me," Michelle directed.

"You have a chance to take a peek at anything preliminarily?" James asked as the three stood in front of the elevator, waiting for its doors to open.

The doors separated, and they entered the old elevator with wood paneling on the walls. "I didn't. Been trying to catch up on other stuff before you guys got here." As the elevator descended to the basement, Michelle and Nelson started casually talking as if they were walking the mall, same as last time. James shook his head at the juxtaposition.

When the elevator stopped and the doors dinged open, James walked past the chatting ladies and exited the elevator. The smell once again smacked him as he stepped into the hallway. James looked up and spotted the double doors to the examination room.

They entered the room and Michelle led them to the front where Mitchard's body lay on a table. Music blasted through the room not quite covering the sounds of power tools echoing throughout.

James stood alongside the table next to Nelson as Michelle began cutting into the body. She took samples of several organs and searched for internal wounds, none of which were found. Prior to working on the head, Michelle tilted it to the side, exposing a mark on the lower left of the neck.

"Whoa! What's that?" James asked.

Michelle inspected it for a few moments. "Not sure. Two small punctures. Almost looks like a bite of some sort. We'll learn more from the toxicology report."

James pulled out his camera and snapped several photos of the marks. They didn't look as clean as an insect bite to him, much more man-made. Once again, his wheels started spinning in a certain direction. James looked over at Nelson, an eyebrow raised.

Nelson nodded, clearly acknowledging what James was trying to insinuate. "That looks like another sign to me. Do we have another serial killer on our hands? Killers don't just leave marks on victims like that in a normal murder. As if this whole thing couldn't get any crazier."

"I don't want to jump the gun, but it sure looks that way," Michelle chimed in.

"What are the odds? I was hoping to wrap this thing up with you today. Tracking down another killer like this is quite a tall task." Nelson responded.

James sat quietly, staring at the marks on the neck, deciding whether to give his opinion. He decided to throw a general assumption, leaving Webb's name out of it. "What if it's a killer who might actually be serving a form of vigilante justice by targeting criminals? I'm just spit balling here, but it could make sense."

"Yeah, and? It's still a killer, James. Sounds like you're suggesting that this is okay." Nelson's tone grew serious as she narrowed her eyes ever so slightly at James.

James rubbed at his forehead, wanting to justify his thinking. "I get that, but tell me you've never worked cases where you wished the suspect would just die? It sounds awful, I know. But sometimes it's the best thing."

Nelson shot a disgusted look in his direction and James realized that he may have said too much.

"I can't say that's ever really crossed my mind. We're going to have to disagree on this one. But if you're right, talk about the complexities of trying to get in the mind of that killer. It'd likely be the opposite of everything we usually investigate." Nelson shook her head.

"Again, just throwing an idea out. I'm not agreeing with killing people or anything like that. Just interesting how karma may be working here," James said, trying to sidestep his comments. "I'm not going to treat this any differently than I would any other homicide."

AN HOUR LATER, Michelle and her partner finished up their exam, stitching the body back together. Tossing a white sheet back over the body, her partner rolled it back to the refrigerator.

"I'll try to have the tox screening run through as quickly as possible so you can get some answers. But as you saw, other than those marks and some defensive injuries, everything looks normal."

"I appreciate you getting this done so quickly for us. Reach out when you have something for me, please." James said with sincerity. Choosing to forgo shaking Michelle's bloody glove wrapped hand, James and Nelson nodded to the ME and made their way back up to the lobby.

James was starting to see why Webb would go off and conduct investigations alone, knowing not everyone would want to follow. He needed more answers to the questions regarding the killer. The feeling of needing closure burned hotter as he walked through the parking lot.

"You heading back to the PD with me?" James asked as they stopped on the sidewalk in front of their respective cars.

"Actually, I'm done here. Got reassigned last night to a case in Manchester, New Hampshire. Wanted to stop in this morning just to get an update before I took off. Glad I had a chance to come to the autopsy. But I feel like I'm leaving you with more of a mess on your hands than when we started," Nelson let out an uncomfortable chuckle, shifting her weight from one foot to the other.

"Nah, it's all good. You helped us solve some massive cold cases and some new ones. I really appreciate your help. I learned a lot following your coattails."

"Come on, James. We both know you have the knack for this stuff. It's just in you. I have the government at my disposal. My job is much easier than for you local detectives. Honestly, most of the local guys I meet want me to do all the work. You have a lot of drive. I was impressed."

James nodded, appreciating yet another compliment from a fellow officer on the same day. "Make sure you keep in touch. Let me know if you're ever down this way again."

"I will. Reach out if you need any help with this case. I can usually cut through some of the red tape for you quicker than making a cold call to the FBI."

"Thanks. But I'm just going to close this case out here and chalk it up to 'who cares, the guy needed to die anyways.'" James gave Nelson the side eye, grinning.

"Not funny," Nelson replied with a deadpan expression, but her eyes twinkled.

James extended his hand, giving a firm shake, feeling truly grateful for the help and new friendship he had formed with Nelson. "Now go see your kids, I'm sure they miss you."

Nelson smiled as she stepped off the curb and opened her door. As she drove away, James stood in the lot, gazing into the sky.

How to handle his next move was bulls eyed into his brain.

THIRTY-SEVEN

WEBB PULLED open the cabinet door, reaching for a mug.

The coffee splashed against the porcelain as he poured himself a piping hot cup of coffee. Leaning against the kitchenette counter at the office, he sipped at his morning fuel. Webb felt incomplete being there. A feeling that brought curiosity and questions into his head.

"Hey Carter, glad you're here already. Can you stop in my office when you have a minute?" Edwards peeked around the corner of the kitchen door. Webb nodded mid sip. Taking a moment to swallow down a little more caffeine, he made his way into his boss's office.

Webb entered the room as Edwards was dropping into the chair behind his desk. Motioning to the seat in front, he said, "Have a seat pal. Want to discuss a few things if you got some time?"

The room felt cold. It was an unfamiliar feeling. One that left Webb feeling like he didn't belong.

Pulling at the wood top of the chair, Webb sat in front of Edwards and rested his foot on his right knee. "Yeah, what's up?"

"Just want to talk about these cases we crushed the past two weeks. You were pivotal in them. You've been such an asset here; I can't thank you enough."

"Not a problem. Just doing what I'm paid to do," Webb said, unfazed.

"I'm sure it must have felt great getting the best of your ex-wife in court the other day. Man! I can't imagine how that victory felt."

The sly, backhanded comment struck a chord with Webb. Edwards clearly knew nothing about him, like everyone else. It served as a reminder to him that after losing Pam, he was a lone wolf, roaming solo through the world. "Yeah, it just feels good to win. Against who, though, doesn't matter to me," Webb turned up the corners of his mouth.

"I got a call from Carmine yesterday. He was ready to throw money at us to keep us on retainer. Couldn't believe we pulled that thing off."

Webb waved his hand in front of his face. "Listen, I'm not interested in doing any more for that guy. That was a one-time deal. This isn't the work you do either. When I started here, your main focus was concentrating on innocent people. Not helping out real shitheads."

Edwards sat back in his chair, crossing his legs and placing his fingertips together. Shaking his head back and forth, he squinted his eyes and pursed his lips. "Ehhhh, I know, but I can't just bat an eye at this, Carter. This is a massive organization that stretches throughout the state. We can really get rich off these guys."

The more Edwards talked, the more it became clear to Webb. This was not the place for him. Now he had a new vision in life, and the direction Edwards was going was against everything he believed in. Helping criminals out so they could re-offend would never be in his plans.

"Won't do it. That was a one-time deal and I have trouble sleeping knowing I did that."

"Carter, come on. I consider myself a man of integrity. I do. But at some point, it's a dog-eat-dog world. I'm just trying to get mine, that's all."

Webb sat back in his chair, drinking his coffee. Whether Edwards represented these people or not, someone will. Webb couldn't hate on the man for making a living. "I have to be honest, Jonny. I've been doing a lot of thinking. I need to take a sabbatical for a while. It's time I clean some things up in my personal life and do what's best for me."

Edwards' head jerked back, and eyes widened with shock. "Wow! I didn't see that coming."

"I know. I'm sorry. I just need to right some wrongs, that's all. I appreciate all you've done for me. You were the only one willing to help me out when no one else was. That means a lot."

"Damn, I guess you've thought about this for a bit now. Seems you've already made your mind up." Edwards rested his elbows on the desk, looking down for a moment before looking back up at Webb. "Listen, you do what's best for you. I get it. Whenever you're ready to come back, there's a place for you here. I'm really grateful to have worked with you."

Edwards stood from his chair, and the two men shook hands.

"Thanks Jonny. I'll be in touch for sure." Webb stood and left the office.

As Webb exited the building, he said goodbye to Ariana, thanking her for the time they had worked together. Turning toward the doorway he stood momentarily. He gripped the handle, pushing it open as he walked outside.

No longer tied down to a job, the days would be filled with his own projects. The sense of freedom overwhelmed him.

THIRTY-EIGHT

HIS KEY SLID into the handle as he unlocked the door to his apartment.

Webb walked in and looked around the emptiness of his home. The room was lit by the sun coming through the windows, but the silence symbolized his aloneness.

He tossed his keys on the counter and pulled open the refrigerator. Stretching to the back of the shelf, he grabbed an IPA, needing more than the contents of a Miller Lite. The can hissed and snapped as he pulled at the tab on top.

Taking a large gulp, he made his way over to the office. Standing in the doorway, the cold aluminum of the can chilled his hand as he looked around the room. The once cluttered room was now clear of his notes, maps, and photos. A room he had spent countless hours in, working toward a resolution, was now clear of any questions.

He stepped into the room, and he sat in his chair, placing his beer on the desktop. Slowly spinning back and forth in his seat, the room felt barren. There was no longer a purpose for the room that had consumed so much of his time.

A large pile of paperwork sat on the top corner of the desk.

Pulling it over, he shuffled through it, reading headlines and looking through photos of past investigations. His hand struck an old, yellowed newspaper which stood out from the rest of the stack. For some reason, it felt as if the paper was reaching out to him. Sliding it from the pile, he found an old article regarding an investigation he once handled. The paper reminded Webb of a chilling case from years ago that had slipped through his fingers. Reading through, the memories of the case came flooding back. Taking his eyes off the words, he stared at the wall in front of him. The victim's face burned into his memory, igniting a flame. Flooded with leads he missed and mistakes he made, now looking with fresh eyes brought a new perspective.

Webb's head became consumed with bringing justice to victims. He stood from his chair and grabbed all his files, tossing them into a box. Shuffling through the folders as he aligned them, he glanced at each, realizing there were multiple cases with unfinished business. The thought of the worst criminals out there getting away with such awful crimes burned his soul.

He snatched the old newspaper article off the desk, folded it up, and placed it in his pocket as a reminder of his purpose. The new clarity in life was welcomed. Having had feelings of emptiness for so long, he finally felt whole. He pulled at the middle desk drawer, which contained a half-smoked box of Camel Crushes. Yielding to his cravings, he picked up the cigarettes and held them in his hand. He tucked the box of files under his arm and walked out of the room.

While passing a closet, he slid it open and reached for a duffle bag full of clothes, slinging it over his shoulder. He slipped his finger through the key ring on the counter and made his way to the door, leaving the apartment.

Webb walked determinedly along the hallway and poked at the elevator button, then descended to the lobby of the complex. His shoes echoed off the tile as he stormed through the vestibule with his eyes on the glass doors. He emerged into the frigid day and took a deep breath, turning his head from side to side at the city in front of him.

While walking toward a metal trash can, his eyes locked in on the cigarettes in his hand; he paused as the camels looked back at him. With a decisive flick of the wrist, Webb discarded the cigarettes, letting go of the unhealthy coping mechanism that had become intertwined with his investigative journey.

Webb walked to his vehicle and carried himself with a newfound lightness. Discarding the cigarettes symbolized the end of one chapter in his life, a farewell to the obsession and self-destructive habits that had consumed him for far too long. With the newspaper article safely tucked in his pocket and the lingering smell of freshly smoked tobacco dissipating, Webb popped his trunk and tossed his bag inside. He slid the box of files to the rear and slammed the trunk door shut. Webb turned and was caught off guard by the person standing behind him.

"Webb. Good to see you again," James said, a slight grin on his face.

Webb stopped in his tracks as he looked the young detective over. He was standing upright and with no fidgeting. Webb could see the confidence in him, something that had changed. Their last meeting was contentious, but he developed more respect for James during the interview. "James, what are you doing here? Did Dealto send you to harass me again?"

James waved his hands, clearly discounting the notion. "No. I just wanted to come chat real quick. I didn't like the way things ended when we met. I should've trusted my instincts on you from the start. Looks like you're heading somewhere though, so have you got a second to chat?"

"Yeah, not a problem." Webb's curiosity was piqued.

"First off, I owe you an apology. You know this case was confusing, and I was just trying to investigate any avenue I had." James threw his hands out, palms up.

There's the apology, now why's the kid really here? Webb thought.

"No need to apologize." He said aloud. "The case got personal for you. I get it. I've got no issue with you. I would have done the same thing."

James nodded and looked Webb in the eyes, flinching his chin forward. "Looked like you were packing up some things in the trunk when I walked up. You taking off or something?"

Webb looked past James, scanning his apartment building up and down. "Yeah. Time to move on. Hard to keep me caged up for too long."

"I hear that. So, what's the plan for you?"

Webb paused, looking James over. He saw a young version of himself standing there. He felt an odd connection to James that they were one and the same. "Not really sure yet. But I feel I have to keep fighting for justice, no matter what obstacles I face. This world just isn't right. Sometimes I feel the hindrances of the bureaucratic approach cause these situations to not end the way they should."

James squinted and appeared to catch the subtle hint. "Sometimes true justice comes in different forms." James raised his eyebrows.

The response seemed to have a deeper meaning than it appeared. Was James on to him?

"I won't hold you up, though. I just wanted to stop by and apologize in person. Feel like I owed it to you." James continued, nodding his head.

"Appreciate that. Standup move on your part. I knew I had you pegged as a good guy right from the start."

Webb reached over, giving a firm handshake of respect to his young, though official, replacement. He was happy to have a man like James doing the work he once had done.

James released his grip and started to walk back toward his car, but stopped and turned to Webb. "By the way, you should really quit smoking, man. That stuff will kill you. Plus, never know where those cigarette butts will wind up." James winked, turned, and walked away.

The comment didn't shock Webb and oddly didn't cause any fear. Webb smiled, knowing James was aware of what he had done. A sense of comradery came over Webb as he felt his lone wolf had an ally. But it was time to continue his journey.

He climbed into the driver's seat and took a moment to appreciate the silence. He felt a sense of liberation and renewal, ready to face whatever might lie ahead.

The engine roared to life. Webb watched in the rearview mirror as his home, his workroom, and the remnants of his old life faded into the distance as he drove away. The once-familiar streets became a blur as he sped towards the main road, leaving behind a part of himself that no longer served his purpose. The weight that had burdened him for so long gradually lifted, replaced by a growing anticipation of what could be awaiting him on his journey to solve the next old case and find closure. The road stretched out before him, a winding path of uncertainty and possibility. Webb was leaving behind the physical space that had once consumed him, as well as the emotional baggage that had held him back. He embraced the freedom that comes with letting go, eager to face the challenges and revelations that lie ahead.

With each passing mile, Webb became increasingly aware of the vast expanse of this new chapter. The road is a bridge, connecting his past to an uncertain future.

The story continues in *Webb of Shadows*, the next Carter Webb thriller. Read on for a sneak peek!

www.amazon.com/B0CV2GFJPG

Did you enjoy *Webb of Deception*? Leave a review to let us know your thoughts!

www.amazon.com/B0CTW44Z1K

WEBB OF SHADOWS CHAPTER ONE

The crackle of the log burning in the fireplace snapped as the ambers from the flame floated forward into the screen. The heat from the flames filled the room while radiating off the walls and oakwood flooring. His nose was filled the smell of cooked bacon as his wife stood in front of the stove.

The Ohio winters were similar to what he was used too, but this winter was colder than years past. His suede Ralph Lauren slippers slid across the floor as he balanced his coffee from spilling over his 'retired' mug. He placed it down onto the end table as he reached his recliner and plopped down. With the local Warren County Times in hand, he pulled at the sides to read today's front page article.

"Do you want an omelet or just scrambled eggs like usual honey?" His wife asked from the other room.

He peered over the top of the paper and thought about not being so predictable, but today wasn't the day. "Just the usual."

His eyes refocused on the article and he shook his head while softly sighing out loud at the garbage he was reading. Since when was a local livestock competition a front page story, he thought to himself.

Ohio felt like Connecticut in a lot of ways, but things were definitely not the same.

The clink of the spatula hitting the plate caused a grumble in his stomach as his wife finished preparing his food.

"Can you grab the salt for me on your way out here too dear?" He could hear her flipping through the cabinets as the doors swung open and clapped shut against the wood frame.

"Found it!" She shouted out. "You'd think after two months of leaving here I'd start remembering where everything is."

He rolled his eyes at the comment he seemed to hear every single morning.

"I was thinking we could shoot over to the local gardening store to get some potting soil. I heard on the news last night that next week might hit sixty degrees. I'd love to get started on my flowers early for once." She said with a hint of excitement in her voice.

"It's still March. Why don't you wait a month so they don't die on you the first week?"

"I think we'll be fine. The weather guy said it's looking like an early spring this year. Besides, I know how much you looove shopping with me."

His fingernails scratched at the stubble on his cheeks as he stared into the wall contemplating the sound of an awful day shopping. "Sure. Whatever you want to do."

She stepped down into the sunken living room as the floor creaked with each step. A soft smile curled upward on her face as he locked eyes with her carrying his morning fuel.

As she laid the plate down, a text message alert pinged from his pocket. With his arm fully extended, he held the phone out in front of his face to focus the words. His autonomic nervous system kicked into overdrive as his blood pressure rose.

"You okay?" His wife asked with a concerned tone.

He cleared his voice and regained his composure as he stood from his chair. "Yea, yea. I just completely forgot I was supposed to meet the guys over at the golf club for breakfast." His body twisted as his back brushed passed her, beelining toward the bedroom. "I'm sorry dear."

"Oh, c'mon Danny. You're retired now. I dealt with you being the mayor for almost thirty years. You promised me moving here would give us more time alone."

The words soared in one ear and out the other like an overactive child who forgot to take their Adderall.

Still briskly walking into the bedroom, he pulled at his flannel pajamas and tossed them in the direction of the laundry basket, hitting the floor just short like always. His fingers flipped through his color coated jogging suits as he pulled at the all black velour black set, snapping the hanger it hung from. He hopped on one foot as he slipped his feet through each pant leg. His toes slid into his crocs while simultaneously swinging the top around his back. With a determined walk and wide eyes, he marched through the hallway.

"When are you going to be back?"

"Soon," he said while pulling a jacket from the coat rack. Clenching at the zipper, he pulled it up securing himself from the cold day outside. He slithered his hand into the pocket and secured a mint, popping it into his mouth to mask to the smell of his morning breath. His wife's eyes beamed through him as spearmint fumes traveled into his nostrils.

"Breakfast with the guys? I'm not doing this again. We've been over this."

He rolled his eyes as an exasperated exhale was released. "Not today. Seriously, I'm not going over that again. Just stop. I'll be back shortly."

The door flung open just as quickly as it closed behind him. His foot flew over the two-step entry way as he hustled through the three car garage. Pulling at the door of his brand new SUV, he secured the grab handle and swung himself into the driver's seat. With his hand gripped to his phone, the frustrated ex-mayor made the call.

"Wow, you've never really been the phone call type." The female voice on the other end replied softly as she picked up his call.

"You told me we'd meet later. It's nine in the morning! You can't keep doing this."

"Geez, relax. You sound a little jumpy this morning."

He sunk his chin into his chest and took a deep breath. Getting into an argument could only cause him more problems. "It's fine," he mumbled into the speaker. "You couldn't have picked a nicer hotel for crying out loud?"

"Just get over here. I'm in room 112."

The phone disconnected as he tossed it to his passenger's seat.

The garage door opened while the engine fired up and car rolled out of its housing. He twisted the knob into drive and began traveling down the long driveway. His wife stood in the window waving with her coffee mug in hand. The disappointment was clear on her face while he flinched his chin giving a half ass goodbye. Eyes locked to the roadway, his home disappeared behind him.

* * *

The car bounced through the pothole filled parking lot of the run down motel. A large cloth with 'JoJos Sleep and Stay' handwritten across it sprawled over the previous hotel logo. He scanned the two-story dilapidated structure looking for her room.

"What a dump," he mumbled to himself as rolled past two people passed out in lawn chairs around empty beer cans outside of a room. At the bottom corner of the building he found room 112 and pulled into a parking space next to a dust covered station wagon. His anxiety flared as he looked at the door. It never gets easier he thought to himself.

The brisk air smacked at his nose as he tucked it under his jacket collar. He squinted his eyes and looked to the left and right. No one in sight.

With his hands tucked into his wool lined pockets, he jogged toward the door. He twisted his head behind him for one last glance, then looked forward and racked his knuckles against the metal door.

The door slowly crept open as he knocked, screeching at the hinges of the ungreased metal. He stepped in, quickly closing the door behind him to avoid being seen.

On top a cheap comforter sprawled across the bed he saw her suitcase. Clothes flung around the room like it had exploded, tossing her contents all over. The sound of the shower running in the rear of the room resonated as each drop struck the tub.

Slowly, he began walking in that direction. His first second step struck the carpet, and he was interrupted by a male voice behind him, stopping him in his tracks. His heart rate sped up as his mind began to race. He paused for moment, then turned toward the voice.

His slowly focused in the dimly lit room, and heart sunk as the man came into focus. He closed his eyes while his head drooped downward.

The water splashing against the fiberglass tub was all that could be heard momentarily before the man spoke. "We need to talk."

WEBB OF SHADOWS CHAPTER TWO

His mouth flung open as he inhaled the dry air that had been circulating for several hours through his car. He released a loud exhale as he yawned in exhaustion from the ten hour car ride. His eyes glanced at the rearview mirror to see the early sun peek over the horizon.

Carter Webb was locked in cruise control as he traveled Interstate 71, making his way out of Columbus Ohio.

The highway was still light with traffic, but the morning workers were soon to flood the interstate. His stomach growled in hunger, and he had a need for caffeine to keep his heavy eyes open. He fought the desire for nicotine as he chomped at a piece of gum. A Chris Stapleton song blared in the background to keep him awake.

He stretched his body up and dug into his front pocket, removing his cell phone. Gripped on both sides of the plastic case, he momentarily shook it back and forth. "Why not," he mumbled.

His finger tapped the screen and facial recognition unlocked the secure device. He scrolled through his contacts, pressing on the name *'Pam.'*

"Well good morning Ms. Mazur. Not even six in the morning and you're up and at it already."

The receiver vibrated as she heavily breathed into the phone. "Yea. Morning spin class. What's up?"

"I just passed through Columbus and reminded me of that diner we loved when you came out here to see me. Thought I'd give you a buzz."

"Yup, I remember the place."

An awkward silence seemed like an eternity after her brief response. "Yea, loved that place."

The heavy breathing continued. "What are you doing in Ohio anyways? Jonny got you on a case out there?"

The muscles in his neck bulged as his hand rubbed up and down them. "Nah. Just got some personal business I need to take care of."

An exhale on the other end blew through as the *"psh"* stung his ear.

"Stopping by to see your girl I assume?"

'No. Just some other stuff I got going on."

The phone muffled and crackled for a few moments before she spoke again. "Listen, I'm in the middle of something. Did you need something?"

"Yea, no. Like I said, was just driving through and thought I'd see what you were up too."

"I appreciate the call. But you can't just ring me anytime you're thinking of our past. You made your own decisions back then and you signed your own name on those papers."

His chest sunk and atoms apple felt like it was going to pop out as he swallowed.

"Of course. Guess I was just bored on this long ride. You get back to your work out. Take care."

The phone pulled down from his ear and pressed end prior to getting a response. He stared down the highway with tunnel vision, as his brain scrambled with thoughts. The blare of the rumble strips rattle his car as his vehicle drifted over them. He swerved back into his lane, sat upright and focused his eyes ahead.

He drove straight through the night without stopping. Not worried about his lack of sleep, it was fuel his body craved. His exit was fast approaching, and it couldn't come soon enough.

Webb cruised down the exit ramp and pulled up to the familiar rural town. He sat at the light, he looked over the area. It was quiet, and the large lots of land reminded him of his time at polygraph school. The farmers were already hard at work, getting their morning duties out of the way for a long day ahead.

He made his turn and passed a green sign that read *Fitchville*. The sign brought back several memories and made it feel as if he never left.

The Olympia Diner sign moved closer as he continued his travels. He pulled into the lot and parked amongst the vacant spaces.

With an empty stomach and increasing need for caffeine, he pulled at the metal handle to enter the restaurant. An old cigarette dispenser sat in the foyer, while Webb grinned at the timeless vending machine. Haven't seen one of those in years, he thought to himself. He pulled at the second door and stepped into the throwback establishment.

The sounds of Kenny Rogers softly played on the jukebox as he walked past the red leather seats bellied up to the bar on his left. With a single row of tables to his right, he made his way to the rear corner booth and sat with his back to the wall. A visual of the entire room was an old habit he couldn't break.

A menu smacked the laminate tabletop in front of him, as he looked up at the young waitress who hovered above him. Her dirty blonde hair was pulled back and her face was clean of any makeup. The maroon blouse adorned the name "Misty" on the tag, as she looked down at him, expressionless.

"Coffee?" She asked with a continuous blank stare.

"Ohhh yeah. Might have to bring the whole pot out to me." Webb said with a laugh. "So, what's good here?"

The waitress reached down, flipping open the menu to the last page. "I make all these pies from scratch. I promise not even your grandma can touch my recipes."

His mouth curled downward, and chin jutted forward while nodding at the woman's brazen comment. "As much as I'm sure that's true, I have to stick with some breakfast for now. I'll take a rain check on that for sure though. If you knew my grandma, you'd know how bold of comment that was."

She shrugged her shoulders and pushed him along. "I doubt that. What will it be?"

"I haven't been out here in a bit, how about some biscuits and gravy."

"I like your style mister. I don't make those, but we got the best around."

Webb smiled and leaned up against the table. "I have to ask, what's with the name Misty? Seems like you're in the wrong profession with a name like that."

"Easy now. I was just starting to like you" She said while staring at the menu on the table. "Everyone around here calls me Ms. T. The name kind of stuck so I went with it."

Webb looked up with squinted eyes, not saying anything.

The waitress cocked her head and sighed. "Aneilka Taronowski. No one even tries pronouncing it. So, Ms. T works for me."

Misty rose from the booth and poured him a piping hot cup of joe, then placed it in front of him before disappearing through the double doors of the kitchen.

Webb pulled at the elastic that secured his files and removed several reports. His hand wrapped around the coffee mug and guzzled down the much needed morning pick me up.

Within minutes, the white gravy smothered over his biscuits slid across the table in front of him. Webb sat back and mouth his mouth salivated.

Misty's eyes homed in on his files as she topped off his coffee.

"You a cop or something?"

"No."

"You look like a cop."

Webb remained silent and dug into his meal.

"What are you working on? You a private investigator or something?"

"Something like that."

Misty didn't respond. She failed to make eye contact with him even once during their interaction. Her demeanor was very guarded, and one he had come across too many times before in his past career.

The loud roar of an engine accelerating through the parking lot interrupted their conversation as an older model Ford pickup truck pulled toward the front window.

Webb looked out at the truck with big "muddin" tires, covered in dry dirt. A small confederate flag swung from the rearview mirror as the truck came to rest.

He tilted his head back toward his waitress, as she locked eyes with the truck that had parked. Her smile had disappeared as her bottom lip quivered. She reached into her apron and pulled off Webb's check. Without saying a word, she tossed it on the table and walked away.

Webb wiped his mouth of gravy and tossed a twenty dollar bill on top of the check. He slipped his files into the folder and resecured them with the rubber band.

The door swung open and caught his attention, as he looked up to the see the operator of the truck enter. His dirty, oversized Timberland boots stomped the floor as he strutted toward Misty standing behind the counter. His thick fleece lined green flannel was unbuttoned, with a pack of Marlboro Reds sticking out the top pocket. His unkempt goatee framed a cocky smile as he approached. He was a larger man, and his body resembled a doughy ex-football player that stopped working out years earlier.

The regulars of the diner kept their heads down and appeared to be intimidated by the man. He grabbed both of Misty's arms at the elbow and pulled her in close as his smile disappeared.

Webb focused on his hands that firmly grabbed her, making it impossible to pull away. The man spoke softly with his face only inches from hers. He couldn't hear the words exchanged, but the visual he observed was an old familiar sight.

He stood from his booth and made his way down the aisle toward the two who stood in between the opening in the middle of the counter.

The man noticed as Webb moved closer. His eyes shifted in Webb's direction with a look of disgust. He released her arms, and Misty took a step back. "You okay?" Webb asked as he moved closer.

She looked away and ignored Webb's attempt to intervene. As he continued toward them, the man thrust his shoulder out into Webb as he passed. Webb remained grounded as the shoulder struck, not causing any inconvenience.

Webb stopped and looked the larger man over, noticing his feet too close together, not in a fighter's stance. Webb knew he could take advantage of the larger man, but the thought of a fight would cause more trouble than benefit. He needed to keep a low profile. Webb ignored the man then nodded goodbye to his waitress as he pushed through and headed toward the exit.

With the two behind him, the male yelled out "Stay away from my girl tough guy!"

"I love you too, buddy." Webb said without skipping a beat as he pushed at the exit door.

He stepped down the concrete stairwell and sat in the front seat of his car that had lost all its heat during his short time inside. The engine fired up to his old beater while he cranked the heat and reversed from his spot.

While rolling past the rear of the truck, a bright yellow bumper stick that read "Fish tremble at the sound of my name" was stuck to it. Webb shook his head in disgust and exited the diner.

WEBB OF SHADOWS CHAPTER THREE

She looked up at the clock, as the silence of the office allowed for a loud click to echo through the room as the second hand made its way around the circle. The room was empty, as it always was at 7:00am. With only two other detectives in the department, Sandra Rinehart was a wolf amongst sheep.

Rinehart stood from her chair and unbuckled her belt. As she unlocked her desk drawer and reached for her duty weapon, the musty scent of the old office struck her senses. It was a small office that only fit five desks. This small and cozy environment should promote cohesiveness amongst partners. But only when partners get along with one another.

She glanced out the window of the one floor police department into the parking lot. Her sergeant and two partners stood next to a patrol car as they laughed while sipping their morning coffee.

Rinehart let out a sigh, rolled her eyes and plopped back into her chair. She slid a coffee pod into her single serve machine on top of her desk. The top snapped down as she began to brew her own caffeine.

With an elastic around her fingers, she pulled back on her long blonde hair and knotted it tight behind her head. Her eyes locked on the email icon as she double clicked the mouse. No new emails meant more time working in the unpleasant environment she once loved.

A loud cackle echoed down the hallway as it grew louder with each passing second. She looked up as her boss and partners made their way into the office. Only fifteen minutes late today, she thought to herself.

"Morning gentlemen." Rinehart said while looking up at the arrogant group.

They ignored her welcome as they broke from the huddle and moved to their desks. Rinehart shook her head and again rolled her eyes. Another day in paradise.

The hot porcelain warmed her hands as she slid the mug off the base. She felt the heat from the liquid as the cup tipped, bringing the highly coveted fuel to her lips.

"Rinehart. I got a case you need to handle." Sergeant Austin said with his eyes still glued to the paper on his desk. His round body jiggled as the out of shape boss seemed winded just trying to get the words out. The thick 70's style mustache covered his lips as he spoke. He'd make a better ventriloquist than an officer Rinehart thought.

"Yes boss, what do you got?" Rinehart said while putting the coffee down as she stood from her desk.

"Missing person." Austin said while holding up the report in one hand while the other simultaneously shoved a glazed donut into his pie hole.

Rinehart tilted her head and slowly inhaled to control the disappointment. "You got it boss. I'll get right on it."

She snatched the report and marched back to her desk. Her designer glasses sat at the tip of her nose as she read the names listed on the first page. "Daniel Paradis? That's a new name. Thought it'd be another one of the regulars."

Austin rubbed his sleeve across his mouth to remove the excess glaze that speckled his mustache. "Yeah. Never know. This could be the big one, ya know?" Austin chuckled as he flipped the pages of his morning newspaper. The peanut gallery followed suit, as they snorted in amusement at the comment.

Rinehart was unfazed by their antics. "Well, my father always told me that life was like a box of chocolates. You never know what you're going to get." Her eyes focused up at her boss and lip inquisitively curved upward. "Or was that, Forrest Gump?"

Austin rolled his eyes and continued his morning paper. The visual disappointment on his face gave her a calming satisfaction. He had continuously given her lackluster cases, but she made it her mission to never let him get to her. Rinehart treated every case as if it was a top priority.

"Hey fellas, let's go grab some breakfast sandwiches. This donut isn't quite hitting the spot." Austin uttered while coughing up a lung into his clenched fist in front of his mouth.

"I'm down. I have to meet up with a snitch in a little while anyways." The detective to her left said, slowly focusing on the word snitch while turning his head toward Rinehart.

She ignored the blatant jab and focused on the report in front of her. The detectives who had only been in the office ten minutes, tossed their jackets back on and made their way out.

"No thanks, I already ate. But you boys have fun."

The office fell silent once again. She looked around at the old wood panels affixed to the walls and the desks that were now unoccupied. The ceiling tiles above were stained, with several missing all together. Not the dream she always envisioned as a little girl, but the investigations is all she cared about. With the three stooges out of her hair, she could focus on the work in front of her. She worked better alone, so they were only doing her a favor.

The missing person case facts seemed common. Nothing stood out to her as she went over the details. Wife reported her husband leaving two days ago and has not heard from him since. The report was only two paragraphs and it lacked further investigative questions that were needed. The first shift officer that took the report was a thirty year veteran. While one would think he would have the experience to gather as much information as possible, Rinehart knew the cop was being lazy. More concerned with making a purchase on eBay than he was doing his job the right way. A theme that was too common in the small 38 man police department.

Rinehart took one last big gulp of her coffee before placing it on her desk and scurrying to the roll call room to catch the officer before he made his way on the road.

She clutched the now rolled-up report through her hands as she walked the dimly lit hallways. In a room just ahead of her, she could see the lieutenant in front of the podium as he addressed the five patrol officers. Rinehart leaned against the door frame and listened to the morning briefing.

The officers stood by seniority from left to right. Their faded cotton uniforms looked more like a deep purple than they did their original midnight blue. Their unprofessionalism and respect for the job was obvious.

"Also, keep an eye out for a late 80's model John Deere tractor. It's dark green that's faded with some rust. Report says it was stolen from Dallas Avenue last night around midnight." The lieutenant said as he addressed his officers.

The senior officer snickered at the comment, as one of them elbowed the man next to him. "Sounds to me like ol Red got drunk again and forgot where he left it." The officers laughed like a pack of hyenas.

The shift commander dismissed the comment and released the men for their tour of duty.

"Detective Rinehart, you here to break one of my officer's balls again?" The Lieutenant said with a straight face.

"No sir. Just got a question for one of them about a missing person." Rinehart said as the officers brushed passed and ignored her existence. Her hand tapped the officer on the shoulder as he attempted to slither by. "Got a second."

He tossed his hands up and rolled his eyes toward the ceiling. "Do I need a lawyer or something?" The grizzled veteran replied.

"Careful. I wouldn't say anything to her bud." Another officer said as his cruiser keys swung around his finger.

The comments breezed in one ear and out the other without a second thought. The officer wouldn't make eye contact and his fingers twisted at the cotton lining inside his pant pocket. Stale smoke emanated from his jacket and a burnt coffee aroma blew in her direction as he spoke.

"Listen, I'm just trying to work this case you handled two days ago. Just have a question about the missing person case you took. Name was Dan Paradis."

The officer pulled his eight point hat off and rubbed at his forehead. His eyes bounced back and forth as fellow first shifters made their way to their cruisers. "Yeah. What about it?"

"Was there anything unusual that stood out to you? You've been doing this a long time. You always seem to pick up good information that the less experienced officers don't." Rinehart said with slight reserve as she tried to provide some positive reinforcement to push him along.

The officer grimaced and exhaled loudly through his nostrils. "You read the report I assume. What do you want me to tell ya? It's all in there. Couple moved here back in the spring from the Northeast. Still had some unpacked boxes laying around. Nothing unusual."

Rinehart bit at her bottom lip, blearily looking through the officer as she attempted to visualize the home. "Okay. Well thank you. Just wanted to make sure. If you think of anything else, just give me a shout."

Empty handed, she turned and made her way back to the office. "Actually, one more thing. Not sure it's important or not." The officer said as she was about to turn the corner. "The wife said there was a car parked a few doors down the night before."

"Did she give a description of the car?"

"Nah. Just sat there a couple hours with its lights on. Probably just some kids smoking a joint or something."

"Why didn't you put that in the report?" Rinehart questioned.

"Eh, must've forgot." The officer shrugged. "The wife seemed like a nutjob anyways. I'm sure you'll figure it out though. I know you prefer investigating our own, but there's only so many of us, ya know?" The officer smirked and raised his eyebrows.

With something to move on, she disengaged in conversation with a clear focus. Her mind began to go down a rabbit hole as she formulated several theories.

Heel to toe racing through the office doorway, she quickly grabbed her car keys off the desk and pulled her radio from the charger. She flung her jacket around her shoulders and exited into the cold winter's day.

Her eyes squinted from the bright sun and her heels feverishly pounded on the pavement. The detective car, a black Chevy Impala, was backed in against a fence. She noticed a paper pressed to the windshield in between the wipers. She pulled at the wiper blade and unfolded the note.

'Watch your six. They're after you.'

Rinehart looked around the lot as her warm breath created clouds around her head. No one in sight. Her fingers crumpled the paper into her fist, and she tossed it to the ground.

She pulled the door open and slid the key into the ignition. The engine made a sputtering noise as her foot pressed up and down on the gas pedal of the outdated Chevy. The car reversed before she popped it into drive and sped out of the lot.

"It'll take more than a little hazing to get rid of me fellas." She whispered.

Enjoying *Webb of Shadows*? Scan the QR code below to pre-order today!

WEBB OF SHADOWS CHAPTER THREE

CARTER WEBB THRILLER SERIES

Webb of Deception

Webb of Shadows (Coming soon!)

ABOUT THE AUTHOR

Joe Lopa, a native of Hartford County, Connecticut, brings a lifetime of unique experiences to his debut crime thriller. Immersed in a family legacy of law enforcement, Joe followed suit, dedicating years to various divisions, notably drug investigations and crimes against children. His intricate understanding of human behavior was honed through his role as a polygraph examiner, a skill that adds depth and realism to his writing.

Beyond his professional pursuits, Joe is deeply committed to his community, investing personal time in mentoring, teaching, and coaching local youth. His dedication is matched only by the support and inspiration he draws from his beloved wife and their three sons. Joe's intimate knowledge of law enforcement, combined with his commitment to family and community, infuses his writing with authenticity and heart, promising readers a gripping and emotionally resonant journey.

Find Joe on Facebook!
https://www.facebook.com/people/Joe-Lopa/61556117731574/

Made in United States
Orlando, FL
01 October 2024